OUT OF SEASON

ALSO BY ANTONIO MANZINI

Black Run

Adam's Rib

OUT OF SEASON

A Novel

Translated from the Italian
by Antony Shugaar

ANTONIO MANZINI

HARPER

NEW YORK · LONDON · TORONTO · SYDNEY

I tawt I taw a puddy tat.

—TWEETY BIRD

HARPER

HarperCollins books may be purchased for educational, business, or sales promotional use. For information, please email the Special Markets Department at SPsales@harpercollins.com.

Originally published as *Non è stagione* in Italy, January 12, 2015, by Sellerio Editore, Palermo.

FIRST U.S. EDITION PUBLISHED 2018.

Designed by Jamie Lynn Kerner

Library of Congress Cataloging-in-Publication Data has been applied for.

ISBN 978-0-06-269649-6 (pbk.)

18 19 20 21 22   LSC   10 9 8 7 6 5 4 3 2 1

CONTENTS

MONDAY

The lightning split the night and froze the white cargo van in a photo flash as it raced at high speed from Saint-Vincent in the direction of Aosta.

"It's starting to rain," said the Italian at the wheel.

"Then why don't you slow down?" replied the guy with the foreign accent.

First the thunder, then the rain, which came down like a bucketful of water tossed onto the windshield. The Italian switched on the windshield wipers without slowing down in the slightest. The only other gesture he made was to switch on the brights.

"When asphalt is wet, becomes slick like soap," said the foreigner, pulling the cell phone out of his jacket pocket.

But the Italian refused to slow down.

The foreigner unfolded a scrap of paper and started punching a number into his phone.

"Why don't you put phone numbers into your directory? Like everybody else does?"

"No directory in phone. All full. And why you not mind your fucking business?" the foreigner replied, punching in the last of the number. The cargo van hit a pothole and they both jerked and bounced.

"Now I vomit!" said the man with the foreign accent, putting the phone up to his ear.

"Who are you calling?"

The other man didn't reply. He heard a sleepy "Hello . . . who is this?" from the receiver. He grimaced and ended the call. "Got wrong," he muttered, angrily punching the keys of the old paint-spattered cell phone. Once he was done with it, he put the phone back into his pocket and looked out the window. The road was full of curves and the black-and-white sign announcing twisting curves ahead only loomed up at the last second. The engine's blown-out head gasket and the rusty muffler emitted a cacophony of noises, like a basket of scrap metal tumbling down a flight of stairs. In the back, the tool box kept sliding from one side of the cargo deck to the other as the van pitched and yawed.

"This is the universal deluge, my friend!"

"I'm not your friend," the foreigner retorted.

Even with the headlights on bright, the Saint-Vincent to Aosta road was completely invisible. And the Italian kept shifting and downshifting, grinding the gears and jamming down on the gas pedal.

"Why you not slow down?"

"Because the sun's going to be up soon. And by the time the sun's up, I want to be home! Smoke yourself a cigarette and stop busting my balls, Slawomir."

The foreigner scratched his whiskers. "My name isn't Slawomir, stupid asshole. Slawomir is Polack name, I'm not Polack."

"Polack, Serbian, Bulgarian . . . you're all the same to me."

"You're a dickhead."

"Why, isn't it true? You're all a bunch of fucking slime-balls. Thieves and gypsies." Then he added: "Are you afraid of some curves?" and he laughed through clenched teeth. "Huh, gypsy? Are you afraid of them?"

"No, I'm afraid of what a bad driver you are. And I'm not a gypsy."

"What, does that make you mad? What's wrong with being a gypsy, anyway? You shouldn't be asha—"

A sudden flat thump interrupted him. The cargo van swerved to one side.

"Fuck!" He tried to swing the steering wheel around in the opposite direction.

The foreigner screamed, the Italian screamed, and the three surviving wheels all screamed in unison. At least until a second tire blew, and then the van lurched forward. It shot through a wooden rail, knocked down the pole with the speed limit sign, and came to a halt against a couple of larch trees on the side of the road. The windshield exploded, the wipers twisted and bent, the engine fell silent.

The foreigner and the Italian sat motionless, glassy eyes

fixed on some distant point while blood oozed from their mouths and eye sockets. Their necks broken, shapeless as a pair of marionettes with their strings cut. Another flash of lightning and the glare caught a still of two dull faces, eyes with pupils made of ice.

The rain drummed down with its demented rhythm on the sheet metal of the van's roof. The wrecked cargo van with its headlights still blazing creaked as it shifted in precarious equilibrium, perched on the roots that stuck out of the dirt. The van gave one last lurch as it settled on the soil, making the lifeless bodies of the two men bounce in their seats.

It had taken three seconds from the first blowout to when the cargo van smeared itself against the tree trunks.

Three seconds. No time at all. Barely a sigh.

THREE SECONDS IS HOW LONG IT TOOK DEPUTY POLICE Chief Rocco Schiavone to figure out where he was. An eternity.

He'd opened his eyes without recognizing the walls, the doors, and the smell of his home.

Where am I? he asked himself, while his sleep-dazed eyes circumnavigated the space around him. The dim light in the room didn't help. He was in a bed, not his own, in a room, not his own, in an apartment, not his own. And most likely, the apartment building wasn't his either. He hoped at least that he was in the same city as last night, the city where he'd been living for nine months now, expiating his transgressions: Aosta.

Seeing the body of the woman lying right next to him helped him put the pieces back together. She was sleeping peacefully. Her hair spread out, loose and black, on the pillow. Her eyes were shut and they trembled ever so slightly beneath the eyelids. She was opening her lips a little, as if kissing someone in her sleep. One leg was uncovered and the foot dangled off the edge of the mattress.

He'd fallen asleep in Anna's apartment! What was happening to him? Wrong! A first false step, a palpable risk of slipping into a comfortable routine! The danger of an unasked-for integration into that city and its inhabitants scared him right down to the roots of his hair, making him sit bolt upright on the mattress. He rubbed his face vigorously.

No, this can't be, he thought. In the past nine months, he'd never once slept away from home. This was the start of the slippery slope, he was well aware . . . and then, before you knew it, you were a regular in a local café, you started striking up friendships with the fruit vendor, the tobacconist, even the guy at the newsstand, until one fine day your barista utters the fateful phrase: "The usual, Dottore?" and you were done for. You automatically became a citizen of Aosta.

He set both feet down on the floor. Warm. Fuzzy. Wall-to-wall carpeting. He stood up and in the half-light of a leaden dawn, as pale as a fish's belly, he ventured toward a chair that embraced a pile of clothing—*his* clothing. A sharp blow to his toes lit up his brain, then a lightning bolt of pain hit him.

He silently threw himself back onto the bed, frantically

grabbing at his left foot, which had kicked the sharp edge of a chair leg. Rocco knew perfectly well that it was one of those ferocious, savage pains that, because God is merciful, do at least have the advantage of being short-lived. All you had to do was clench your teeth for a couple of seconds and it would all be over. He cursed in silence, he didn't want to wake the sleeping woman. Not because he was particularly solicitous of her sleep, but because if she did wake up, he'd have to engage in a serious discussion and he had neither the desire nor the time. She ground out a couple of mysterious words between her lips, then turned over and went on sleeping. The pain in his foot, sharp and merciless, was starting to fade, and soon it was nothing but a memory. Fully awake now, he put both hands on his face and flashes of the evening flicked before him, as if his eyes had been transformed into a slide projector.

A chance encounter with Anna, the best friend of Nora Tardioli, his now ex-girlfriend, at the Caffè Centrale. Her usual smile, her usual feline gaze, her eyes tip-tilted, the eyes of a murderous she-cat, the usual getup of a dark lady of the provinces. Glass of wine. Idle chitchat.

"You do know, don't you, Rocco, that Nora expects you to call her sooner or later?"

"You do know that I'm not going to call Nora ever again, right?"

"You know, you two haven't spoken since her birthday."

"You know, that's something I do intentionally."

"You know, Rocco, she really cares about you."

"You know, Nora is having an affair with the architect Pietro Bucci-Something-or-Other."

Laughter from Anna. Raucous, slashing, mocking laughter, which made Rocco horny as hell.

"You know, you're wrong there. Pietro Bucci Rivolta is mine."

Anna jerked her thumb toward her chest, making the silver necklace that dangled over her neckline jangle.

"But why are you so interested in me and Nora?"

"Because you're making her suffer."

"There's nothing else I can do. Evidently, I'm not what she needs."

"Why, are you saying that you know what Nora needs? It isn't much, Rocco. Nora isn't asking for much. She'd be happy with the basics."

Anna ordering two more glasses of wine.

Then another two.

"Shall we go?"

The street. Dim lights. The entrance to Anna's building, not far from Rocco's.

"I live around here."

"Then it won't take you long to get home."

Anna smiling, her eyes dark and glistening. Her eyes tip-tilted as usual. Still the eyes of a murderous she-cat.

"You don't like me one bit, do you, Anna?"

"No. Not one bit. Oh, God, I guess you're not a complete loss, physically speaking. Fine sharp nose, smoldering dark fake-Latin-lover eyes, you're tall, you have nice shoulders, and plenty of hair on your head. But you know what? I wouldn't even board a cable car with a guy like you, just to get up to the ski slopes. I'd wait for the next car."

"Well, don't worry, it's not a risk you're about to run. I don't ski. See you around."

"Maybe so . . . but I hope not."

He lunges at Anna. He kisses her. She lets him. And with the hand behind her back, she opens the front door.

Going upstairs.

And they fuck. Forty-five minutes, maybe fifty. And for Rocco, that's one for the record books.

Anna's breasts. Her hair, loose and black. Her muscular legs.

"I do Pilates."

Her arms, firm and shapely.

"That's the Pilates, too."

Exhausted and sweaty, both sprawled on the bed.

"Girl, I'm too old for this, you know."

"So am I."

"What about the Pilates?"

"It's not enough."

"You're very pretty."

"You're not."

They both laugh.

"Water?"

"Water."

Anna getting out of bed. Firm ass cheeks. Rocco thinking: Pilates again. She goes into the kitchen. He knows it because he hears the sound of the refrigerator door. She comes back to bed.

"Next time will you tie me up?"

"I'll handcuff you, actually. That's more my line of work."

Rocco guzzling from the bottle of mineral water. Anna showing him her paintings, which hang on every wall in the apartment. Flowers and landscapes. Which she paints, to fill her endless afternoons of boredom. He falls asleep like a child as she shows him a Tuscan marina.

HE QUICKLY GOT DRESSED. UNDERWEAR, TROUSERS, shirt, Clarks desert boots, jacket—and with a catlike step he left the bedroom and Anna's apartment.

THE AIR OUTSIDE WAS COLD, PARTLY BECAUSE OF THE rain that had fallen all night long, and the sun had not yet appeared. But a glow on the horizon announced that it was going to be a beautiful day. He looked up and saw a very few clouds grazing lazily in the midst of the sky.

He pulled out his cell phone and glanced at the time. Six fifteen.

Too early to go get breakfast but too late to go back to sleep. His house keys jangled in his pocket, as if suggesting a shower before heading over to the café on Piazza Chanoux.

HE WALKED ALONG QUICKLY, HIS SHOULDER BRUSHING the walls like a cat out late, striding past the two cross streets that separated his apartment from Anna's, and finally returned home.

As was to be expected, the apartment was empty. For

that matter, even Marina wasn't there. She wasn't in bed, she wasn't in the living room watching some pre-dawn newscast, nor was she in the bathroom taking a shower or in the kitchen making breakfast. It was as if she'd heard him come in. As if Marina had seen the unslept-in bed and had understood that Rocco hadn't come home that night. For the first time in all these months, he'd slept away from home, and maybe she hadn't liked the new development. So now she was sulking and refusing to show herself.

Without bothering to look around, he slipped into the bathroom and turned on the hot water. He took off his clothes and stepped into the shower, shampooing his hair and running the water over his body for several long minutes. He only stepped out of the shower once the steam had turned the bathroom into a Turkish hammam. He cleaned the mirror with the flat of his hand and his face appeared before him, in all its dingy squalor. Bags under his eyes, reddened eyelids, wrinkles over his cheekbones. He snarled and took a look at his teeth. He wished that Marina might pop out of that blanket of dense steam. But no such luck. He picked up the bar of shaving soap and began the process of shaving.

BY EIGHT O'CLOCK, HE WAS AT THE CAFÉ ON THE PIazza, the second obligatory destination of the morning. Then he walked from there to police headquarters. All of this without even noticing that, high overhead, instead of clouds there was now a clear blue sky.

He stealthily entered the office. He avoided the questions from Officer Casella, who was standing in the doorway, and hurried down the hallway to avoid meeting D'Intino or Deruta, the two officers he'd dubbed "the De Rege Brothers" in honor of the Piedmontese comics, a pair of dumb-and-dumber buffoons from nearly a century ago, repopularized by Walter Chiari and Carlo Campanini when Rocco was just a kid, hunched over in the living room—which also served as his grandmother's bedroom—watching the old black-and-white television set.

Before starting a day at work, Rocco needed to smoke a joint, and in order to do that, he necessarily had to sprawl comfortably in the chair at his desk with his office door closed, in silence. Absolute silence.

He went in and sat down at his desk. He pulled out a joint. A little stale, but still acceptable. After just three tokes, things already started to go better. Yes, the temperature was going to change and, yes, all he had ahead of him was a quiet day in the office.

Someone knocked at the door. Rocco rolled his eyes. He stubbed the joint out in the ashtray. "Who is it?"

There was no answer.

"I *said*: 'Who is it?'"

Still no answer. Rocco got up and threw open the window, to eliminate the stench of cannabis.

"Who is it?" he shouted again as he strode toward the door.

Still not a word. He opened the door.

It was D'Intino, the Abruzzese officer, who was waiting silently like a watchdog.

"D'Intino, is it too much trouble for you to say your own name?"

"No, why?"

"Because for the past hour I've been shouting, 'Who is it?'"

"Ah. Were you talking to me?"

"Well, were you the one who knocked at the door?"

"Of course."

"When someone knocks on a door and, on the other side of the door, someone asks who is it, who do *you* think they're talking to?"

"I don't know . . ."

"Listen, D'Intino, I don't want to ruin a day that actually seems to have gotten off on the right foot. So, I'm going to make an effort to be nice and try to figure out what's wrong. Shall we just start over?"

D'Intino nodded his head.

"So now I'm going to close the door and you knock again."

He suited action to words. He shut the door. He waited ten seconds. Nothing happened.

"D'Intino, you have to knock at the door!" he bellowed.

Ten seconds later, D'Intino knocked at the door.

"Good. Now, who is it?" Rocco shouted.

No answer.

"I said: Who is it?"

"Me."

"Me who!?"

"Me."

Rocco opened the door again. D'Intino, as expected, was still standing there.

"All right, now, me who?"

"But, sir, you knew it was me."

He smacked him flat-handed on the back, three times. D'Intino hunched his neck deep down into his shoulders, and took the smacks from his boss with faint objections. "Yes, but I said it was me because you'd already seen me, sir, right? And so I said to myself, why shouldn't I . . ."

"Stop!" shouted Rocco, reaching up and placing his hand over the policeman's mouth. "Enough is enough, D'Intino. We've determined that it was you who was knocking. Now tell me, what is this about?"

"A bad, bad crash on the state highway."

"So what?"

"Two dead."

"Well?"

"The highway patrol wants to know if we can come."

Rocco put his face in his hands. Then he shouted: "Pierron!" He couldn't take anymore of D'Intino, he needed to talk to someone with an IQ higher than that of an orangutan.

Ten seconds went by and the face of Italo Pierron, the best officer he had, peered in from a side door. "Yes sir, at your orders!"

"What's all this about a crash?"

"On the state highway from Saint-Vincent . . . a cargo van. There are two fatalities."

"So take D'Intino and go, thanks."

"Well, actually, I . . ." said D'Intino, pointing to his ribs.
"What?"

"Dottore, my ribs still hurt pretty bad."

A month and a half before, D'Intino had been the target
of an assault that had resulted in a broken nose and a devi-
ated septum. Then, as if that hadn't been enough, he'd fallen
into an open road-construction pit, fracturing a couple of
ribs, which were still painfully tender. The video feed from
a security camera that happened to record the attack on
D'Intino and Deruta—Deruta being the 230-pound-plus officer who was running neck and neck with D'Intino for the
prize of biggest idiot at police headquarters—had made the
rounds of the building, as well as the district attorney's office. It had become a cult favorite among the cops and mag-
istrates of the high mountain valley. That few minutes of
film with the two bumbling cops trying and failing to arrest
a couple of drug dealers was trotted out any time anyone
in the office felt their morale droop. Judge Baldi watched
it obsessively, Judge Messina, three times a week with his
whole family. At police headquarters, Italo Pierron and Deputy Inspector Rispoli enjoyed screening it in the passport
office, which had also become the secret venue for their love-
making. Lately, even Police Chief Andrea Costa had become
one of the video's audience of fans; at the sight of the ordeals
facing two of his officers, he doubled over, laughing until the
tears came. The only one who seemed immune to the comic exploits of that silent three-minute black-and-white clip was the
medical examiner, Alberto Fumagalli. Every time he watched
that short feature, he grew sad and came close to weeping. But

there was no need to worry too much. Fumagalli's emotional health had been seriously damaged anyway by all the time he spent with corpses, and especially by a latent and insidious manic-depressive pathology lurking deep within.

"But what about the highway patrol?" Rocco asked with exasperation. "Aren't car crashes their business?"

"Actually, it was the highway patrol who called us. In part because it was a single-vehicle accident. Just the cargo van. No other cars involved. But there's something that doesn't add up. So, they want us."

"What a pain in the ass!" Rocco shouted, and took his green loden coat down from the coat rack. He put it on and shut the door.

"D'Intino, if you're not fit for duty, would you tell me why you continue to come into police headquarters?"

"I take care of matters involving papers."

"He takes care of matters involving papers," Rocco repeated in a low voice to Italo. "Did you get that? He takes care of matters involving papers. Come on, Italo. Or are you unfit for duty due to some random dysfunction?"

"No, I'm not. But I would remind you that Deputy Inspector Rispoli is home with a fever of 102. We can't count on her."

Rocco looked him up and down with a cold gaze. "And neither can you. Am I right?"

Italo blushed and looked down.

Without another word, Rocco started toward the exit.

The love affair between Italo and Caterina was something he still had difficulty swallowing. Deputy Inspector

Rispoli was one female he'd been keeping his eye on for months now. And to see her snagged away like that, from right beneath his nose, had undermined his self-esteem.

While he strode rapidly toward the main entrance, Rocco Schiavone turned to look at Italo: "Do you get a kick out of always sending D'Intino to my office?"

"Some people smoke a joint, other people send D'Intino to their boss to get the day off on the right foot." And he laughed.

Rocco decided that the time had come to exert pressure where it mattered and get D'Intino sent off to some god-forsaken police station on the slopes of the Maiella Massif. It was his own health that was at stake.

In May, the world is lovely. The first daisies push up, dotting the meadows with white and yellow, and flowers spew colors from the balconies like so many tubes of tempera paint crushed underfoot.

The same was true of Aosta. Rocco looked up at the sky. It seemed that the clouds had finally gone away to summer somewhere else, while the sun caressed the mountains and high meadows, making that wonderful palette of colors glitter and sparkle. And it did Rocco Schiavone's mood a world of good. He'd been waiting for that spectacle for a long time, since the end of September of the year before, when he'd been set down, bag and baggage, at the police headquarters of Aosta. He'd been transferred there as punishment from the Cristoforo Colombo police station in the outlying

EUR neighborhood, a prosperous residential and business district, of his hometown, Rome. There had been months of intense cold, of snow, rain, and ice, and they had cost him no fewer than ten pairs of Clarks desert boots, the only kind of shoes he ever wore.

If he looked carefully, there were still a few clouds riding high above. But they were bright white and were scudding along; at the very most they'd stop to linger awhile among the mountain tops. Nothing to worry about.

"So you see, Rocco?" Italo asked him. When they were speaking privately, he addressed him on a first-name basis.

"What?"

"You see that spring comes to Aosta, too? I always told you so. You should have believed me!"

"It's true. I'd given up hoping. All these damn colors. Where were they until yesterday?"

Italo pressed the gas pedal to the floor. As they raced off down the street, Rocco patted all his pockets. "Fuck!" he blurted, and plunged his hand into the officer's jacket pocket. He grabbed his cigarette pack. Chesterfield. "I know that one of these days you're going to surprise me and instead of this crap you're going to have a pack of Camels."

"Dream on!" Italo replied.

Rocco lit one and put the pack back in Pierron's pocket.

"What do you say, Italo? Shall we go get some lunch in the mountains?" suggested the deputy police chief.

"Where?"

"I'd like to go back to Champoluc, to the Petit Charmant Hotel. The food is unbelievable there."

"Well, why not? Let's see how quick we can get done, right?"

"A car crash is nothing serious. What can there be about it that's so mysterious? They're all such dummies up around here." And he took a drag on his cigarette.

It was quite a cheerful scene outside the window of their squad car. Even the trees seemed to be smiling. Without all those pounds of snow weighing down their branches, making them look like weary nonagenarians, crushed to the ground with the burden of age. Now they were reaching for the sky, young and new, fresh, taut, straight, and limber.

Rocco remembered the night he'd just spent with Anna. He felt something tingle between his legs. "It's really spring!" he said, stubbing out the cigarette in the car's ashtray.

THE BLAME FOR THE CRASH WAS PUT ON TWO WORN old tires that had blown out on a curve, so that the Fiat cargo van had smashed head-on into a pair of larches. Carlo Figus and Viorelo Midea, driver and passenger, had been killed instantly. All that remained of the two bodies was a pair of bloodstained sheets that had been used to cover them. Rocco Schiavone and Pierron were chatting with the officer from the highway patrol.

"So are you going to tell me what doesn't add up? What's so strange about this wreck?" asked Rocco.

"More than strange, it's something very serious," said

Officer Berruti, mirrored sunglasses and white teeth, looking like he'd just stepped out of an episode of *CHiPS*, the old TV series from the seventies.

"What is it?"

"The cargo van has stolen plates. Not its own plates."

Schiavone nodded. He gestured for Berruti to go on. "So, to make a long story short, according to the registration, the cargo van belongs to Carlo Figus, the guy who was driving, but the plates on the van are completely different."

Another highway patrol officer came over to talk to them; this one was slightly overweight and had a sharp, wide-awake look on his face.

"Ciao, Italo!" He knew Pierron.

"Ciao, Umberto."

"Well, Dottore, the plates that are on this cargo van were reported as stolen in Turin on February 27th. They belong to a certain Signor Silvestrelli, and are supposed to be on a Mercedes A-Class, not a Fiat Scudo cargo van. This cargo van ought to have license plate AM 166 TT on it."

"And I'm guessing that AM 166 TT isn't out on the roads somewhere else."

"Nope, not at all!"

"Oh, what a pain in the ass," Rocco murmured under his breath, rolling his eyes skyward.

"What did you say, sir?" Berruti asked, solicitously.

"Oh, what a pain in the ass!" Rocco said again, looking the officer right in the eyes. "What a pain in the ass! It was all going too well, far too smoothly. An accident, some paperwork, and we're done! And instead these two assholes have stolen plates. What pieces of shit!" After kicking a small rock, Rocco left the three cops exchanging glances.

"So you'll take care of notifying the families?" Umberto asked Italo.

Rocco, who was just a few yards away, swung around: "Of course we'll take care of it, Italo. This isn't a car crash with a little bit of paperwork, this is a theft and it's our job."

"Thanks!" Umberto replied, happily. "If there's anything you need . . ."

"You guys stay right here, fill out all the paperwork that's required, and don't let me see you again. I have to go see Fumagalli in the morgue, goddamn it to hell!" Then, cursing under his breath, he headed off toward the squad car. The two highway patrol officers looked over at Italo. "Is he always like this?"

"No. He's in a good mood today. If this were a murder, then we'd be laughing out of the other side of our mouths. Believe me. Ciao, Umberto! When are you going to give me another chance to beat you?"

"Any time. Eight ball or billiards?"

"Billiards."

I CAN'T SEE ANYTHING.

Are my eyes still closed?

They're open. They're wide open and I can't see a thing.

Am I still sleeping?

I'm not sleeping. I know I'm not sleeping. My head is spinning, it's spinning around like crazy. My temples really hurt. The blackness is turning gray. It's not dark out anymore. But I still can't see. What do I have over my face? What is it? A spider web? No, you can see through spider webs. No, this is a dark veil of some kind. Dark and made of threads. Black threads. Disgusting. It's filthy and disgusting. If I close my eyes, my head spins around. I have to keep my eyes open and peer through this disgusting black veil that's hanging in front of my face.

She was laboriously dragging her thoughts along, heavy as they were, still drenched in slumber and headache. She tried to take off the blindfold hanging in front of her eyes. But her hands wouldn't move. Frozen in place.

They won't move. My hands won't move! I have a black cloth on my face and I can't take it off because my hands won't move.

She strained, tugged once, twice, but her wrists were fastened tight.

Am I trapped in my bed, with my head stuck in my pillowcase? Why would I be trapped in my bed? What the fuck am I thinking? Maybe I'm still sleeping, it's still dark out and soon I'll wake up and go get breakfast.

Her temples were pounding regularly, like dead bells. A subterranean pain, continuous and dull.

It must be night time. I can't hear the road. And I can't hear Dolores making breakfast or Papà walking in the hallway.

Those were the familiar sounds of home. And here there was nothing but silence.

I'm sitting down. On the bed?

She tried to stand up but failed.

Is my back tied to the wall? To a wooden plank?

She tried to move her legs.

They wouldn't move. They were fastened tight, just like her hands. Her ankles were nailed in place. Is this some kind of paralysis? Am I paralyzed? No, my fingers will move. And I can move my feet. But my ankles are fastened tight. As are my wrists. Is this a nightmare? I'm going to wake up now, I'm going to wake up now, I'm going to wake up now.

She tried to hop by jerking the chair along, but nothing happened.

What the fuck do I have on my face? A blindfold? A blindfold, for sure. And on the other side of it I can see . . . what is that? It's a wall. A gray wall. This isn't my bedroom. My room is yellow, this room is gray. And where are my Coldplay and Alt-J posters? It's all gray in here. Gray and filthy. But I can see. So it's daytime now. But if it's daytime, why isn't anyone coming to wake me up?

"Mamma?" she shouted. And the sound of her voice frightened her. She tried again, still louder: "Papà?"

It was getting harder and harder to breathe and there wasn't much air. That disgusting blindfold in front of her face was cutting off most of the air, and every time she tried to draw a breath, it touched her lips.

"Mamma? Papà?"

It was no good.

She was wide awake, and she wasn't at home. She couldn't move, she couldn't see anything, it reeked of mold, and she was all alone.

Chiara started crying.

CARLO FIGUS'S LAST KNOWN ADDRESS WAS ON VIA Chateland. Rocco had sent Officer Scipioni over to deliver the sad news and see if he could wrangle a relative of any description to take over to the mortuary. Rocco had decided to send Officer Antonio Scipioni solely and simply out of necessity, seeing that Inspector Caterina Rispoli was bed-bound with a fever of 102, and Italo Pierron was out tracking down Viorelo Midea, the other man killed in the crash. That meant the deputy chief had no one else but Officer Scipioni on regular duty in Aosta since December. He didn't know him well, but at least he knew he wasn't a mental defective like Deruta or D'Intino or, say, Casella. He knew the man was half-Sicilian, the other half of his family tracing its descent back to the Marche region, and he'd always struck Rocco as well-organized and alert. Rocco had never heard arrant nonsense spilling from his lips and he hoped he could include Scipioni among the reliable officers at police head-quarters. Having another man he could count on would be a plus.

The deputy chief was waiting at the front door to the morgue, smoking a cigarette, when he saw the unmistakable figure of Alberto Fumagalli, the medical examiner from Livorno, loom into view through the pebbled glass. As was their custom for the past nine months now, neither man said hello. Alberto looked straight up, grimaced, muttered something, and then nodded his head in Rocco's direction. "So are you going to come in after you're done with that?"

"No. I'm going to wait out here. A police officer should be here soon."

"Who? The one who always throws up?"

"Italo? No. Another one. He's bringing a next of kin to identify the body."

Alberto looked him in the eyes. "Do you want to know something right away or should we wait till you're done with your cigarette?"

Rocco took a deep drag. "Just tell me."

"He died happy."

Rocco stepped closer to the medical examiner. "What's that supposed to mean?"

"The Italian? He died happy."

"So how do you know that? Did he tell you so?"

"He certainly did."

"Get to the point. This isn't the day for it, and anyway I can't stand talking to you in the first place."

"Yessir. So you want to know how he was able to tell me? Come on, I'll show you."

So there was no way around it, he'd have to take in the sight of the two corpses. He flicked away the cigarette and followed the medical examiner.

● ● ●

IN THE AUTOPSY ROOM, THERE WAS THE USUAL ODOR of rotten eggs mixed with food gone bad and the reek of a harbor. On the gurneys lay the two bodies. Alberto walked over to them. "No, I'll spare you the cadavers today. What you're especially interested in is right here . . . in the microscope, come on." And he pointed to the eyepiece. He lowered his eye to it and adjusted the focus. Then with a smile he made way for Rocco.

"What do you see?"

"What do I know? Round things, sort of white and sort of purple . . . I don't know, it looks like one of those blots that psychologists use. . . ."

"They're called Rorschach blots and they don't have anything to do with this. What you're seeing on the slide is a swab that I took from the Italian's penis."

"What a dick. . . ."

"That's right, also known as the dick. And do you know what you're observing there?"

"You just told me, didn't you?"

"No. What you're observing is *Gardnerella vaginalis*."

"I don't know that that is, but from the name we shouldn't find samples of it on male genitalia, should we?"

"Outstanding! Gardnerella is a microorganism, and many women have it and just live with it. But if it proliferates too abundantly, then we start to see those off-white secretions, which by the way, also produce something of a stink, you know? And. . . ."

"Cut to the chase, Alberto. So what you're saying is that this guy got busy right before being killed in the crash?"

"That's right. And if we calculate that these two were killed no later than four a.m., shall we say he must have done it not even an hour before that?"

"Are you asking me?"

"No, I was making a statement with a question mark. It's a very chic thing to do these days, because it's like saying: I want to hear your opinion, but in any case, I'm right. And anyway, I'd be glad to give this mysterious woman who gave this poor man the last joys of sex a shot, but the shot I'd have in mind would be a shot of metronidazole."

"Are you thinking of a prostitute?"

"From the looks of these two, I'd say so."

"By which you mean?"

"Have you taken a look at their faces, Rocco? If the two of them wanted to get laid, they either pulled out their wallets or else they headed home for a hand of solitaire. Do you want to take a look at them?"

"For today, the Gardnerella will suffice."

OFFICER SCIPIONI WAS ESCORTING A MAN OF SOME indeterminate old age down the hallway. Arm in arm with the young policeman, the old man was moving forward one tiny step after another, toward the door of the morgue, staring straight ahead at some fixed point before him.

"Deputy Chief Schiavone, this is Carlo Figus's grandfather. The only other relative is the victim's mother, but she can't leave her apartment, she has diabetes . . . both her legs were amputated."

"Okay, well . . ." said Rocco, helplessly throwing his arms wide.

"This is Signor Adelmo Rosset, Carlo Figus's grandfather. Adelmo, this is Deputy Chief Schiavone. . . ."

The man barely looked up. His eyes were light blue and seemed to be immersed in a dense, sticky liquid. He didn't change expression, he just slowly moved his hand to his pocket, pulled out a handkerchief, and wiped his mouth.

"He doesn't talk much," said Scipioni.

"I see that. But is he up to this?"

"I don't know. I think he is. Carlo Figus's mother, who would be Adelmo's daughter, says that he can hear perfectly and understands everything, isn't that right, Adelmo?"

Like a centenarian tortoise, the man turned his wrinkled neck toward Scipioni. He slowly flashed a smile that revealed three surviving teeth. Then he shut back up like a flower at sunset.

"So what should I do, Deputy Chief?"

"Let's get going. Fumagalli's waiting." Rocco reached out an arm and offered it to Adelmo, who clutched it tight and, escorted by the two policemen, walked toward the glass partition. Rocco knocked three times loudly, and the aluminum Venetian blinds were pulled up, revealing Fumagalli's face. The medical examiner on the other side of the glass had the cadaver all ready for viewing. He gestured to Rocco, as if to ask, "Shall I uncover it?" and Rocco nodded, never once looking away from Adelmo. The old man's face reflected off the glass and as chance would have it, the reflection matched perfectly with the position of the cadaver's face in the other room. Fumagalli uncovered the corpse. The face of Carlo Figus took the place of his grandfather's face. Adelmo looked for a few seconds. Then he slowly reached out a hand until his fingertips came to rest on the glass. He turned toward Rocco. His gaze lay somewhere far away, immersed in liquid, but a tear welled up in one eye and ran down his cheek, plopping into a deep wrinkle as if it were a dry river bed. Adelmo trembled as he looked at Rocco. There was no need of anything more. The deputy chief nodded to Fumagalli to cover up the dead body.

"Antonio," he said to the officer, "take Signor Rosset home."

Scipioni nodded. "Come along, Signor Adelmo, let's go. . . ." The old man took his hand off the glass partition. His fingerprints vanished in a few seconds, reabsorbed by the chill of the glass. He seemed bewildered, as if someone had just awakened him from a bad dream. Then he grabbed Scipioni's arm and headed back down the hallway with very slow, cadenced steps.

Rocco needed a drink.

HE'D MADE A PHONE CALL TO ALERT JUDGE BALDI. Baldi in turn had ordered him to come into the district attorney's office, but the deputy chief had declined the invitation with the excuse of official duties. At the very latest that afternoon, he'd promised the judge, he'd come in to talk. That stupid crash was threatening to turn into an unbroken series of bureaucratic pains in the ass that would make your hair stand on end. And right now the only thing he wanted to do was watch his ice cubes melt in the preprandial spritz that Ettore had brought to his outdoor table. The utmost calm reigned over Piazza Chanoux. There were two city constables on the pavement outside the *La Stampa* newsroom, chatting at their leisure with a woman and her black toy poodle, three workers on a ladder busy changing a streetlamp lightbulb, and Nora striding swiftly toward his table.

"Oh fuck me . . ." Rocco said under his breath. The woman was heading straight for him, there were no two ways about it. Her eyes were level and her stride was determined. The hope that an unexpected sprained ankle might stop her vanished when the deputy chief noticed that Nora was wearing running shoes. There was still one slender, vanishing possibility: a lightning bolt. But that looked unlikely; there was only a blue sky overhead. Nora reached the table. Without a word, she pulled out a chair and sat down across from Rocco, without once taking her eyes off his.

"Can I order something for you?" asked Rocco in a faint voice.

"Anna? With her of all people?" the woman roared.

"Who told you?"

"Aosta is a very small city."

"Well, your informant got it wrong."

Nora narrowed her eyes. "Really?"

"Really."

"The bakery that I use and that Anna uses is right across the street from Anna's apartment, and the baker told me that he saw you sneak out at six something in the morning like a thief. Is that enough?"

Why lie? Why start trying to come up with excuses, frantically treading water? After all, sooner or later Nora was bound to find out. Maybe he'd have told her himself.

"All right then, Nora. Anna."

"My close friend . . ." but she was talking to herself more than to Rocco.

"Well, actually, I don't know if you can say friend. . . ."

"You're right about that. All things considered, I should thank you. With one simple move, you cleared up two things. One is that our relationship isn't going anywhere, and two, to describe whatever it is I have with Anna as a friendship is, to say the least, overstating the matter."

"I'd say so."

"In fact, I don't know whether to be more pissed off at you or at her. What hurts most? The betrayal of a love story or a friendship?"

"Are you asking me?"

"No, I'm just thinking aloud. But after all, between you and me it wasn't really so much of a love story."

Rocco took a deep breath. He looked Nora in the eye. "I guess it wasn't."

"Did you do it to humiliate me or to take revenge?"

"Revenge? For what?"

"You assumed that the architect and I. . . ."

"Just forget about that, Nora. No revenge. I did it because I wanted to and before I knew it, I was in bed with her.

More or less the same reasons that were driving your friend. Nothing more than that."

"Could there have been a less depressing way of putting an end to this thing?" Nora asked, and this time her eyes were gentle, large, and vulnerable.

She'd done it, she'd made him feel like a piece of shit.

"Maybe so, Nora. Maybe there was a time when I would have known how to do this better. There was a time, like I say. But we're talking about ages ago."

"I have a hard time believing that," and a tear that had been welling up for a while slid down her cheek. Nora wiped it away with an impatient swipe of the hand.

Why did people stubbornly keep dragging him by the hair into life? Why couldn't they just let him live out these last few years before old age as unhappily as he wanted to, in the vacuum he'd created around himself, and which nothing would ever be able to fill again? That's what he wondered as he gazed into Nora's eyes: Nora, whose only crime had been to cross paths with him.

"You see, Rocco? I know, you've always been perfectly clear with me. You never gave me a lot of illusions, even if I went on hoping. You can hardly blame me, can you? The days went past and I said to myself: just be patient, Nora. It's a relationship built on a sliver of onion skin. Put any extra weight on it, so much as an ounce, and it'll give. The whole thing will break. So I waited. What, is there a law against that? But it's only today, sitting here in front of you at this little café table that I ask myself: what was I waiting for? What are you ever going to pull out of your magic top hat? What could a man like you ever have that would make a woman like me keep waiting? Nothing. Aside from a bed, we never had anything in common. Now I'll feel terrible for a while, for a while I'll spend most of my time at home, I'll cry all over myself for a while. Then I'll go out, go to the hairdresser, maybe even buy a new dress, and I'll start living again. Hopefully without you in my head. But there's just one thing: is there any hope that you'll fuck up for the umpteenth time and they'll transfer you to, oh, I don't know, the farthest Barbagia district of Sardinia?"

Rocco thought it over, reflecting seriously. "Yes. There's always hope of that happening."

"Well, it'll be a fine day when it happens." And at last Nora smiled. "Are you going to finish that?" she asked Rocco, grabbing his glass of iced spritz. Rocco didn't have a chance to answer. The cocktail of aperol, prosecco, and tonic water had already drenched his jacket, while two ice cubes had found their way down the front of his shirt.

"Have a nice day!" Nora exclaimed with a smile and strode, with the victor's posture, away from the café table and the bar on Piazza Chanoux.

Rocco got to his feet. He untucked his shirt from his trousers and let the ice cubes fall to the ground. Two tables away, the only other customer watched him, expressionless. He let a smile appear briefly on his lips, then went back to his newspaper. After all, it's a well-known fact, there's nothing more ridiculous than the misfortunes of others.

Ettore was already out the door. "Should I bring you another, Deputy Chief?"

"Forget about it, Ettore. I need to get back to the office. Enjoy your lunch!"

No surprise, really. Everything had gone exactly as it was supposed to. Everything was predictable. Everything was obvious. Still, somewhere something was bleeding. He just hoped it was a flesh wound, nothing serious, and if it was going to leave a scar, it might be a small one, and practically invisible.

As soon as he walked into police headquarters, Deruta came rushing toward him, loaded down as usual with mysterious papers.

"Deputy Chief? Deputy Chief, excuse me . . ." then he froze. He started sniffing like a bird-dog.

"What the fuck do you want, Deruta? This isn't the day for it."

"What happened to you, sir? You reek of candy."

"A pack of Charms melted in my pocket."

"But you're all wet!"

"You do have a certain spirit of observation. You ought to think about joining the police. Now, is there something urgent you wanted to tell me, or were you only interested in busting my balls here in the middle of the hallway?"

"Yes. About those two men killed on the state highway to Saint-Vincent. Pierron called in. He says he needs to speak with you, and that it's urgent."

"Where is he now?"

"On his lunch break."

Rocco nodded and strode briskly to his office.

HE OPENED HIS ADDRESS BOOK AND SEARCHED FOR A phone number. He dialed it.

"Heddo?" the stuffed-up voice of Caterina Rispoli answered after the third ring.

"Caterì, it's Schiavone."

"Hello, Debudy Jief."

"How are you? Do you have a clothespin on your nose?"

"No, I've got a vever of 102. . . ."

"Great. Could you put Italo on?"

There was a pause. Soon, Officer Pierron's voice rang out from the receiver.

"Yes?"

"I'd recommend you disinfect the receiver first, otherwise you'll get the flu, too."

"Don't worry, I got a flu shot."

"Whatever you say. So, you wanted to talk to me?"

"Yes . . . how did you know I was . . . okay, anyway . . . concerning the other man killed in the crash. Viorelo Midea. All we know is that he was a resident of Bârlad, in Romania. No address here, though. What should we do?"

"We'll send a letter to the embassy, we'll write to the next of kin, what the fuck do I know? Is there anything else?"

"Yes. I found out where he worked."

"And would you perhaps care to tell me?"

"At the Posillipo Pizzeria. I know the place. It isn't far from police headquarters."

"We need to head over there."

"Right now?"

"Of course not, take your time, hold on, let me check my appointment book. How about July 13th? Do you have anything planned?" and he hung up.

CHIARA WAS STRUGGLING TO BREATHE. EVERY TIME she inhaled, the bag over her face clung to her. Her cheeks and her foreheard were covered with sweat, her tears were as sticky as flypaper. She hadn't moved in hours. Her temples continued to hammer her cranium, steady and pitiless.

SHE'D SCREAMED UNTIL HER VOICE WAS GONE. BUT no one had answered, no one had come into the room. Through the cloth she could clearly see that gray wall with the shelves stacked with old objects. Plastic bags, paint brushes caked with tar, saw blades with rusty teeth. She must be in a garage or an abandoned warehouse.

She was starting to remember.

The night before.

She'd gone out for the evening with her boyfriend, Max, and with Giovanna. Alberto, Max's cousin, was going to come down from Turin and join them. They had made an appointment to meet at the pub at seven that evening. From there they were going to go to Sphere, on the road that went up to Cervinia. Chiara didn't really feel like it, she'd have preferred to just be alone with Max but Giovanna was crazy about Alberto. And all day long Giovanna had pestered Chiara in sixteen different languages to spend the evening together. "At least that way," Giovanna said with a smile, "if he jilts me I won't be alone and I can cry on your shoulder." But jilting Giovanna wasn't a material possibility. Chiara knew that, as did Max and half of Aosta. The only one who didn't seem to know it was none other than Giovanna. Five foot seven, a brunette with silky straight hair—not curly like Chiara's who had to spend at least an hour every morning untangling it. If you then added to the silky hair a pair of emerald-green eyes and a body that made the rest of the high school drool helplessly, it truly became difficult to understand the source of that insecurity. That's just the way Giovanna was. Sonia, Paola, and Giovanna—the three prettiest girls in the school—were also the most insecure. She wasn't, though. Chiara was strong. She had a family behind her, a father and mother who loved her and, most important of all, who counted for something in Aosta. Chiara Berguet was a leader. She knew it; when she spoke, all her girlfriends listened. And though her eyes were small and her hair was curly, that hadn't kept her from laying waste to a field of hearts. At school, all the boys were crazy about her, and there wasn't a protest march, a school occupation, a field trip, or even a simple skiing trip that didn't orbit in some way around the second desk, third row, in class Five B.

Alberto had arrived. Handsome, twenty-two years old, with his leather jacket and smooth black hair. He had eyes for no one but Giovanna, even a blind man could have seen it. After three beers and a couple of aperitifs, they'd gone to Sphere. Where they danced and went on drinking like idiots.

And then . . .

What the hell happened? How the fuck much did I have to drink? At least three gin tonics. My face in front of the restroom mirror. Me vomiting. Me vomiting a lot, though. Giovanna talking to Alberto under the strobe lights. Max chatting with a couple of southern bumpkins in their thirties. Who are they? The smoke from the cigarette rises straight up toward the black night sky, chilly and starless. I'm outside the discotheque. I'm smoking a cigarette and everything is spinning. Max takes me home. The key in the door lock. Darkness. But what did I do after that? Chiara, try to remember! Try to remember. Nothing. Pain. Nothing but pain.

Along with the headache, she was starting to feel another source of discomfort. Between her legs.

What is it? A snake? A venomous snake slithering up and down? A snake with red-hot skin? Get this bag off my head. Free my hands! I need to touch myself, scratch myself, grab that snake. It's burning me.

POSILLIPO PIZZERIA WAS ONLY OPEN FOR BUSINESS IN the evening. When Rocco and Italo knocked at the glass door covered with credit card stickers, a man with an enormous belly slowly took shape from the darkness of the interior. He immediately won himself a name straight out of Rocco's

imaginary bestiary—he frequently amused himself by finding similarities and physical affinities between people and
animals. Standing before him was an Atlantic puffin, or *Fra-
tercula arctica*. A prominent nose, a tiny little mouth practically lost in the chubby cheeks, and small eyes set far apart
in the face. The high-arching eyebrows gave him the expression of a beggar in the street. Unlike the northern sea bird,
this man had a straggly little beard that tickled his chin.

"Hi there!" he said as he opened the door. "We're closed
at lunchtime," and he dried his hands on an apron he wore
tied around his waist.

"Schiavone, Aosta police headquarters. Could we talk to
you for a minute?"

"Why, of course. Come in, come in, make yourselves
comfortable," he said as he made way for the two policemen.
"Can I offer you anything?"

The Neapolitan accent seemed more like a costume put
on for his Valdostan customers than an authentic cadence.

"No, nothing, thanks."

"Then at least can I get you an espresso?"

"Sure, thanks."

"Please, make yourselves comfortable at this table, and
I'll be right back. Do either of you smell something sickly
sweet, like candy?"

Rocco and Italo exchanged a glance. Italo spoke up in
response: "A pack of candy melted in the deputy chief's
pocket."

"Ah," said the man and vanished behind a double door
that presumably led into the kitchen.

Rocco and Italo made themselves comfortable at a table in the middle of the dining room.

"But let me tell you, Rocco, just to be clear. More than Charms, it smells like honey lozenges. Strange, what does a spritz have to do with honey?"

"Are you trying to be funny?"

"No."

"You're trying to be funny. And it's not your best move."

"I swear to you I wasn't trying to be funny."

"Then wipe that idiotic grin off your face."

The pizzeria, which had been decorated and furnished by some expensive architect in perfect Amalfi Coast style, lost all its elegance thanks to the hundreds of photographs and posters of S.S.C. Napoli that the proprietor had put up everywhere, undoubtedly without consulting whoever had designed the place. The usual Vesuvius, Pulcinella eating a bowl of spaghetti, and Totò just about everywhere, as well as the jersey from the S.S.C. Napoli 1989–90 championship.

"Speaking of relations with the opposite sex, you didn't go have sex with Caterina while she has the flu, did you?"

"What are you thinking? Of course not. I just took her some chicken soup."

"I doubt that very much."

"Poor thing, she's sick as a dog. The last thing she'd want to do is have sex."

"The last thing she'd want, maybe, but not the last thing you would."

"Here you are, a couple of espressos the way they make them at Gambrinus, on Piazza Trieste e Trento," and the

Atlantic puffin set down the tray with the two demitasse cups on the table. While Italo was sugaring his espresso, Rocco looked at the man: "I'm Deputy Chief Schiavone. Can I ask what your name is?"

"Domenico Cuntrera. They call me Mimmo!"

"Mimmo, so does this place belong to you?"

The man looked around with a glance of satisfaction: "Let's say it does."

"Let's say it does?"

"Yes, it belongs to me and another friend of mine, but he just helped me out with some money at the beginning. But back in the kitchen and serving at table there's no one but Domenico Cuntrera, known to his friends as Mimmo." And he pounded his chest. "So, gentlemen, what can I do for you?"

"Where are you from? And don't tell me Naples, because you're not Neapolitan."

The man smiled. He scratched his nose. "You're perceptive."

"It's my job."

"I'm from further south, Soverato, in Calabria. Ever been?"

"No. But I'll guess that it's better for marketing if you pretend you're from Naples."

"Yeah, a little. But there is one element of truth: I've been an S.S.C. Napoli fan ever since I was a *guaglione*." He made a great show of using the term for "kid" from Neapolitan dialect.

"Who the hell cares?" Rocco retorted flatly, drank half

his espresso, then set the demitasse cup down in the saucer, looked Domenico right in the eye, and said: "Viorelo Midea."

"What has he gotten up to?"

"Does he work here?"

"Yes, sure he does, three times a week he waits tables. What's he done now? *Che fice?*" he asked in Calabrian dialect, having abandoned his Neapolitan accent by now.

"He's dead."

Domenico's eyes opened wide. "He's . . . he's dead? But how?"

"In a crash," Italo specified, after draining the last of his espresso. "Early this morning."

"But he didn't even have a driver's license!"

"There was another guy behind the wheel. A certain Carlo Figus. Ever heard of him?"

"Carlo Figus, Carlo Figus? No, never have. Where did it happen?"

"On the road to Saint-Vincent."

"So, what, they went to the casino?"

"We have no idea where they'd gone. But they had a stolen license plate."

Rocco lit a cigarette.

"Actually, you know . . . there's no smoking in here," but the deputy chief ignored the proprietor of the pizzeria.

"How long had he been working here?"

"For a year. Jesus . . . I'm sorry to hear it."

"I'll bet you are. What can you tell us about him?"

"Little or nothing. I know he lived near here, on Via Voison. He had roommates."

ANTONIO MANZINI

"Was he married? Did he have children? Family?"

"No, not married, and no kids. A few relatives, he must have, because every penny that he earned he sent home."

"Please give me the exact address."

"Via Voison . . . where the gray apartment buildings are. I don't remember the street number, but it's the only one with yellow shutters on the windows. He lived there, on the third floor. With another guy. A Moroccan, I think. But I don't know what his name is. Ahmid something. They're all called Ahmid. But let me tell you, I don't know if he still lives there. That Viorelo was always moving. For two months, I even let him stay in a camper I have in a garage."

"What a fucked-up life," said Rocco.

"Oh yeah. Right you are. What a fucked-up life."

"But do they at least make a decent pizza or is it as fake as Domenico and the espresso that he makes?" asked Rocco as soon as they were back in the car.

"It's not bad."

"Like I'm asking someone from Valle d'Aosta . . . what could you possibly know about pizza? To judge from the building and this SUV parked outside, business is going swimmingly."

"I couldn't tell you. Whenever I've been here, the place is always half deserted."

"Then maybe he's a big winner at the casino."

"So where are we going?" Italo asked, putting an end to the pointless discussion.

"Back to the office. I still need to get lunch."

"At this hour of the afternoon, the most you can hope for is a panino in some café." And Italo put the car in gear.

"Now, that's one thing I miss, a proper Roman *tramezzino*. This is a perfect day for a *tramezzino*. But we'd have to be in Rome to get a decent *tramezzino*."

Oh God, no, thought Italo. Twice weekly he was forced to sit through Rocco Schiavone's usual cantata for nostalgia and tenor.

"The *tramezzino* is serious business, Italo. You can't joke around with the *tramezzino*. White bread, strictly white bread. The fillings allowed are tuna, artichoke, tomato, chicken salad, spinach, and mozzarella. Personally, I don't like shrimp and cheeses and, least of all, prosciutto. If you ask me, the *tramezzino al prosciutto* by rights belongs in the category of the *panino*. And the mayonnaise must be homemade, light and pale yellow. Most important of all, the *tramezzino*—and you need to get this into your head once and for all, Italo—the *tramezzino* must be kept fresh under slightly damp tea towels. If you walk into a café and you find *tramezzini* wrapped in cellophane, turn and leave! Those aren't *tramezzini*. They're corpses, rotting carrion! A proper *tramezzino* must be stored under a damp cotton cloth. Article Three of the Constitution."

"Article Three of the Constitution? What are you talking about?"

"The Roman Constitution. You want me to recite the first two articles? Article One: Don't go around busting people's chops. Article Two: Never drive on the Lungotevere—the riverside parkway that runs along the Tiber—on a Saturday evening. And then, of course, Article Three: A proper *tramezzino* must be stored under a damp cotton cloth."

"Did you write this Constitution?"

THE AFRICAN WAS NAMED ZERSENAY BEHRANE. Zersenay, not Ahmid. And he wasn't Moroccan, he was Eritrean. The building wasn't on Via Voison and the only correct detail was that the shutters were yellow. Zersenay spoke excellent Italian and shared the apartment with two other Eritreans. But he hadn't seen Viorelo Midea in months, didn't know what had become of him or where he lived now. The only thing that Rocco and Italo got out of the visit was a delicious *tsebhi,* the renowned beef and chicken stew with lentils and *teff* bread. They ate it from a common plate with the other tenants. In order to return the hospitality Rocco sent Italo out to get an ice-cold six-pack of beer. When they left the building with yellow shutters, their stomachs were full and their heads were spinning slightly.

"Don't you think it's wonderful that in the middle of the Alps we've had a typical Eritrean meal?"

"True, Italo. It's wonderful."

"The only thing is I have no idea where Eritrea is."

"On top of Ethiopia and underneath Sudan."

"Is Sharm El Sheikh anywhere around there?"

"Jesus, Italo, go take a look at a globe."

• • •

"WE REALLY FUCKED UP BIG TIME."

"True," Rocco replied.

"I've been trying to call Nora since this morning but her phone is turned off. If there's one thing I regret, it's that I ruined my friendship with her for a piece of shit like you."

"Will you do me a favor, Anna?" asked Rocco. "Just call me every day, these compliments of yours are a shot in the arm for my self-esteem."

"If you ask me, the two of us are never going to lay eyes on each other again."

"Okay, even though Aosta isn't exactly a huge city. It could happen. We even live near each other."

"I swear to you I'll turn the other way and cross the street to avoid you."

"Just make sure you look both ways when you cross the street. I wouldn't want to have you on my conscience."

"Go fuck yourself, Rocco."

And Anna hung up.

Someone knocked at the door.

"Who's busting my balls?" he shouted. There was no reply. It was quite likely that this was D'Intino. He got up and went to open the door. The officer from Abruzzo was standing at the door, waiting.

"D'Intino, can't you get it into your head? I ask who is it and you're supposed to answer me. That's what people do when they knock on a door."

"Deputy Chief, this came for you." And he handed a package to Rocco.

"What is it?"

D'Intino leaned forward and sniffed at the deputy chief's jacket.

"Sir, I smell something that's kind of sickly sweet. What is it?"

"Mind your own fucking business. Well?"

"The personal effects of Viorelo Midea. There's a watch, an old cell phone, and a bunch of keys. What should we do with them?"

Rocco turned his back and walked to his desk. "Pierron!" he shouted.

D'Intino looked around. "He's in the other room . . ." he replied.

"Pierron!" Rocco shouted even louder.

"Here I come!" he heard from the far end of the hall. Italo stepped around D'Intino and walked into his office. "D'Intino, why are you standing in the door? Come in or get out!" he said to the officer. Then he turned to Rocco: "Tell me, deputy chief. What is it?"

"This is Viorelo Midea's cell phone. It wouldn't be a bad thing to know what numbers he was calling. Contacts, et cetera. But these keys look like they go to an apartment."

"Yeah, but who knows where it is."

Schiavone's eyes lit up. "D'Intino, get Deruta and both of you report to me immediately!"

D'Intino snapped to attention and hurried off.

"What have you got in mind?" Italo asked Rocco.

"Watch and learn."

Not even two minutes later, Deruta and D'Intino were

standing facing the deputy chief, practically at attention, ready for their instructions. "All right now, friends, officers, partners," Rocco began. "Now, you know that unfortunately Chief Inspector Rispoli isn't well."

"Yes, she has the flu," D'Intino specified with a note of satisfaction in his voice. The De Rege Brothers detested Deputy Inspector Rispoli.

"That's right. Very good. I have a mission I was planning to entrust her with, given her notable deductive skills as well as her steel-trap memory. But now I can't."

"Eh, no, you can't, no," Deruta added, redundantly.

"And so I'm going to entrust this mission to you two. It's a very difficult assignment, and also very, very dangerous."

The two policemen were extremely attentive. Leaning against the bookshelf, Italo was enjoying the scene without any idea of what the deputy chief was driving at. Schiavone was holding up the bunch of keys that had belonged to Viorelo. "Do you see these?"

"Keys!" said D'Intino, practically hypnotized.

"Very good. Keys. They belonged to Viorelo Midea. Now I need you men to find out what door they go to."

The two policemen exchanged a glance.

"How are we supposed to do that?"

"I told you. It's going to be difficult, arduous, virtually impossible. But I'm going to give a starting point. Write this down!"

Deruta rushed over to the desk, grabbed a sheet of paper and a pen and bent over, ready to take down a note.

"What about you, D'Intino, aren't you going to take notes?"

"I remember everything in my head."

"Maybe so . . ." Rocco heaved a dubious sigh and shot a glance at Italo. "All right then, start from a building on Via Kaolak . . . the gray apartment houses. The first ones you run into heading that way from here, with yellow shutters. Viorelo used to live on the third floor there, until four months ago. You start asking around there, talking to the neighbors."

"But can't we go ask the inhabitants of that apartment where this Viorelo lived?"

"No. In fact, if word gets back to me that you've gone and bothered my Eritrean friends, I'll ship you off to Perdasdefogu. You got that?"

"Crystal clear," said Deruta.

"Where's that?" D'Intino asked Deruta, who answered: "Far, far away. . . ."

"All right then, the two of you, go investigate. Without causing a fuss, without being noticed, check all the keyholes. Try the keys, try them, try and try and try again, and when you're done, bring me Viorelo's place of residence!"

D'Intino's eyes opened wide: "What do you mean, bring me?"

Deruta flew into a rage: "God damn it to hell, D'Intino! Bring me is a manner of speech, he doesn't expect you to break down the apartment and haul it over! Forgive him, Deputy Chief." Then, still shaking his head, he finished writing his note.

"Get started right away. This is going to be time-consuming and difficult. Can I count on you both?"

Deruta looked at him seriously: "Certainly, sir. After all, this week I don't even have to put in shifts at my wife's bakery."

"Very good, Deruta."

"Do we still need to report to Rispoli?" Deruta asked as a last detail. He seemed slightly annoyed.

"No," said the deputy chief. "This time, you're reporting directly to me!"

Deruta's chest swelled with pride, and D'Intino smiled, his eyes glistening. They took the keys, saluted, and hurried out of the office.

"If you ask me, they might even succeed," Italo commented.

"So they might. But one thing is certain. They're going to be out on the streets, and we'll be able to work in peace." Just then, the phone rang. "Sure enough, there you go." Rocco lifted the receiver. "Schiavone here."

"This is the chief of police!"

It was Costa.

"Would you tell me what's going on with this fatal crash and this stolen cargo van?"

"Not the cargo van, it's the license plate that's stolen. But it doesn't seem to be of any importance. I'll send up the documents right now . . ." and he gestured to Italo, who rolled his eyes, ". . . and that way you can take a good look for yourself. Excuse me, right now I need to hurry out to Frang . . . *ertz* scary and set off a security diode."

"I don't understand."

"They're waiting for me right now at the reinforced concrete foundations where they found the cargo van."

"Huh, I still didn't get it. Anyway, you get going. And keep me posted. Ah, Schiavone, one more thing!"

"Yes sir."

"Nice notch in your belt. My compliments."

"What are you referring to, sir?"

"You know and I know what I'm referring to. That's a damned fine woman. Take care."

"Just satisfy my curiosity on this. Do you go to the same bakery, too?"

"Exactly!" said Andrea Costa in English, and put down the receiver.

"And I thought that up here in Aosta people basically minded their own fucking business."

"Wrong. One of the many clichés that you southern Italians believe about us in the north. And anyway, thanks for sticking me with having to report to the police chief."

"No, you're going to have Casella do the report. What you're going to do now is take Viorelo's cell phone to someone in the telecommunications police and get him to extract all the numbers."

"All right. Excellent. But one thing. Why are we so focused on these two losers?"

"The license plate, my friend. You don't go roaming around Aosta with a stolen license plate just so you can drive up to Saint-Vincent and get laid."

"And get laid?"

"I'll explain later. Think of it like this: Why would some-one go around with stolen plates but on a cargo van that he actually owns? Because he's afraid of running into a check point? I doubt that. If they stop him, he's done for. No, he's afraid of pictures and footage caught by close-circuit video cameras. Why? What is he planning to do? Certainly some-thing crooked. Do you follow me?"

"Certainly."

"An armed robbery, a burglary. . . ."

"Or maybe they're just afraid of the speed cameras."

"And you think they'd be willing to risk hard time be-hind bars to avoid a 200-euro traffic ticket?"

VIA CHATELAND 92, THE RESIDENCE OF CARLO FI-gus, was a five-story apartment building erected at the be-ginning of the eighties and forgotten in the years since. What leapt to the eye of any casual observer were the stark black horizontal lines at the elevation of each floor, intersecting with other vertical lines which instead descended from the roof, giving the impression that they were many branches of climbing ivy chewed up by the passing winters and by the decades of neglect. But upon closer examination they proved to be cracks, some of them quite deep, that had carried away substantial chunks of plaster. Carlo Figus lived on the third floor. When Rocco and Italo knocked at the door, a woman in a wheelchair answered. Carlo's mother. The face was gray and the hair yellowish with drab roots. She wore purple eye-glasses and an old cardigan with the face of Mickey Mouse stitched over the heart. Her hands were small and white, and she looked at the policemen with large dead nearsighted eyes from behind the thick lenses. "Excuse us, Signora . . . we're from police headquarters . . . may we?" asked Rocco.

The woman nodded her head without adding a word and skillfully reversed her wheelchair, allowing Rocco and Italo to come in. But once they were through the door, they couldn't go much further than a foot or so. The house was packed with clutter. Newspapers, bags full of clothing, pillows, a junkyard filled the rooms almost to the ceiling. What furniture there was lay beneath a tsunami of various objects that seemed ready to engulf the tenants from one moment to the next. There was only a single path through, a trench in the midst of the accumulated garbage, and the woman threaded that path in her wheelchair. She rolled along and waved for the policemen to follow her. Italo and Rocco walked along the ravine through the dump, looking around them but unable to come up with any coherent thought. They'd never seen such a thing, and as policemen they were accustomed to some absurd sights. There was even a fragment of a mannequin: the head and arms poked up from the rubbish. It looked like the victim of a shipwreck gasping before going down for the third time in that sea of detritus. Panes of pebbled glass, the occasional book, a PC, a drum, toy soldiers, and papers—a never-ending expanse of papers and newspapers.

The hallway led to a living room, and there the piles of objects were stacked against the walls, leaving a space of twenty or thirty square feet. Two small armchairs upholstered in green corduroy stood at the center of the clearing, along with an old television set sitting atop what must once have been a bookshelf, and a small table with two demitasse cups and a sugar bowl. All around was a delirious cornucopia of trash that even covered the one and only window in the room: newspapers, plastic objects, a deflated air mattress, a section of a glider seat, vases, bowls, pipes, a clothes rack, even a chalkboard. The stench of mold, mushrooms, and wet dirt blighted the apartment. Italo was already starting to turn pale. Rocco, on the other hand, simply sat down in one of the corduroy armchairs.

"Do you want an espresso?" were the first words out of the woman's mouth. She had a faint voice.

"No, Signora, thanks though. I imagine that you know why we're here."

The woman nodded. "My father came back not even an hour ago. Now he's in his room, asleep. Do I need to wake him up?"

"Absolutely not."

"Who'll pay for it?" the woman asked suddenly, looking at the two policemen.

"Who'll pay for what?"

"For my Carlo's funeral. Who'll pay for it?"

Italo looked at Rocco. "The town administration, Signora. You'll see, we'll do things right. Isn't that so, Italo?"

"Yes!" the officer agreed.

"But who'll help *me*, though?"

To answer that question, you either needed to have the shameless verve of a member of parliament or the sheer brass of a card cheat. Rocco was neither one nor the other. So he said nothing.

"Carlo used to bring home some money when he was working. He was a bricklayer. But he couldn't always find work. Sometimes he could. Sometimes he couldn't. Is there a pension?"

"Is there?" Rocco asked, looking at Italo.

"Yes!" the officer agreed again.

"I've got social security. My own and my Papà's. If we put both checks together, we can come up with 800 euros. But the rent, the utilities. Me and Papà both need our medicines. It's not like I can make it without my medicines. Just take a look." And she pulled up the blanket that was covering her legs. Or really, the two stumps that were all that remained of her legs. "Without my medicines, I can't live."

"No, Signora . . ." said Rocco. "But now we'll be able to do something, won't we?"

"Yes," said Italo. By now, Italo had fallen into a trance, and he could only express himself in sentences of one word. It was up to Rocco to carry on the conversation. He couldn't hope for any more help of any kind from his officer who stood there, stiff and motionless, eyes wide open.

The woman covered herself up again and sat there, staring at her lap. "My legs. They were beautiful once. Do you want to see?" Without waiting for an answer she spun her wheelchair around and pushed it forward toward a heap of curtains, discarded sheets, and bathroom cabinets. She leaned forward and started rummaging through that pile of junk in search of something.

"But seriously, Signora, it's all right, don't worry, we believe you!" said Rocco.

"Yes," said Italo.

"We believe you. Let's talk about Carlo now, please."

"I've got it here somewhere," and without waiting for a response, she rolled out of the living room. Rocco looked at Italo. "Are you starting to feel unwell?"

"Yes."

"Do you need to leave?"

"Yes."

"All right then, go. Wait for me downstairs. We'll see you in ten minutes or so."

"Yes," said Italo. Then, without any change of expression, he did an abrupt aboutface and headed straight for the hallway and the front door. A deafening noise came from another room. Followed by silence.

"Everything all right, Signora?" Rocco shouted. But there was no reply.

Then Rocco heard the front door of the apartment close, which meant that Italo had survived the trek and found his way out. At last Carlo's mother came back to the living room. Empty-handed, though.

"I can't find them anymore. They were my high school photographs. I can't find them."

"Don't worry. You're fine. You're fine just like this."

The woman burst into tears. She turned red and hid her face in her hands. "Why?" she asked, sobbing. "Why?"

But Rocco didn't know what she was referring to. Whether it was Carlo, or her life, her disease, or just the fact that she couldn't find those pictures. Or maybe it was all four things together.

"I was supposed to die first, and only then Carlo could die. That's how it works. That's how life is supposed to be. Children are supposed to die after their parents. But instead, what happened? I'm still alive. Why am I still alive? My father is alive, and my son isn't?"

The deputy chief felt the urge to light a cigarette, but he refrained. A stray spark in that place could set off a blaze of biblical dimensions.

"I really liked Elisa. She was a good girl. And she loved Carlo. But then she went away. And Carlo never found another one like her. Are you married?"

"Used to be."

"It's wrong to break up. If you're together, you can help each other. But not when you're alone. This isn't a world for people to be alone, you know? You should go back to your wife."

Rocco nodded.

"They'll evict me from here, won't they? I'll be evicted, and my father with me," the woman said now.

"Why?"

"Now who'll give me the money for the rent? Who'll pay my bills? And what about when Adelmo dies? Then what will I do? How can I live? Look, all I have are these!" and from the pocket of her cardigan she extracted a handful of crumpled scraps of paper. "Just these."

"What are they?"

"Coupons . . . for Mimmo's pizzeria. And I can't even get there in my wheelchair."

Rocco looked around. He didn't know how things went in cases like these. Maybe she'd get a place to stay in public housing? With subsidized health care? He'd never asked those questions before.

"Carlo managed to bring in at least 800 euros a month, you know?" she said, as she daubed at her eyes and nose with a rumpled handkerchief she kept in the sleeve of her moth-eaten cardigan. "Carlo was a good boy. He was a painter and he knew all about plumbing, too. Do you want to see his room?"

"No, Signora. No." Rocco stood up. "I have to go now, but I promise you that I'll talk about your situation with those who are in charge of these things. I promise."

"Are you leaving already?"

"I have work to do."

"Will you come back to see me?"

"Yes," he promised. What else could he do?

"Maybe if you call first, I can tidy up a little."

Rocco smiled. He reached out his hand to say goodbye to the woman who instead, unexpectedly, leaned her head toward the palm of the deputy chief's hand. Rocco took a deep breath and caressed her hair. She looked up at him, her eyes still wet with tears, and took his hand, pressing it against her cheek. "*Arrivederci*, Signore."

"*Arrivederci*, Signora Figus."

"It's Signora Rosset. Figus was my husband."

"*Arrivederci*, Signora Rosset."

The woman released her grip. Rocco turned and, stepping around mountains of rubbish, found the front door of the apartment.

THE SNAKE HAD TURNED INTO A BILLION CRAWLING ants and Chiara could feel them marching and biting everywhere.

Black ants, red ants, with enormous scissoring mandibles slicing into my flesh. I have them inside me. They run up and down, running and running with matches flaming in their claws, burning and biting. Water. I want water. I need water. I swallow . . . saliva and dust. But I have to be careful not to throw up. If I vomit with my face in this bag, it's all over. What should I do? It hurts . . . it hurts! And it stinks. The bag stinks of mud, mold, and saliva. My saliva. My old saliva. Please, please, please, my hands. I have to scratch, I have to get this bag off my head, I have to breathe. It hurts inside me. Those fucking ants, get them off me! Get them off me! I want ice. Lots of ice on my pussy. Then it would be all better. I want to get up, run and run, run away. Dive into the sea. Under water. Emitting a streamer of bubbles. In the cold water that caresses everything and puts an end to the pain. I'm underwater, letting bubbles stream away. I'm running out of breath. I'm running out of breath. I come back to the surface. I'm suffocating. I need to get this bag off my head. Right now!

She shook her head three, then four times. But it was no good. The bag wouldn't come off. With every sudden movement, it seemed to her as if her brain was slapping like jelly against the walls of her skull.

She started crying again.

Why? Why am I here? What happened to me? What did I ever do?

She wept and talked. And the more she talked, the more alone she felt. And the more alone she felt, the more she wept.

Like Grandma in the coffin. With the handkerchief under her chin. Grandma, what's wrong? Do you have a toothache? Grandma . . . what a big nose you have . . . and what big ears you have . . . now they're going to shut you up in there, Grandma, and no one is ever going to speak to you again. No one will ever pat your cheek again, no one will look at you or think about you. Where have you gone, Grandma?

Was this what it was like to die? She couldn't say. You don't think about that kind of thing when you're not even twenty.

Am I dead? No, I'm not dead. I can feel pain, and behind the bag over my head is a wall, and I'm tied up. No, I'm alive and I hurt all over, and I'm burning all over too. No, I'm definitely not dead.

But you'll die, a hidden voice said to her. A dull, faint voice, soulless, genderless.

You'll die right here, tied up like a salami . . .

I'll die. I'll die here, all alone.

She compressed her lips to hold back her tears. Which were no longer tears of desperation or impatience. They were now genuine tears. And those hurt even more. Because they dripped down her cheeks all by themselves, like a mountain stream.

Chiara is dying, Chiara is dying, that voice said again.
In six days it would be her birthday. She'd be nineteen.

CARLO FIGUS WAS A MISERABLE WRETCH. VIORELO
Midea was maybe even worse. In the cargo van, except for
a few tools, there was nothing of any particular interest.
"Maybe I'm getting it wrong. Could I just be obsessing about
this license plate? You might have been right after all, Italo."

"What do you mean? That they were afraid of getting a
fine?"

"Maybe so. Maybe that's all it was about." Rocco got up
from the desk and stubbed his cigarette out in the ashtray.
"Oh well, see you tomorrow. Are you going over to Caterina's?"

"Yes. Her fever's dropped a little."

"Then she'll be coming back to work!" said Rocco
enthusiastically.

"It's dropped a little, I didn't say she was all better."

The deputy chief grabbed his loden overcoat. "Be well,
Italo."

"I'm coming with you." The officer switched off the table
lamp that stood on his desk.

"Excuse me?" Scipioni had poked his head into the room.

"What is it, Scipioni?"

"I didn't want to intrude. But they sent these down from
upstairs!" and he handed a sheet of paper to Rocco.

"What is this stuff?"

"Those are the numbers from Viorelo's cell phone. Or
actually, they're the last three numbers he called. They're

still working to extract the earlier ones. That guy deleted them all."

"What about the directory? Did he have any numbers in his directory?"

"Only a dozen or so, and they all had Romanian prefixes. If you'd care to take a look."

Rocco glanced at the sheets of paper. Then he handed them to Italo. "Do you mind putting them on my desk? I'll take a look at them tomorrow."

The officer did as requested. "Thanks, Scipioni. Have a good evening."

"Same to you."

THE SUN HAD SET IN A SARABANDE OF PINK CLOUDS, making it clear that the next day it would once again shine in all its springtime potency. The day was coming to an end and the only thing Rocco desired was to wander around Aosta a bit before going home. That was something he enjoyed now that the weather allowed it: wandering aimlessly, with no particular place to go. Just strolling to get a breath of fresh air, look at the faces of the passersby, the dogs trotting on their leashes, stopping to buy a pack of cigarettes from a vending machine. He felt the urge to call Seba down in Rome to see if there was anything interesting going on. Something new that might bring in a little cash. But he was too tired for that. He just wanted to look at the buildings, the Roman arch, and the faces of the people, the sky that had turned so blue it verged on violet, the mountains that, for the first time since he'd come to Aosta, seemed to smile benevolently.

"*Do you know how to do these?*" *Marina asks me.*
She's sitting on the sofa. She has the weekly puzzler in her lap. Now she has this new obsession. She does the diagramless crossword puzzles, the ones without black squares, in case you didn't know.

"*No, I don't know how to do them,*" *I tell her. And it's the truth. The best I can do is connect the dots or ink in the spaces. And read the funny jokes.*

"*Easy to understand. Eleven letters.*"

"*Clear?*"

"*Eleven letters, I said!*"

"*Crystal clear?*"

"*So you're just a dope,*" *she says to me.* "*Eleven letters. It starts with a p and ends with an s.*"

"*Precise, no, that's seven letters. Jesus, Marì, what the hell, I don't know.*"

"*Well, in the meantime I'll do the across clues. Aren't you going to eat?*"

What would I eat? The fridge is empty, there's an echo in there. There's a frozen pasta alla carbonara. "*There's a frozen pasta alla carbonara.*"

Marina shakes her head and in the meantime she writes.

"*Perspicuous,*" *she says, all of a sudden.*

"*What?*"

"Easy to understand was perspicuous. I'm going to write this on my notepad, too. Nice word."

Easy to understand. So what is she trying to tell me? *"So what are you trying to tell me, Marina?"*

"Nothing. Just that it's easy to understand."

Just wait and see, she's referring to last night, to the fact that I didn't come home. But no, she can't be referring to that. She knows it. That's low, material stuff, suitable to me, to someone with both feet solidly planted on the ground, on the floor, not someone who's part of the air, of the things that rise and are carried away by the breeze.

The pan is sizzling now. I toss in the contents of the bag. Steam rises into the air. And with it, the chemical aroma of the carbonara. Even though this yellowish mess is to carbonara as a tractor is to a Ferrari. I know how to make proper carbonara.

"Do you remember, Marì?"

"Of course. . . ."

"The first night. I told you that I was a wizard at making pasta alla carbonara."

Marina laughs. God she has a lot of teeth. The light gleams off them, and if I look carefully, maybe I can even see myself in them. That was the worst carbonara in history. *"You ate it out of pity, didn't you?"*

She laughs and she doesn't answer. That's what she's always done. When Marina laughs, there's no room for anything else. Only the laughter. And fair enough. When you laugh, you laugh and that's that. It's the only moment of liberty left to us, after all. When we laugh.

She's not here now. She's not on the couch anymore. She's

not at my side while I eat my chemical carbonara. Maybe she's in bed, maybe she's in the bathroom, or more simply, maybe she's just gone out.

And it hurts.

Is it the absence that hurts? No. What hurts is the loss. Which is different from absence. The loss knows what it lost. Absence might just be a vague sensation, a silent, disembodied feeling of something that's missing, something that I lack, but that I don't really know anything about. Loss is what I feel, because I know perfectly well. And it's much worse than absence. Because what I knew and held in my hands is gone now. And it's never coming back. It's the same as the difference between Ray Charles and Stevie Wonder. Stevie was blind from birth, Ray went blind. Ray knew what it was to see, Stevie never did. Ray felt loss. Stevie felt absence. Stevie is doing better than Ray ever did. I'd bet my own eyes.

How long had it been since she'd had anything to drink? Time had lost all meaning and direction. There was no longer any light in the room. Her headache had gotten worse. And the ants kept marching up and down. Every now and then they seemed to stop but then they resumed their race.

Pain was added to pain. She'd gotten used to breathing slowly but her body had become a stiff mass pierced by pinpricks.

I need to sleep. If I sleep, it all gets better. If I sleep, I no longer feel the ants, my temples, the fire.

I need to pee. Still? Again?

She *had* to pee. She'd been holding it for a good long while, but now she couldn't resist.

What am I going to do? It hurts too badly. Please, I'm begging you, come take this hood off my head. Come let me breathe. Come give me water.

Thirst and the need to pee at the same time. That had never happened to her before.

I have to pee. Now. Maybe that way I'll be able to drown all those damned ants. Maybe I'll be able to put out the fire. For sure, if I pee I'll put out the fire and I'll drown them.

Go on, do it, what do you care? Pee on yourself, said the little voice. *It'll all be over in a flash.*

Sitting down? I'm supposed to pee on myself sitting down? I'll get all dirty. It'll be such a mess. I can't do it. I really can't just pee on myself.

It was a nightmare that had haunted her nearly every night her first few years of life. She'd wake up with the terror that she'd wet the bed. But that was an ancient thing, done now and finished. She hadn't thought she was going to have to go back there.

Come on, hurry up, it'll only take a second.

She kept holding out. But she wouldn't be able to much longer. She was about to explode, she had to give in.

What about the smell? The smell will kill me!

She compressed her lips and let go. She could feel the rivulet caress her thighs and slowly run down her legs, to her calves and then into her shoes. Then Chiara started crying again.

She peed on herself! She peed on herself! Chiara peed on herself. The voice made fun of her. *Ha ha ha . . . for shame, for shame, for shame, eighteen years old and she pees on herself!*

"Shut up! Shut up!" she shouted through her tears. "Shut up!"

Isn't your mamma here to clean up after you? Where's Dolores? Did they leave you all alone?

"You need to shut up, I told you!" she shouted, her voice choked by sobs.

Now it's all sticky, isn't it? It's sticky and it smells . . . worse than a stable . . . so what are you, a cow?

"Leave me alone," said Chiara in a tiny, faint voice.

I don't want to listen to you anymore. Go away. Get out of here. And the ants haven't budged. They're still right there. And it burns worse than ever. I need to sleep. If I can sleep, the pain will go away, the stench will go away, and I can breathe. And when I wake up again, I'll see Mamma and Papà.

Or whoever it was that brought you here.

Who?

It's not as if you got here under your own steam.

A little water. Just a mouthful. One tiny mouthful and I'd be fine, I could sit here and be a good girl.

Water? You want a little water? How much would you pay for a glass of water? Would you give me your ticket to see Alt-J?

"I'd . . . give you . . . my house. . . ."

Her head stopped pounding, Chiara's eyelids sank shut, and the girl dropped into a deep, dark pit.

TUESDAY

He'd only been sleeping for an hour or so when the intercom crackled. Rocco sat bolt upright, his breath caught in his throat. He looked around wildly. He was in his bed. In his bedroom. At home. Outside the sky was inky black. What could have awakened him? It was the second squawk from the intercom that cleared up his doubts.

"Well, fucking hell . . ." and he looked at the time on his alarm clock. A quarter to one. "Who is it?"

He got out of bed and, walking barefoot, made it over to the intercom. Hiking his boxer shorts up a little, he lifted the receiver. "Who is it?"

"Deputy Chief?" came a man's voice. "I'm sorry about the time. This is very urgent."

"Can I ask who this is?"

"Pietro Bucci Rivolta."

"Who?"

"Pietro Bucci Rivolta. We met at Nora's party."

Oh no, not fucking *this*, thought Rocco. The architect. The one who he'd thought was Nora's lover and who, instead, was Anna's. What does he want? No! Some jealous tantrum at one in the morning was more than he'd be able to take. "What's going on?"

"It's very important . . . I know it's late, and I hate to bother you, but. . . ."

"Well, you've already bothered me. I'll come downstairs. Give me five minutes."

He went back to his bedroom and quickly got dressed.

A DARK WIND HAD SPRUNG UP, DRIVING THE TEMPERА-ture down. The street was deserted. Pietro Bucci Rivolta was bundled up in his heavy jacket. On his head he wore a checkered flat cap. As soon as he saw Rocco come out of the street door, he walked over to him with a broad smile. A sign that he was here on a mission of peace. "Sorry to bother you," he said, extending his hand. Rocco clasped the hand and shook it. "But this is something that's not letting us sleep."

"And now it's not letting me sleep either. What's happened?"

"First of all, how's Nora?"

"Fine . . . I think she's fine." The question had caught him off guard. The architect was certainly taking the long way round. The question he'd been expecting was: how's Anna?

"Give her my regards when you see her. But I came here to tell you something very important. You're a policeman, and a very good one from what Anna tells me . . . do you remember Anna?"

Rocco put a vague expression on his face, as if he were searching in the drawers of his memory for who knows what object he hadn't thought of in years. "Nora's friend? With dark hair, right?" he asked, blushing at the squallid panto-mime he was putting on. But also proud of the fact that Anna considered him a good policeman in spite of everything.

"Exactly. And it was Anna who told me to come see you. I apologize again for the time of night. But I think it's very serious."

Rocco Schiavone looked at the architect. He felt like a piece of shit in the presence of this man—so innocent, dis-tinguished, well-dressed and groomed and easy on the eyes.

"I need to talk to you, Schiavone. Can I buy you a drink?"

"At this time of the night? Where are you going to find anything open in Aosta?"

"Ettore is still open. There was a bachelorette party."

"All right." With a yawn, Rocco bade a farewell to his night's sleep which was now well and truly gone.

"Hold on a second," the architect told him. He turned and waved his hand. The passenger door of a Mercedes parked a short distance away swung open and a girl with long hair got out of the car.

The young woman shut the door behind her and, hands

plunged deep into the pockets of a skimpy short jacket, came walking over to Rocco and the architect. She wore a pair of ankle-height light hikers. As soon as she reached the two men, she smiled. "Hi."

"My daughter. Giovanna," said Bucci Rivolta.

"Hello," Rocco said. And looked at her. She was an unreasonably beautiful young woman. So beautiful that you couldn't even really class her among other beautiful young women. By all rights, she needed to be promoted to the category of Lovely Creatures, superior beings that have nothing in common with common mortals.

"The reason I'm here," said the architect, " . . . is for her."

Ettore had brought over a couple of glasses of white for the grownups and a Coke for Giovanna. It had been the architect's choice to sit at the table farthest from the door. He too was a regular at the café, since his office was on the piazza. And he'd probably even witnessed the jealous scene that Nora had made, if he'd chanced to look out his window. Who could say? Rocco still hadn't entirely digested the idea of the enormous difference between a city of forty thousand and a metropolis of more than four million.

"All right, then, Dottor Bucci Rivolta. . . ."

"Pietro."

"Okay. Pietro, what's happening?"

"Giovanna, tell him."

The young woman, encouraged by her father, took a sip of her Coke, set down the glass, and looked at Rocco with her emerald-green eyes. She brushed back her long smooth hair and started talking. "The fact is, I think there's some kind of problem with Chiara."

"Who is Chiara?"

"She's my best friend. Last night, we went to Sphere."

Rocco's eyes were twin question marks.

"It's a discotheque on the road to Cervinia," Giovanna explained.

"It was me, Chiara, Chiara's boyfriend Max, and Max's cousin, Alberto, who came down from Turin."

Rocco gestured as if to say, "Go on."

"It was a very nice evening out. At the end of it, Max took Chiara home, and Alberto came with me."

Rocco looked at the architect who looked completely unruffled. He was listening to his daughter.

"Alberto took me home and then went over to Max's house to sleep."

"And up to here . . ." said the deputy chief.

"Exactly. Except, today Chiara didn't come to school."

Rocco shrugged. "That happens. Maybe she's sick."

"No. Because today there was a test in Italian. The final. And this year we're having the full array of finals. So Chiara couldn't possibly miss that class. I just assumed she must be sick, myself."

"And did you try calling her?"

"Yes. Her phone has been turned off since last night. So I went over to her house. But she wasn't there."

"What do you mean?"

"Her mother told me that she wasn't there. I asked her

where Chiara was and she told me that Chiara was at her grandmother's."

"I imagine," Rocco said, "that you went and talked to the grandmother as well."

"That would have been difficult," the architect butted in, "since, of Chiara's two grandmothers, one died six years ago and the other one lives in Milan."

"Then maybe she went to Milan. I don't really see the problem here," said Rocco, who was starting to run out of patience.

"She wasn't at her grandmother's in Milan. I called," said Giovanna. She finished her Coke and looked at the deputy chief again. "Chiara's grandmother is at Abano Terme. The housekeeper told me so."

"Well, listen to the way I'm guessing it went," said the deputy chief after draining his glass. "Chiara spent the whole day with her boyfriend, Max, and then dreamed up a lie to tell her mother to keep from getting caught. She turned off her cell phone to keep her parents from catching on and, this morning, that is, a few hours from now, you'll see her back at school, happy and well rested."

"No, sir. Max hasn't seen her since last night either."

"Tell him, Giovanna."

The girl looked at her father. "Chiara has a cell phone, an iPhone. And it has a case with the American flag on it. I saw her cell phone on the table by the front door at the villa when I was talking to her mother."

Rocco nodded. The architect looked him in the eye: "An

eighteen-year-old who's willing to go without her cell phone for a whole day?"

"It's even worse than that," added his daughter. "I know she had the cell phone last night at the club. So she definitely went home. But where is she now?"

"I think there's an answer. And I believe. . . ."

"That's not all," the architect interrupted the deputy chief. He put a hand in his pocket and showed Rocco two colorful stubs of cardboard.

"What are these?"

It was Giovanna who answered the question. "Tomorrow night there's an Alt-J concert in Milan. Chiara and I have been waiting for it for months now. Chiara wouldn't dream of missing Alt-J, for anything in the world. Do you know how long it took me to find these tickets?"

"All they ever talked about was this concert, Dottore. Believe, something's not right. What it is, I can't say. But I don't like this one little bit."

"In other words, you think that Chiara is now a missing person."

"Chiara is a missing person," Pietro Bucci Rivolta agreed, "and her parents won't say anything about it. I've known Pietro and Giuliana for years. I've worked with them, too. I came up with some excuse and dropped by their villa at nine thirty. Pietro wasn't in, and Giuliana wouldn't show her face. I just had a chat with the Filipina. Their daughter's cell phone wasn't on the side table where Giovanna had seen it earlier, and what's more, the Filipina suddenly burst into tears for no good reason. Trust me, Schiavone, something's not right."

The deputy chief stood up from the chair. He took two steps toward the door. He spread both arms wide. "This family. . . ."

"The Berguets?"

"Exactly. Tell me more."

"Pietro and Giuliana Berguet have a daughter, Chiara, and a company, Edil.ber. Construction. Like I told you, I worked on a couple of projects with them. They build houses, apartments, bridges, they even worked on the airport. . . ."

"That was a brilliant piece of work," Rocco commented.

"Right," Pietro admitted. The airport had been a notorious boondoggle, a veritable bridge to nowhere. "In other words, they're builders."

"Are they rich?" asked the deputy chief, who was starting to come up with an idea.

"Very."

That word, "very," was a punch to the gut for Rocco. "In that case." He pulled out his wallet. He paid the check. "What time is it?"

"Almost two in the morning, Dottore."

"All right, let's put this down in the official record," Rocco said with a solemn demeanor. "At two in the morning on a Tuesday in May, Deputy Chief Rocco Schiavone, stationed in Aosta now for nine seemingly endless months, has been saddled for the umpteenth time with an authentic pain in the ass of the tenth degree!" he said in a loud voice. Pietro and Giovanna stared at him in bafflement. They had no way of knowing—as everyone who had worked or had dealings with Rocco Schiavone since September knew—that the deputy chief had a ranking all his own of the things he classified as pains in the ass. That is to say, the duties and run-of-the-mill daily occurrences that upset him and made his life a hell on earth. Italo Pierron was actually collecting an encyclopedic list of them which he planned to post on the glass-front bulletin board at police headquarters to make sure everyone was clear what they should and should not say to the "boss." The hassles or pains in the ass started at the sixth degree and rose from there in a clear hierarchy. Among the least dire, that is to say, in fact, pains in the ass of the sixth degree, there were plumbers or bricklayers who tended never to live up to a promised schedule, the multiple zeroes in bank routing numbers, motorcyclers without mufflers, old pens that were out of ink when you needed to jot down an urgent note. Pains in the ass of the seventh degree included dogshit on sidewalks, losing your place in a book you're reading—back when Rocco still read books, anyway—and the barbarous fad of finger food. Among the pains in the ass of the eighth degree he included letters from the tax authorities—though after Rocco brought a lawsuit against an Equitalia employee, those letters had become rarer than a snow leopard—having to attend Mass, something he hadn't done since 1980, sand in clams, wine that tastes of cork, and having to eat lunch later than two o'clock. The ninth degree included all the furies of the weather, be they tropical downpours, bitter cold, snow, wind, storms, and hail, and then idiots in general, having to go vote, and tooth decay. But reigning sovereign and imperial over all was the pain in the ass of the tenth degree, the worst that life could thrust upon him: the murder case that duty chose to hang around his neck. And on that early Tuesday morning in May, Rocco had just realized that before him there now loomed, immense and undeferrable, a pain in the ass of the tenth degree.

When they stepped outside it had just started raining.

"Do you want a ride home?" the architect asked.

"Home? What for? After all the stable door is wide open and the horses have bolted. Just take me to police headquarters, if you would."

He climbed into the architect's Mercedes and they headed off to the office.

It was 2:12 a.m.

STANDING AT THE DOOR WAS OFFICER CASELLA. A smile appeared on his face the minute he saw the deputy chief: "Sir? What are you doing in the office at this time of night? Couldn't you sleep?"

"No, I couldn't. And if I'm not sleeping, someone else shouldn't be either. Where are Deruta and D'Intino?"

"I have no idea. You sent them out to scour the city, and if you ask me, they're both at home, fast asleep."

"Wake them up and tell them to get moving!"

It wasn't any real need for the comical duo that drove the deputy chief to issue that order; it was a thirst for revenge, plain and simple.

"Should I tell them to come to headquarters?"

"No, tell them that they haven't reported in to me and that what we need now isn't for them to rest, it's for them to get out there and hunt down the thing we talked about."

"I'll convey that message!" Casella said as he picked up the receiver.

ROCCO STRODE INTO HIS OFFICE. HE GRABBED THE phone. After a substantial number of rings, someone picked up on the other end. "He . . . hello, who is this?"

"I hear that your voice sounds much better, Inspector Rispoli. Did you take the clothespin off your nose?"

"S . . . sir, is that you?"

"Yes, it's me, and it's two twenty in the morning. Has your fever subsided?"

"Last night, that is, a couple of hours ago, I had a temperature of . . . 99.5."

"So what is it? Are you taking antibiotics?"

"No, echinacea. I'm using homeopathic treatments."

"Do they work?"

"They do with me."

"I cured a cold once with bryonia. Have you ever tried it?"

"Excuse me, sir, but are you calling me . . . to find out how I'm feeling at two twenty in the morning?"

"Well, what if I was?"

"I'd consider that show of personal concern for my health to be the mark of a person with a badly warped psyche, if you want my sincere opinion." Caterina was starting to wake up.

"It would, wouldn't it? But actually, I'm not. I'm really

trying to track down Italo. Who's right there beside you, isn't he? Tell me the truth."

A series of noises could be heard, followed by Italo's voice rising from the depths like some obscure underwater creature. "Yes, sir. . . ."

"You need to come to police headquarters."

". . . at two in the morning?"

"At two in the morning. Something very bad has happened."

"Am I allowed to know what it is?"

"No. It's a surprise."

"Is this a tenth degree?" Italo asked in a very small voice.

"A full-blown case of it, Italo, my friend, a full-blown case. And there's no time to lose."

"WHAT ABOUT HER GRANDMOTHER IN ABANO TERME?"

"I called the hotel. She checked in alone, without any granddaughter accompanying her, as I expected."

"Yes, but what are we going to do about it at three in the morning?"

Rocco put out the umpteenth cigarette of that nightmarish early morning. "We have two alternatives. It's up to us to decide what to do. The first option is to wake up the judge and request authorization to put bugs on the phones, talk to the chief of police, and then to the family, and thereby expose the girl to an incredible risk because some journalist might happen to be at police headquarters or at the district attorney's office."

"True. The favorite sport at district attorney's offices everywhere is scattering confidential information to the four winds." Italo lowered his head as if trying to come up with a solution. Then he looked up again, with an uncertain expression on his face. "What's the second alternative?"

"We could go pay a call at the Berguet residence."

"At this time of night?"

"At six o'clock."

"And what are we going to do until six o'clock?"

"There are lots of things we can do. But I'd need Caterina. Does she still have a fever?"

"A little. But maybe she could come into the office. What about D'Intino and Deruta?"

"For now, I've just made sure they're awake and I've sent them out onto the street."

"But why?"

"Because I hate them. Now come with me, we need a Trojan horse."

"A what?"

Rocco didn't bother to reply. He'd already grabbed his loden overcoat and now he was striding briskly out of the office, leaving all the lights on behind him. Italo Pierron at this point had no choice but to follow him.

SCHIAVONE HAD PARKED OUTSIDE THE HOUSE IN THE village of Porossan, a little villa that dated back to the twenties. Made of stone and wood and abounding in flowers, it was surrounded by a forest of fir trees. It was covered with climbing wisteria vines that reached up to the second story and, in just a few days, were certain to explode their purple blooms like rifle shots. That was the lovely residence of the Berguet family. Plunged in darkness at four in the morning. Rocco and Italo walked over toward a dark blue car.

"What are you planning to do, Rocco?"

"Is that Giuliana Berguet's Suzuki Jimny?"

"Yes it is, as registered with the motor vehicles department," Italo replied. "Why do you want to know?"

"A very nice little car, too expensive, and frankly not my personal favorite. It's noisy and it doesn't handle all that well. It originated as an off-road vehicle, and, truth be told, it does pretty well on rough terrain."

"Rocco, I don't want to buy the car, I want to know what we're supposed to be doing here at four in the morning!"

Rocco offered no reply and instead simply inserted a pointy metallic object into the car's door lock. He pulled open the door and gave Italo a big smile. "Follow me with the squad car," and he climbed behind the wheel of Giuliana Berguet's vehicle.

As he was heading back to his own car, Italo heard the roar of the Suzuki engine echoing through the silence of the predawn hour. Shaking his head, he thought how clear it was that Rocco Schiavone had missed his true calling.

AFTER A HALF-HOUR DRIVE ON THE STATE HIGHWAY 26, they arrived in Saint-Nicolas. Rocco braked. He got out of the car. He found a rock and smashed the two headlights.

"What, has he lost his mind?" Italo muttered under his breath as he waited in the squad car.

Rocco walked over to the car, wiping his hands.

"What did you just do?" asked Italo.

"Those bastards! They stole a car and left it broken and abandoned twenty miles outside of Aosta. Luckily that friend of yours from the highway patrol, the one who always beats you at pool, what's his name? Umberto?"

"Yes."

"Well, he just happened to find it up here. He got suspicious because someone clearly vandalized it. What a stroke of luck."

Italo looked at Rocco blankly. "But you damaged their car!"

"Aside from the fact that they have insurance, remember, they're wealthy builders. It's just a rough guess, but I'd say that they have the 400 euros to get it fixed. Now, give Umberto a call and tell him the whole story. This Umberto is a smart guy, right?"

"A very smart guy."

"So he knows how to keep a secret?"

"Does he really have a choice?"

Rocco thought it over for a handful of seconds. "No, I don't think he does. There's always a nice busy intersection down in Secondigliano where they need a traffic cop. Come on, give him a call, maybe while you're driving us back into the city. Can you do both things at the same time?"

"I think so. And I believe I could do both things and

chew a stick of gum, too. But I still don't understand exactly what it is we're doing. . . ."

"It's a Trojan horse!" and with that, the deputy chief slipped his hand into Italo's pocket and grabbed his cigarette pack. He grimaced at the sight of it, but lit one anyway.

AT SIX IN THE MORNING, INSPECTOR CATERINA RISP-oli entered Rocco Schiavone's office wrapped in a scarf that left only her eyes uncovered. She smelled fresh and clean, with a whiff of eucalyptus ointment. Standing next to the deputy chief was Officer Scipioni, with a day's growth of whiskers. Italo, on the other hand, was seated at the desk.

"Hello . . ." Caterina greeted the three men in a faint voice.

"You look like a Berber," Rocco said with a smile. "Please, go ahead and take a seat, and forgive me. . . ."

Caterina sat down next to Italo. Rocco didn't miss Italo's apprehensive glance.

He really loves her, he thought to himself.

The deputy chief rubbed his hands together. Outside, a faint morning light was dawning. "Very good, now that we're all here, I need you to listen to me. There's something very grave that only we four in all of police headquarters can know. I have grounds to believe that a young woman named Chiara Berguet has been kidnapped."

Scipioni and Rispoli stared wide-eyed. Caterina even threw in a cough or two.

"But of course, there has been no official report lodged. Now, how was I planning to proceed?"

"I imagine without saying anything to the district at-torney's office or the chief of police?" suggested Antonio Scipioni.

"Very good, Antonio. But if you don't mind, if there's one thing I hate, it's rhetorical questions."

"Did I do that?" the policeman asked with some embarrassment.

"Yes. You just did. In this working group, rhetorical questions are prohibited. But let's go on. Now then, I need you, Caterina, to get me all the information you can find about Edil.ber, the family's construction company. Revenue, payments, financial situation, everything."

Caterina nodded.

"Antonio, stick close to Caterina. In the field. If you need to go pay a call on someone, first inform me, then, seeing that our Inspector Rispoli is feverish, I want you to go instead. Is that clear?"

Antonio Scipioni nodded without speaking. He still hadn't fully understood this thing about rhetorical questions.

"Italo and I, on the other hand, are going to focus on the family. And we'll do our best to come up with something."

"What if a fellow officer starts asking questions?" Caterina asked.

"Invent something, anything. You're working for me. You're trying to find documents for a financial investigation, a tax inquiry. . . ."

"Suspicious transactions for expenditures incurred by the city commission for public works in the context of the special-track financial police operation along the Swiss border?" Scipioni tossed out.

Rocco looked at him seriously. "Strictly in the investigative venue with appropriate jurisdiction, of course!" he added, and then slapped him on the back. "I always knew I could count on you, Antonio! Now I'll send you up some hot coffee and pastries from the café. You can all work right here, out of my office. There's just one thing. That desk drawer that's locked absolutely *must* remain locked, are we clear?"

Rispoli and Scipioni nodded. Rocco reached into his pocket and tapped the joint that he had just taken from that very same drawer ten minutes earlier. He knew that without it, the day wouldn't get started right. Together, he and Italo finally left the office.

HE HAD LAIN IN AMBUSH FOR A GOOD LONG TIME. Motionless, alert. Then he'd seen it stick its head out from the thorn bushes next to the house. A leap, but it had simply been too quick for him, and it had hidden in a crack in the wall, too small for him to get into. He lingered a little longer but he quickly tired of waiting and went to crouch by the soot-encrusted window of the old farmhouse. He'd looked inside. Who knew? Maybe the mouse had hidden inside. But he saw no mouse. Instead, there was a girl. In the middle of the room. She was fast asleep, seated on a chair with her back pressed against a cement column. Her hands were bound to the backrest and her head was black, without eyes or a mouth. He scratched behind his ear. The nettles had stung him as he lay in ambush. He carefully licked his paws, first the left one, then the right. He sniffed at the air. He stood up, stretched, and left that old house behind, trotting briskly across the meadows. The bell hanging from his red collar tinkled with each step. Good for snakes. But it was still early in the season. Snakes come out in summer.

His house was on the other side of the hill. But he didn't feel like going back there. He walked along calmly, brushing past dandelions, gentian plants, and clover. Moss-covered stones surrounded by daisies. There was a bounty of them. He sniffed. A fox had passed by. For sure. Keep an eye out. High above, a crow cawed a couple of times. He had reached the top of the hill. He could see the garden of his house and the roof with the iron rooster. A lizard went darting past ahead of him. He didn't so much as deign to glance at it, while the lizard, frightened, dove under the mossy rock and hid.

Genghis Khan was just one year old. And there was something that was luring him far from there, from the four comfortable walls of home. It couldn't be to hunt that disgusting mouse or to chase after stupid, darting lizards. No. If it hadn't been for this strange sensation, he'd have already caught the mouse at least ten times. Instead it was a somnolence mingled with lust. That May day, Genghis Khan could smell a different perfume. A perfume of flesh and flowers, something wild and something sweet.

"Genghis, where were you? Mamma made you your breakfast!"

The old woman had put the dog's bowl down on the ground. But the dog had no interest in eating. There was that smell, and a pressure right under his tail was pushing him to get moving. With a single leap, he sailed over the fence and headed straight for the road.

"Genghis, breakfast!"

"Can't you see that he smells a she-cat in heat? Let him go. He'll be back when he's sown his wild oats!" the old man replied with a smile as he was putting away the fruit crates in the yard. "Lucky boy!" and he shot a glance at the patch of orange fur that was darting across the lawn.

His wife looked at him and smiled.

THEY'D EATEN BREAKFAST AT ETTORE'S CAFÉ, AND they'd sent a thermos full of coffee and four pastries up for Caterina and Antonio. Rocco had smoked his joint, Italo had smoked a cigarette, and now they were finally outside the Berguet residence. It was twenty minutes to seven. Umberto from the highway patrol was there waiting for them.

"Good," said Rocco as he got out of the car, "it's more credible with Umberto here, isn't it?"

"Sure," Italo muttered. He'd left the car windows open. The upholstery reeked of cannabis. "What's up with the joint?" he asked Rocco.

"It's good for me. It opens up my nervous system, it puts my heart at peace with this piece-of-shit day, and it gives me the strength to go on living. Is that enough?"

"Yes," Italo replied.

With long strides, Rocco walked over to Umberto. He shook his hand and asked: "So you've been fully briefed?"

"Certainly, sir."

"Do you have Berguet's phone number?"

"Yes."

Rocco handed him his cell phone and the registration of the automobile. "Here you go. Now, if you would, let's start our little skit." And the three men headed over to the front door.

A good solid minute went by before someone came to answer the door. A Filipina in a white-and-red striped uniform, not much more than three feet tall, looked out seriously at the three policemen.

"What is it?"

"Is Signora Giuliana Berguet at home?"

"What do you want?"

"Police. We need to talk to her."

"Right now, Siniora is sleeping."

"You go and wake up?" Rocco asked with a smile.

"I don't know, because if she is sleeping, maybe she not want to be waked up."

Rocco heaved a deep sigh. "Let me have first and last name?"

"Of Siniora?"

"No, of you! Your name!" and he pointed to her.

"Dolores."

"Dolores, go wake up the Siniora. Don't you see that the Siniore, by which I mean me, is starting to get really really impatient?"

The Filipina seemed to reel slightly, then she stepped to one side and let the policemen through.

"Wait here," said the housekeeper, and her sandals flapping against her feet, she toddled off through a door.

The architect's touch in the furnishings could be seen everywhere, even in the scent of cinnamon that wafted through the air. A classical, slightly heavy-handed style, made up of fabrics, cloth on the walls, brocades, gold-leaf mirrors, and large Persian carpets. A revisitation of the Grand Hotel des Bains, but still, it had its allure. On the walls, a succession of early nineteenth-century landscapes, some of them so darkened by the passage of the years that it was no longer possible to distinguish colors or brushstrokes. Over the glass door to the living room, a sixteenth-century nativity enjoyed pride of place, and no doubt it alone was worth more than the whole villa.

Italo and Umberto looked around. "Not bad, eh?"

"I'd have to agree," said Rocco. "A little overdone, but you can see why."

"Are those marble floors?"

"Venetian marble," Rocco specified.

"What about that?" Umberto pointed at an inlaid desk.

Rocco took a closer look. "That's a bureau Mazarin. It might be walnut. And it looks like an ivory inlay."

"Expensive stuff?"

"Probably less than 20,000 euros," said Rocco smugly, as the two policemen gulped back their saliva.

"How do you happen to know these things, Deputy Chief?" Umberto asked.

"My wife used to like them."

"And now she doesn't like them anymore?" the highway patrolman asked innocently. Italo jabbed an elbow into the man's ribs. Umberto failed to understand the reason why, but refrained from asking any further questions.

Dolores came back, glaring sullenly at the policemen. "Siniora arriving now."

"Thanks, Dolores. All the best," and the woman went through a swinging door that must have led to the kitchen.

"Deputy Chief," Italo began—in the presence of other policemen he used more formal terms of address—"why are we doing this?"

"Look around, catalogue details and impressions, and listen carefully. That's the work we need to do."

Distractedly, Rocco walked over to a wood-and-marble credenza set directly across from the front door. He pulled open a drawer. Inside he found Chiara Berguet's cell phone, the one with the American-flag case. In a silver platter, there was some change, a bunch of keys with a fob in the shape of the letter M and a curious plastic plug, a gilt paperweight, a little bundle of rubber bands. On the shelf, in order, next to a cordless telephone, were a stack of bills, a typewritten sheet of paper signed by the mayor of Aosta, and a notepad.

Italo watched his superior officer rummage around in those objects. He thought he saw Rocco take a pale green scrap of paper off the notepad and stick it in his pocket. Just in the nick of time, because Giuliana Berguet appeared at the living room door. Skinny and tall, curly hair, linen trousers and a long-sleeved T-shirt. She was smiling but beneath the layer of makeup that she'd just put on, it was possible to glimpse a hundredweight of circles under those eyes. The eyes themselves were dead, scared, and they pointlessly tried to give themselves the confident, unruffled demeanor of the grand mistress of the castle. Her cheeks were ashen, their only color the synthetic hue of the foundation, and slightly hollowed and haggard. At a rough guess, she hadn't slept in many dozens of hours, and looked as if she might faint from one moment to the next. "Gentlemen, what can I do for you?"

"Deputy Chief Rocco Schiavone, Aosta police head-quarters." And Rocco extended a hand in Umberto's direction. Umberto handed him the registration from the car. "Do you own a blue Suzuki Jimny with license plates . . ." and here he read from the registration, "DD 343 AF?"

The woman nodded. "Why?"

"Our officer from the highway patrol found it . . ."

"Where did you find it?"

"Up at Saint-Nicolas . . . a little the worse for wear," said Umberto.

"But how could that be?" asked Giuliana Berguet. "I hardly ever use the car but . . . my brother-in-law Marcello does, and I'm sure that yesterday he parked right outside in the street. . . ."

"And this morning it was all the way over in Saint-Nicolas," said Rocco. "Now we have our suspicions. . . ." and he let the phrase linger in the silence of the hallway as he carefully observed the woman's face. She was swallowing and clutching her left hand so tightly with her right hand that she was cutting off the circulation. "What . . . what do you suspect, Deputy Chief?"

"That this car might have been used in an armed robbery carried out last night at a jeweler's down in the city." Giuliana nodded. And it seemed to Rocco that she heaved a sigh of relief. "Is your husband at home?"

"No!" Giuliana replied as promptly as a little kid shouting, "Tag, you're it!" And as if determined to contradict her, a man emerged from the other side of the hallway. Rocco, Italo, and Umberto turned to look at him. "Who are these gentlemen?"

"They're from the police," Giuliana hastened to reply. "They found the car in Saint-Nicolas. It seems that last night someone stole it to use it in a jewelry store robbery."

"And what makes you think so?" asked the man, turning his eyes to the policemen. Rocco took a step toward him: "Deputy Chief Schiavone, Aosta police headquarters."

"My pleasure. I'm Marcello Berguet. I'm the Signora's brother-in-law, her husband's brother."

"Ah, so you're the one who used the car last night?"

"Certainly, I almost always use it. And I'm sure that I parked it in the street outside last night. Aosta may have a lot of problems, but parking isn't one of them . . ." he said with a smile. "Anyway, what makes you so sure that the car was used in an armed robbery?"

"A closed-circuit video camera filmed the whole robbery. They plowed into the plate glass window using the front of the Signora's car."

"Well, how do you like that?" said the man. "Well, we

were all here last night. And I swear that I parked it right downstairs in the street."

"I know that," and Rocco smiled. "I know that, and I don't have any suspicions that you might have been involved in a jewelry store robbery. In short, I hardly think you need to fence stolen jewelry, do you?"

Giuliana and Marcello both laughed, though their laughter was forced. "No, no, I'd say not."

Rocco looked over at the highway patrol officer: "Thank you for your help, officer, you may go now!"

Umberto, faithful to the script, gave the deputy chief a snappy salute, smiled at Giuliana and Marcello, and then left the house.

"In any case," Schiavone resumed, "Signora, I'm going to have to ask you to come with me to police headquarters. There are a few boring routine procedures we're going to have to get out of the way. You've been the victim of a felony crime, after all. I hope to make you waste as little time as possible."

"But, you understand, I have something to. . . ."

Giuliana looked over at her brother-in-law, who froze in place, unsure what to do next.

"No, I can't come with you. I mean to say, first I have some prior commitments. Can I . . . can I catch up with you down there a little later?"

"Signora Berguet," Rocco said patiently, "I'm not inviting you to a cocktail party. This is something very different, let me assure you."

The woman chewed her lip. Then she looked at the

policemen. "I can't come. I have a very important appointment. At ten o'clock."

"We'll certainly be done by then. Trust me," the deputy chief insisted.

"I . . . I have to stay at home, is that clear?" the woman said. And she sat down on a Louis Something-Or-Other settee that creaked under her feather weight.

"Why is that, Signora? Are you not feeling well?"

Giuliana put her hands over her face and started shaking her head. "No, I'm not feeling well. I'm not feeling well at all!" It was a cry of despair, heartbreaking, so piercing it raised goose bumps. Her brother-in-law hurried to her side and tried to comfort her, but Signora Berguet, in the throes of a burst of rage, threw her head back and glared at Rocco, her eyes red with weeping. "I'm only leaving this house with my lawyer. I'm calling him this minute and I'll ask him if this is normal police procedure. Barging into a person's home at seven in the morning to drag them off to police headquarters! I'm the victim here, let's make that clear! My car was stolen, it's not like I stole it myself! Why would I have to come downtown? No, Deputy Chief, I'm not coming. Go ahead, file a criminal complaint, handcuff me if you must, but I'm not willingly setting foot outside this house!"

Rocco smiled. He gestured to Italo to head toward the front door. He seemed satisfied. "Whatever you say, Signora Berguet. I can see that you're on edge and tired and I don't want to make life any harder for you than it already is. Can't I do anything to help you?"

Rocco's question fell into a pool of the utmost silence.

Italo had opened the front door and was standing on the threshold, waiting for his boss and looking back at Giuliana, who was in turn looking at Marcello, who was watching Rocco. The deputy chief had the feeling that the woman was about to shout: "Yes, you can do a great deal for me! Bring me back my daughter!" Instead, it was the brother-in-law who replied: "Thanks, deputy chief, but there's nothing you can do. Believe me."

Suddenly the phone rang and the sound rang through the whole house. Giuliana Berguet started as if someone had touched her with a live electrical wire. She was staring at her brother-in-law, who mopped the sweat off his lip. Imperturbably, Rocco observed them. At the third ring, the woman stood up: "Excuse me," she said, but Rocco was faster. He handed her the cordless: "Here you are, Signora."

Giuliana grabbed the telephone, which Marcello in turn tore from her hands and, finally, on the fifth ring, answered, turning his back to them and striding out into the hallway, toward the living room behind the glass doors. "Excuse me," he said. But Marcello never reached the living room. He suddenly turned around and shouted into the receiver: "No, I'm not interested in a single contract for electricity water and gas!" and then hurled the phone into a cozy, upholstered armchair. "These call centers . . . they're intolerable, don't you find?"

THE SKY HAD CLOUDED OVER. ITALO WAS DRIVING IN silence and Rocco had already lit a cigarette. "Don't tell me that it's starting to rain again?"

"Eminently possible," Italo replied.

They drove through the intersection, leaving the Berguet home behind them. On the side of the road, at the intersection with the state highway, Umberto was waiting for them on his motorcycle. Italo pulled over. Rocco rolled down his window. "Electricity water and gas?" he asked.

"Nothing better occurred to me." And Umberto gave the cell phone back to the deputy chief.

"It's fine. Thanks, Umberto. You were very helpful."

"Glad to be of service, sir. If you need anything else, give a call whenever you like. Ah. And what about the Signora's car? Shall we take care of it?"

"Yes, if you could. Thanks."

Umberto smiled and revved the BMW motorcycle: practically popping a wheelie, he vanished around the curve.

"Not at all bad, this Umberto."

"We went to high school together."

"And what do the two of you do?"

"Nothing much. We play a few games of pool now and then. We're both fixated on sports betting. He follows the soccer championships, basketball, skiing. . . ."

"And do you win?"

"So far, we're up by 400 euros. Not bad, eh?"

Rocco made a face.

"You feeling pessimistic about this, Rocco?" Italo was no longer talking about the online sports betting site, SISAL.

"Does that strike you as a normal reaction for a normal phone call? And does it seem to you that the Signora had a normal reaction at being asked to come down to police head-quarters? It doesn't strike me as good at all."

"So you're saying that her daughter . . . ?"

"No doubt about it."

"EDIL.BER BELONGS TO PIETRO BERGUET, WHO OWNS a 75 percent share. The rest of the company belongs to his brother Marcello, who doesn't actually work there, though. He's a math teacher at Aosta's scientific high school. The company builds apartment buildings and private houses but also larger public works. They were one of the contractors who worked on the airport, built a highway interchange, and renovated Fort Bard . . . they're competing for some public works the regional government is getting ready to assign." Caterina Rispoli reeled out like a hypnotic mantra all the information she'd been able to assemble in a few hours' work. "Their total annual profits are twelve million euros, they have twenty full-time employees plus an assortment of specialized workers under contract. Bricklayers, carpenters, and so on."

"In other words, they've created jobs and prosperity for a fair number of people," Antonio Scipioni concluded.

"Yes, but I found a couple of articles from the past few months," Caterina went on. "Things aren't actually going all that well."

Rocco stepped away from the window. He was observing the black clouds that were gathering in the sky over Aosta.

"What do you mean?"

"The papers are talking about a downturn. Workers locked out of the plant, delayed paychecks, the usual cheerful array of things."

"And then what happened?"

"Then apparently everything turned out for the best, or at least I didn't find any more articles."

"I need to go have a chat with this Pietro Berguet. Does anyone have a suggestion about how to do it?"

"Could you dream up another criminal complaint like you did with his wife?" Caterina suggested, and then blew her nose into a Kleenex.

"Or else a regular audit?" asked Antonio Scipioni.

"An audit of what?" Schiavone objected.

"I've got it!" Italo shouted. "Carlo Figus, the worker killed in the crash the other night. Let's say that we have indications that he worked for them, and then we can just go and ask a few questions."

"That's a good idea. Nice work, Italo." Then he shot a glance at Caterina Rispoli. "Inspector, if you're not feeling up to it, you can certainly go home."

"No no, I'm better. And after all, to tell the truth, staying home bores me." She shot off the first smile of the day, which illuminated her face. Even in this state, brutalized with the flu and a cold, Caterina Rispoli was a purebred, an outstanding woman. With the sweetness of a mother and the diabolical mischief of an older sister.

"Sure you're not making a foolish mistake?"

"Positive, Deputy Chief."

"Speaking of foolish mistakes. An hour ago we heard from D'Intino and Deruta," said Officer Scipioni.

"And where are they?" asked Caterina.

"They have a key and they're trying to figure out what door it goes to," Rocco explained.

Caterina's eyes opened wide. "A needle in a haystack?"

"Worse. The hair of a cow in a stampeding herd," Rocco corrected her. "And what did the two of them want?"

"Nothing, you know how much they hate me. They wanted to talk to you and they wouldn't tell me anything. He said that you ordered them to report only to you."

"As per their instructions. Okay, who cares about the De Rege Brothers. Shall we go, Italo?"

"Where?"

"To the offices of Edil.ber, what's the matter with you, feeling sleepy?" He stood up. He grabbed his loden overcoat. He stuck a hand in the pocket. "Ah, Caterina. Did you ever play this game at school?" He handed her a scrap of paper.

"What game, sir?"

"With a pencil? You rub the edge of the graphite point over it, and a phrase emerges?"

"Certainly, me and my friends would do it all the time in school. We'd write secret messages on a sheet of paper and throw it away, keeping the sheet of paper from underneath so that the pen left a deep but invisible impression. Then if you rubbed a pencil on top of it, you could read it."

"Very good. Would you take a look at this and see if there are any secrets on this little sheet of paper?"

Italo recognized it. It was the scrap of pale green paper that Rocco had taken off the notepad at the Berguet residence.

Caterina blackened it with her pencil. "Huh . . . there are some numbers. And there's a word . . . hold on," she squinted to see better. "Huh . . . Deflan, I think it says Deflan."

"What's that?"

"Hold on . . ." The inspector hurried over to Rocco's computer. She started typing. "It's a pharmaceutical. Let's see, it's an anti-inflammatory. Used to treat rheumatism, gastric inflammation . . . it says here: treatment of pathologies of inflammatory origin."

"Okay, well obviously the doctor must have prescribed it for the woman or her husband," said Italo.

"What about the numbers?"

"Nothing that resembles a phone number."

"Oh well, that was a dud. Let's go, Italo."

THE OFFICES OF EDIL.BER WEREN'T FAR FROM THE airport. They were in a modern office building made of glass and mirrors. A large white gate led into the company parking area. Rocco and Italo left their car there. They started walking toward the central building when the deputy chief noticed something on the metal fencing. A white banner fluttering in the wind. He walked over to it and unfurled it to show Italo. It was just a tattered section of torn protest streamer. It could be read clearly, "We've Had It With . . ." and then, "Our Jobs!" At the end of the phrase were the initials of a trade union. That was all that remained of a recent demonstration.

The two policemen went back toward the building made of glass and mirrors, opened the door, and entered the offices of Edil.ber.

Facing the front door, they found a panel that indicated the location of the various offices with an array of arrows. Executive offices were on the second floor.

When the elevator opened, they found themselves looking out into a small round lobby. On the white walls hung photographs of projects undertaken by the company. Hangars, bridges, buildings. And sketches of projects. The sound of footsteps was muffled by the navy-blue wall-to-wall carpeting. A powerfully built woman who looked about sixty came walking toward him.

"May I help you?"

"Deputy Chief Schiavone, Aosta police headquarters."

The woman gulped.

"Who's in charge here?"

"Who's . . . Dottor Berguet. Pietro Berguet. Can I ask the reason for your visit?"

"No, you cannot. Where is he?"

The woman pointed at a door with "President's Office" written on it, in fire engine red.

"Will you announce us or shall we just go on in?"

The secretary snapped out of it and went to knock on the door. She opened it slightly, stuck her face in, said something, and turned to look at Rocco and Italo.

"Go right in," she said, and stood aside to let them pass.

INSIDE THE ROOM WERE TWO MEN. ONE WAS SITTING on a white leather sofa, the other stood in front of the plate glass window and was nervously smoking a cigarette. Rocco took a wild guess and turned to the man who was smoking. "Hello, Schiavone, deputy chief of police, Aosta."

The man standing by the window came toward him, stretching his mouth into a ceremonial smile. His face was tense, he had dark circles under his eyes, his tie was undone and, though he clearly wore a first-rate suit, it was rumpled and creased. When he was relaxed and rested, he was probably a handsome man, with light-colored eyes and a dark, curly head of hair. But now he looked more like a heavily used cleaning rag. "I'm Pietro Berguet," he said, crushing his cigarette out in the ashtray that already contained a small mountain of crumpled butts. He extended his hand, and Rocco shook it. His palms were sweaty. "And this is Dottor Cristiano Cerruti, vice president of the company," he said, pointing to the man sitting on the sofa. Cerruti didn't even bother to stand, limiting himself to a faint, desultory smile. He wore a well-tended little beard, the kind that requires hours to keep neatly trimmed and aligned, like a grass tennis court at Wimbledon. His suit, too, needed pressing. "What can I do for you, sir? My wife told me that you stopped by my house this morning. Is this still about the stolen car?"

"No. At the police department we're masters of multitasking, aren't we, Pierron?"

"Certainly."

"Just think, Dottor Berguet, my officer here is capable of driving, making a phone call, and at the same time chewing a stick of gum."

Pietro Berguet looked at Rocco Schiavone as if he were a visitor from another galaxy.

"And since we're masters of multitasking, we have more than one problem to solve. Now then . . ." Rocco reached out a hand and Italo handed him a sheet of paper. "Did Carlo Figus work for you?"

Pietro Berguet thought it over for a moment. "Hold on, just like that . . . I wouldn't really know. Shall I ask human resources?"

"If you would."

"But why do you want to know?" asked the president as he picked up the telephone that sat on his glass desktop.

"He's been in a crash and now he's dead. It happened last night. On the road to Saint-Vincent."

Pietro Berguet opened both eyes wide. "I'm sorry to hear that. Fabio? Listen, does Carlo Figus work for us?" He sat and listened in silence. "Thank you . . . thanks, Fabio." And he hung up.

"Yes, Carlo Figus worked for us for a couple of years, from 2001 to 2003. But this is a terrible thing. How did it happen?"

Rocco looked at Italo. He was tired of talking and he left the job to his subordinate. The officer began: "The accident was caused by old tires. The van had a blowout and slammed into a pair of trees. He was killed instantly."

Pietro Berguet nodded. "Oh, *Madonna mia*."

"Right. It was our duty to inform you."

"But he doesn't work for us anymore," Cristiano Cerruti broke in, still sitting with his ass parked on the sofa. "So technically we could say it's no longer any of our concern. Please convey our condolences to the family."

"Forgive me, I don't remember your name."

"Cristiano Cerruti. Now would you care to explain why you're asking all these questions about that poor guy?"

"Certainly. Of course. Since he had a stolen license plate on the van and a criminal record, I'm investigating the man. Do you think that's all right, or should I have come to ask your permission?"

At last, Cerruti snapped to his feet, as if instructed by some internal command. "Do you have a warrant from a judge?"

Rocco burst out laughing. "Do you hear, Italo, how much trouble the television causes?" and then he focused on Cerruti's face: "I don't need one. You strike me as tense and a little on edge, Dottor Cerruti. My own experience suggests that you'd be well served by taking a seat and counting slowly to ten." Then he addressed the president of the company: "Dottor Berguet, do you mind if I go and have a brief chat with this Fabio in personnel?"

"Why of course not; it's Fabio Limetti," said Pietro with

a sigh of relief, clearly glad to see that the two policemen
had decided to be on their way. "Be my guest, absolutely,
let me ask my secretary to accompany you." He opened the
door. "Ines!" he called, and the dumpy woman in her early
sixties reappeared in the hallway. "Please see the gentlemen
down to Limetti's office. I'd appreciate it, thanks."

The woman nodded and extended her arm, pointing the
opposite way from the elevator. "Gentlemen, if you'd care to
follow me."

"Are you planning to stay in your office, Dottor Berguet?" asked Rocco.

"Certainly. Of course. If you need anything at all, you'll
find me here."

"What about you, Dottor Cerruti?"

"For sure," the man replied, sitting back down on the
sofa.

"Good. I have a feeling we'll be seeing each other again."
And he said it very seriously. He wanted it to sound like a
threat. And in fact, a threat is what it sounded like.

FABIO WAS A YOUNG MAN IN HIS EARLY THIRTIES,
fair haired, pale, with a pair of enormous blue eyes without
eyelashes, which gave him a slightly stunned, innocent expression. He was calm and cooperative, with a small, faint
voice, almost a woman's voice. He handed over the file with
Carlo Figus's pay stubs and even left the two policemen
alone in the room to read through the files.

"But what are we looking for?" Italo asked.

"You just continue to keep an eye on the parking lot. If Berguet leaves, we'll go after him." Rocco was leafing through the papers. "So, where is the blond boy? I have a couple of questions to ask him."

As if to grant the deputy chief's every wish, Fabio opened the door with a paper cup in one hand. "Ah, my good Fabio, you're exactly who I need right now. I see here that the payroll accounts are handled by the Vallée Savings Bank."

"Certainly. It's the bank that we've always worked with."

"Excellent. And are the company's accounts all there?"

"There and at the Banca Nazionale del Lavoro. But mostly there. The engineer also has his personal account there."

"What about you? Where do you keep your savings?"

"Me what, Dottore? With what they pay me, it's a miracle if I make it to the end of each month."

Rocco and Fabio enjoyed a hearty laugh and gave the matter no more thought. Italo continued to keep an eye on the parking lot. "But are things going better now?"

Fabio looked at the deputy chief. He hadn't understood the question. Rocco clarified the concept. "I mean, are things going better here at Edil.ber? Is there enough money now?"

"Ah!" Fabio said, his smile returning. "Yessir, much better now. For the past month now, the payments have been regular and reliable. Certainly, it happens from time to time, a shortage of funds, a lack of liquidity, delays in payments, suppliers knocking at the door. But now it seems that things have leveled out."

"In other words, you're receiving your paycheck."

"Well, I did last month. Let's keep our fingers crossed for this month, too," Fabio replied, in his mezzo-soprano voice.

Then the deputy chief got to his feet. "Thanks, Fabio, you've been helpful. Extremely helpful."

"NOW I WANT YOU AND ANTONIO TO TAIL PIETRO Berguet and the other guy, with the trim little beard."

"Cerruti?"

"That's the one. Make sure you don't lose them."

Italo shifted to a higher gear and accelerated. When they entered Aosta they were doing sixty. "Should I leave you at headquarters?"

"Yes."

"But we're not going to inform the judge?"

"When the time is right. And time, my friend, is not on our side."

Not even three minutes later, the squad car screeched to a halt in front of police headquarters. Rocco got out. There was a clap of thunder and it started pouring down rain, as if a giant hand had turned the shower knob. "Fucking hell . . ." muttered Rocco, as he ran to take shelter in the front door. Casella was still standing in the entrance. "But isn't anyone going to take over your shift?"

"Sure, another guy is coming down, a guy from Naples. Then I can knock off. Ah, deputy chief, D'Intino and Deruta came by. But there's no news."

"What did you tell them?"

"What you told me to say, sir. To just keep searching without ever stopping."

"Did they look tired?"

"Tired? They looked like two of those thingamajigs, there, what do you call them? The little bears with black circles around their eyes?"

"Raccoons?"

"Exactly. A couple of raccoons, considering the circles they had under their eyes." And Casella burst into laughter, confident that he was on comfortable terms with the deputy chief. But Schiavone shut down that illusion abruptly: "Casella, what the fuck do you have to laugh about? Are you interested in being sent to keep Deruta and D'Intino company?"

"No, sir."

"Then cut the laughing." And he left him standing there at the entrance.

As he went up the stairs he ran into Scipioni, who was hurrying down them. "I'm going to join Italo, deputy chief."

"Good, but make sure you take two different cars. You need to be able to move independently. Give each other the relief and stay in constant contact with me or Inspector Rispoli."

"Yessir. And thanks."

"For what?"

"For the trust you've placed in me. Desk work really

doesn't suit me." And he vanished, with a handsome smile on his lips.

When Rocco opened his office door, Caterina Rispoli wasn't there. He took advantage of the opportunity to get another joint out of the drawer. Then he picked up the phone. "Architect? This is Deputy Chief Schiavone."

"Yes, sir, deputy chief. . . ."

"What school does your daughter attend?"

"The scientific high school on Via Cretier. Why?"

DID I SLEEP? DID I DREAM? WHERE AM I?

Still here. Still bound to the chair, still with a hood over her head. She inhaled all the air she could. She still wasn't used to the stench of that dark, filthy fabric that clung to her face. She craned her neck, pushing back with her head. The back of her head touched the column against which the chair rested. That it was a column was something that had already become clear to her. As was the fact that she was bound to a chair. She continued to twist her neck.

If you bang your head harder against the wall, you can crack it open, and you'll be done with all this misery.

The little voice again. But Chiara was determined to pay it no mind.

What about down below? Does it hurt? Does it hurt?

Not as bad. Down below it was hurting a lot less. She could still feel the pain, but like a memory of what it had

been before she fell asleep. How many hours had it been?
She couldn't say.

I can see the metal shelves. All of that rusty junk on
them. Now there's a little light.

She rested the back of her head against the cement
column again and then let her head fall forward. Her face
slammed against the rough cloth, which no longer followed
her movement. She tried again. No good. The bag remained
immovable.

It's hooked onto something. It's stuck . . .

She tried once again to press the back of her head
against the hard cement. Then she snapped forward. The
hard, smelly bag wouldn't budge.

What is it stuck on? A nail? Some snag? Yes! Yes!
"Yessssss!"

The first piece of good news.

I just need to slip down lower. As low as I can go. That
way I can get it off my head. That way I'll be free to move.

She needed to try as hard as she could. It would be hard,
but she could do it.

She clenched her abdominals and pushing back slightly,
tried to lower her torso. She could feel her face rubbing
against the canvas. A good sign. That mean her body was
moving while the hood remained stationary.

She arched her back, tugging hard on her stomach muscles. She managed to gain a few inches, but it still wasn't
enough.

Lower. She needed to slide even lower.

She pushed her chin down as far as she could. She glimpsed a piece of silver duct tape around her chest.

That's what's fastening me to the chair! The duct tape. Over my tits! If I can just get the duct tape over my breasts . . . there! I did it! I did it! It's looser now and I can move to one side. And get lower. And then I'll be able to get this stinking bag off my head.

But make sure you don't sweat.

The little voice was back now.

If you sweat, everything's going to get sticky and then nothing will slide, you'll be jammed in place!

"I'm not sweating! I'm not drinking and I'm not sweating," she shouted.

What's that got to do with it? You peed in your pants, and now for all you know, you're sweating.

"Go fuck yourself!"

Don't sweat . . .

The voice was right. She had to keep from sweating! If she sweated, her T-shirt would stick to her skin, it wouldn't slip anymore, and the duct tape would stay there, over her breasts, nailing her to the spot like an entomologist's insect pinned in place. She had to be very careful. Move slowly, without any sudden jerks.

You're thirsty, and if you get too thirsty, you'll fall asleep. And then you'll die, won't you?

"Quit messing with me!" she shouted.

She started inhaling the stinking air again, puffing up her chest so she could slowly slide lower, and then exhaling all the oxygen and straightening up suddenly. It was no good. The duct tape remained stuck on top of her breasts.

It's pointless. You can't do it. You're ridiculous. You have small breasts, but you still can't do it!

She tried again. Inhale air, puff up the chest, slide down, exhale the air, come back up. She was certainly sweating.

My head. It's spinning. I feel like puking.

But Chiara didn't stop. Three, four more times.

You can't do it!

Then it suddenly happened. The silvery duct tape rose toward her shoulders until it was just inches from her throat. She gained some distance.

"That's it!" Chiara shouted. "I did it, you asshole! You asshole!"

She stopped to catch her breath. Now she had to make sure that the bag was still anchored.

Please, please, please . . .

She could move her torso. And so she lurched to the right, contracting her abdominals once again and toppling over to the side. She jerked once, twice, felt a stab of pain on her left side, but didn't give up. And then, at last . . .

Air!

There was a gust of wind on her cheek, as if someone had opened a window. She breathed as deep as she could, holding the clean, fresh air in her lungs. Her head was spinning, but that didn't matter, it was almost pleasurable. Her cheeks and forehead felt cooler.

I'm free! I'm free! I can breathe real air! It's so good!

By now, the hood must be behind her, attached to a nail or a projecting section of the column. She could imagine it sagging pendulous like a chicken skin. She spat onto the floor the stench that had been constricting her for hours, the dust that she'd been forced to swallow. And finally, she took a look around.

A room measuring about a hundred square feet. In front of her were metal shelves covered with old equipment and tools. On the left, a wall with a dripping sink. She wished she could hurl herself against that dirty, rusting faucet and lick every drop. On the right was another wall with a window up high. She could see the clouds. And an orange cat that had been watching her for who knows how long.

"AND WHERE IS THIS MAX?"

"In room 4A," Giovanna replied, fluttering her eyelashes over the emerald glint of her eyes. "What about Chiara? Have you found her?"

Rocco shook his head. "No, Giovanna, still no news. Now go back to class. I'm going to ask the principal to let me speak to this Massimiliano Turrini." Rocco turned to speak to the principal, a man of about sixty who had stood, arms crossed, leaning in the doorway of the front office the whole time Rocco had been questioning Giovanna. "Dottor Bianchini, I need to speak to Massimiliano Turrini, in room 4A. Shall I go up, or will you have him called down?" The principal didn't reply. He waited until Giovanna had left the room, then he strode over to Rocco Schiavone with quick, short steps. "Listen, Deputy Chief Schiavone, I'm happy to cooperate, but you do realize that I'm going on trust and nothing more here, don't you?"

Rocco looked at him. He'd already catalogued Eugenio Bianchini, principal of the high school, in his mental bestiary. He was a specimen of *Sorex araneus*, also known as a common shrew. An enormous upturned nose, and underneath it a short, bristly mustache like that sported by Bristow, the famous British buying clerk featured in the cartoon of Frank Dickens, small dark eyes behind a pair of round eyeglasses.

"Excuse me, I'm not sure I understand what you're driving at, Dottor Bianchini."

"I'm trying to tell you that we're holding regularly scheduled classes here, and I wouldn't want your presence to frighten or alarm any of my students. Are we sure that all this is really necessary?"

"Yes."

"But shouldn't I be looking at a sheet of paper signed by a judge?"

"No."

"Listen, Deputy Chief Schiavone, I'm going to make this very simple. Max Turrini has had some problems, I know that and we all know that."

"I don't."

"Well, to make a long story short, every so often he sells things he shouldn't strictly be selling. As far as that goes, of course, even I. . . ."

"That's not why I'm here. Max Turrini's drug dealing

will be the subject of another visit I intend to pay your high school."

"Let me insist on this point. He's a sterling young man, his father is a respected physician, and you need to proceed very cautiously. He's a slightly questionable. . . ."

"A slightly questionable what? He deals drugs, so? Listen, thank you very much, but believe me, I'm here for entirely different reasons. And I'll use velvet gloves, trust me."

The principal grabbed Rocco by the arm: "I'm required to be discreet, but also to protect my students."

Rocco looked at that pale, dainty little hand that was clutching at his biceps. The principal immediately released his grip.

"Bianchini, as far as that goes, you're also required to protect your own personal safety."

The principal was nonplussed. "I don't understand what you're trying to say."

"Let me see if I can make it any clearer." Rocco stood up from his seat. He was a good foot taller than the principal. "It's not as if this morning I had nothing better to do with my time and I just said to myself: Rocco, why don't you stroll over to the high school and ask the kids some questions, to help pass the morning?"

Dottor Bianchini was breathing slowly. He could now sense a growing wave of aggressive hostility in the policeman he had before him. Still, he remained the principal of a high school, and he certainly had no need to listen to the orders being given him by just any old deputy police chief. At least not after twenty years of orders imposed upon him by his beloved spouse, Signora Bianchini, née De Cicco, and by his mother Rosa, eighty-seven years old, and still filled with all the vim and energy of the legendary cyclist Fausto Coppi on the Pordoi Pass. "You know what I say, Deputy Chief Schiavone?"

"No, what do you say?"

"That if you want to talk to Massimiliano Turrini, first I want to see. . . ."

Rocco interrupted with a sudden gesture. For a moment, Bianchini was afraid the man was about to slap him.

"How old is Massimiliano Turrini, a.k.a. Max?"

"Twenty, I believe."

"And he's a senior?"

"That's right."

"Well then, Einstein is no longer a minor. If you don't mind, in that case . . ." and he stepped around the principal and left the office.

But the shrew had no intention of letting himself be bypassed so easily. "You can't just pop into a school without a warrant, without so much as a scrap of paper from police headquarters or the district attorney's office and expect that. . . ."

This time Rocco whipped around, grabbed the man by his lapels, and glared straight into his eyes: "Listen, asshole. I'm going to tell you something right now, and it would have been better for your health if you'd never heard it, but seeing that you insist, here it is. I'm trying to save the life of one of your students, Chiara Berguet, who's in trouble as deep as the deep blue sea. And if this particular piece of information starts circulating around town, there's a good chance that the girl won't make it. Is that all clear to you now, or do I need to get rough?"

"You . . . you've already gotten rough," Bianchini stammered. Rocco let go of him. He adjusted his jacket for him. "You don't know anything and I never said anything. If we manage to save Chiara's life, then part of the credit will go to you, and that will only be possible if you stop getting in the way and busting my balls. Have I made myself clear?"

Bianchini nodded.

"So should I go to the classroom, or will you have him come here?"

"I'll send a hall monitor. Wait in the administrative office." And he hurried away.

MASSIMILIANO TURRINI, A.K.A. MAX, BUT DUBBED Einstein by Rocco, compensated for his lack of scholastic talent with a shameless, Apollonian beauty. He stood six foot three, blond as an angel—that is, if angels really are— deep, soulful dark eyes. His teeth, straight and dazzlingly white, were set in his soft, fleshy lips. He had a prominent nose but, far from clashing with the rest of his face, it gave it a stroke of virility.

"So all four of you were at Sphere."

"That's right, my cousin Alberto with Giovanna, and then me and Chiara. We danced and got up to some trouble. But Chiara had too much to drink."

"How do you know?"

"Because at a certain point she disappeared. I walked around the club trying to track her down and I found her in the bathroom throwing up. I took her outside, I got her some fresh air, let her smoke a cigarette. Anyway, these things happen, right?"

"Of course."

"And then nothing, commissario."

"Deputy chief, Max, it's the third time I've told you. . . ."

"Ah, right, you said that. Then, nothing else, I took her home and I left."

Rocco took a cigarette from his pack and lit it. Max stared at him, eyes bulging: "Deputy Chief, you're not allowed to smoke in here!"

"True. And you know what I heard? That at school, you're not allowed to peddle drugs either."

Max dropped his gaze.

"Have you stopped?"

The young man just nodded his head.

"Tell me something. Do you steal pharmaceuticals from your father's clinic?"

Max smiled naively, then scratched his blond hair.

"Sometimes, yes . . . Rohypnol, Stilnox, you know, light drugs that trip you out. Only . . . I swear to you, I don't do it anymore." And he crossed his forefingers in front of his lips and kissed them twice to drive home the point.

"Well, Max, now I want you to think hard. When you took Chiara home, did you see her go inside?"

He thought it over for a short while. "No, she got out, she walked to the door, and I left."

"That is, you didn't wait to make sure she got the door open?"

"No. Why?"

"Just because, Max. That's what you're supposed to do when you see a young woman home. Didn't your Papà teach you that?"

"No. I don't talk much with Papà."

"Right. All you do is empty out his medicine chest. What about with your Mamma?"

"No, she never told me that."

"Fuck!" Rocco stood up. He opened the window to throw out the cigarette. Outside it was still raining. "Doesn't it ever stop?"

"Do you know that last year in Aosta we got snow in May?"

"Do you know that if it happens again this year, I'll commit a murder?" The deputy chief shut the window. "All right, Max. Go back to your class. How are you doing this year?"

"What do you mean, how am I doing?"

"I mean, how are you doing in school?"

Max thought it over. "Ah, how am I doing . . . great. I'm taking math, physics, and chemistry."

"Which is quite impressive, seeing that you're attending scientific high school."

"You know something funny? My math teacher is actually Chiara's uncle."

"Marcello Berguet?"

"What do you say, should I see if Chiara can put in a good word for me?" Then he seemed to stop and think it over. "Deputy Chief, why are you asking me all these questions about Chiara? Yesterday Giovanna was asking me about her too."

"When was the last time you talked to her?"

"Sunday night."

"And since then?"

"I called her twice but the phone was turned off. So I texted her on Whatsapp. But she still hasn't replied. Do you know anything?"

"I think she might have gone to stay with her grandmother in Milan."

"What are you, crazy? Her grandmother is basically in a coma!"

"Right, maybe you're right. Take care of yourself, Max. And take my advice. No more strange business dealings."

The young man got up from his chair. "I swear!" He opened the door but didn't walk through it. "Dottor Schiavone, do I need to worry?"

"Maybe so, a little."

Max looked at the policeman, then bowed his head. "Has something happened to Chiara and you don't have the nerve to tell me? Is she dead?"

"She's not dead, Max. Don't worry. You'll see, she'll turn up safe and sound."

"Well, that's a relief. Will you call me if you find out anything?"

"Of course. If anything, I'll leave word with your secretary."

Max failed to grasp the irony. "I'll keep calling her. She'll have to turn her phone back on eventually, no?" And with his gleaming white smile, he vanished behind the door of the principal's office.

SHE'D TRIED TO COAX THE ORANGE CAT CLOSER. BUT it had just gazed at her for a few minutes, then it had turned and vanished without another thought for her.

Cats aren't like dogs.

The little voice was right. A dog would have barked. And barked and barked. And maybe someone would have heard it.

Don't you need to pee?

Of course, I need to pee.

Even though she hadn't had anything to drink in who knows how long. She looked down at her legs. Bound to the chair. Her skirt hiked up and on the flesh of her thighs, the foam from the urine that she'd peed on herself hours ago.

My stockings? Why don't I have my stockings? I had them on before! I don't like to go around without stockings.

The tidal wave of pain down there took shape again. Not as strong as before, but still quite distinct. Chiara shut her eyes. She waited for that impact wave to subside.

"Is anybody there?" she shouted. "Oh!" Her voice was hoarse and weary. "Please!"

If they brought me here, there must be someone around, right? There must be someone.

No. There's no one. No one at all.

"Shut the hell up! I'm trying to think!"

Kidnapped. Someone kidnapped me and brought me

here. But you bring water and food to a kidnap victim. Even if it's in a dog bowl, you don't just abandon them, do you?

There was nothing on the floor. No bowl, no containers. And the old wooden door had a chain that fastened it tightly through a hole in the wall.

"Is anyone there?"

If you ask me, things will only get worse if someone does show up.

"Worse than this?"

Yes.

Soon my father will get here. He'll take care of things. Right, Papà?

The rustling of tree branches in the wind. Then a sudden gust of water. It was raining outside.

Think about it: what would happen if the cellar flooded?

"Fuck you!"

You'd drown like a rat.

She hauled on both arms with all her strength. But, aside from sawing the straps binding her deep into her wrists, she obtained no other results.

I'm not going to die here, I'm not going to die here. I'm not going to die.

Are you sure?

THE VALLÉE SAVINGS BANK OCCUPIED AN ENTIRE OF-fice building on Via Frutaz. And on the ground floor of that building was Branch Office No. 1. With his loden overcoat and his hair drenched with the rain that for some time now was refusing to yield to the sweet-smelling month of May, Rocco Schiavone tried to enter the bank through the revolving door. But midway through, the door clicked to a locked position, trapping him. An expressionless voice ordered him to leave keys and other metallic objects in the lockers supplied for that purpose. Rocco did as he was told. He kept only his cell phone with him. But the door froze again. Behind the bulletproof glass, the security guard rather brusquely waved him back to the lockers. Rocco rolled his eyes and put his cell phone in the locker, too. But now the door froze in place for a third time. Once again, the guard waved him back. Rocco threw both arms wide, as if to say: "I don't have a thing left to put in the locker." But the security guard wasn't interested in discussing the finer points. Indifferent to Rocco's objections, he waved him back to the row of lockers. The deputy chief reached into his pocket. He pulled out his wallet. He pressed his police headquarters identification card against the glass and urged the security guard to come closer to read it. Then, since it was impossible to make himself heard through all that bulletproof glass, he pointed to his mouth and carefully and visibly enunciated the string of words, "I'm-from-the-police-and-if-you-don't-open-this-fucking-door-I'll-kick-your-ass-black-and-blue." And then he smiled. The guard nodded to show that he'd understood and went over to press a button next to the revolving door, which finally spat the deputy chief out into the bank. "What the fuck, do I have to strip bare naked to get in here?"

"Maybe you have a chain," the security attendant tried justifying himself.

"I don't have a chain."

"Any metal plates in your bones?"

"I have one in my balls. Could that be it?"

The guard didn't answer.

"The director. I need to talk to her immediately."

The man pointed to a door to the side of the tellers' windows. "Third office down the hall."

"Thanks."

"Please forgive me, I'm just doing my job."

"No, you need to forgive me. I'm just doing mine, too."

He turned to look at the tellers, with the lines of customers waiting. Sitting in the waiting area was Anna, looking at him. Rocco tried flashing her a smile. He saw her write something quickly on a sheet of paper. Then she held it up so Rocco could see: "There's no getting away from you, is there?"

Rocco narrowed his eyes. He read the message. Then he held both arms out helplessly and went through the door that led to the offices.

"DOTTOR SCHIAVONE, I'M SO HAPPY TO MAKE YOUR acquaintance," Laura Turrini began; she was the director of the bank branch, a distracted forty-five-year-old.

"Dottoressa Turrini . . . let me ask you something. Is your son Max Turrini, Class 4 A?"

"Oh my lord! What's he gotten up to this time?"

"Nothing, nothing. It's just a coincidence."

Laura Turrini took a deep breath and blew away the

clot of anxiety that had just gathered in her trachea. "That's good, what a relief. My husband and I were thinking of sending him to boarding school, you know?"

"That way, instead of just peddling his father's barbiturates, he'll go directly to working for the Medellin cartel. . . ."

"Please, take a seat." And she pointed to the little office sofa. "Can I get you an espresso, a mineral water?"

"No water, thanks, what's falling from the sky is more than enough," and he pointed to the window that was weeping thousands of rainy tears.

Laura smiled and sat down next to the policeman. Her elegant skirt suit was a color that fell somewhere between pink and lavender and clashed violently with her pale skin and her freckles. Her blonde hair was the fruit of a talented hairdresser's efforts. Laura's hair had lost its original color years ago. Her dark eyes darted this way and that. They transmitted messages, retreated shyly, smiled. Laura Turrini spoke with her eyes. And at that particular moment they were focused on Rocco's face. "You know what? I've heard a lot of people talk about you. Rumors circulate here in Aosta. I hear you're very good at your job."

"So it would seem."

"You just have one shortcoming. You don't have an account with our bank." And she broke into laughter. She had the same perfect teeth as her son. She let the laughter go on a little too long, as if showing off her array of molars and incisors. Who knows how many times she'd practiced that pose in front of the mirror. Neck bent slightly back, head held high, chin thrust forward, and lips opened wide to display the entire double arch of teeth.

"That's true. I don't have an account here." Rocco came right to the point. "What can you tell me about Edil.ber?" And Laura Turrini's smile flickered out. "What do you want to know?"

"Do you have their accounts here?"

"Let's just say that this bank is a point of reference for them."

"Lines of credit?"

"Certainly. We have always supported Edil.ber. But may I ask just why all these questions?"

"We're trying to understand what happened a few months ago, all the problems they were having with their workers."

Laura nodded, smoothing her skirt over her knees. "Yes. They were having difficulties meeting payroll. Edil.ber was running late on getting paid by their clients, but then, thank God, it all worked out."

"Were you the ones who financed Edil.ber?"

Laura paused. "Yes," she replied.

"I know that you aren't required to answer me, but can you tell me how much money you gave Edil.ber?"

"You said it yourself. I can't answer that."

"So I'd need a judge to make you answer?"

"I think that's right."

Rocco nodded. "But you can tell me how many years you've worked with Pietro Berguet's company, can't you?"

"Certainly. At least four years."

"Is Pietro the brains of the company?"

"I'd say so. But Engineer Cerruti, too. They're a tight pair, they work well together. Cerruti hasn't been working for the company very long, but he's immediately distinguished himself."

"What about Pietro's brother? Marcello?"

"Marcello? Marcello is a teacher, and he doesn't work for the company. In fact, you know something? He teaches my son. He only has a percentage of the company. He's on the board of directors, but he doesn't make any major decisions."

"Do you know the Berguet family very well?"

"Certainly. Giuliana and I have been friends since high school. Our children, as you must know, are dating."

"Tell me something, Dottoressa Turrini. Have there been any major transactions on the Berguets' personal accounts in the last few days?"

"I can't answer that question either."

"Does he enjoy good health, economically speaking?"

"No comment."

"Again with the judge?"

"Again with the judge, Dottor Schiavone."

"You haven't lied to me today at all, have you?"

She opened her eyes wide. "How dare you ask such a thing?" Laura Turrini practically shouted.

"Well, then, let me thank you and apologize for the intrusion. I hope you have a good day."

Rocco got to his feet, and so did Laura Turrini. Rocco thought she seemed very relieved that that interrogation disguised as a pleasant chat was over.

• • •

HE HATED POLICE ISSUE CARS. THEY ALWAYS HAD clutches that were slow to disengage, mysterious and worrisome percussions inhabited the engine compartment, there was never a cigarette lighter, the seats were uncomfortable and swaybacked from overuse, and the windshield wipers left streaks on the glass because of the worn rubber. He was taking the car back to police headquarters to switch it out with his own, but Beethoven's "Ode to Joy," the ringtone of his cell phone, burst out at a louder volume than the noise of the raindrops drumming on the car's sheet metal roof.

"Tell me, Italo."

"Well, listen, sir. . . ."

Listen, sir, thought Rocco. Italo wasn't alone.

"Go ahead. . . ."

"Maybe it's nothing, but Pietro Berguet just left Edil.ber and went into a shop."

Rocco turned on his blinker and pulled over. "He must have gone in to buy something, right?"

"I doubt that. It's a children and babies boutique. All sorts of things for kids. It's called HeyDiddleLiddles!"

"HeyDiddleLiddles? What the fuck kind of name is that?"

"How am I supposed to know? I didn't name the place."

"What does he have to do that's so urgent in a kids' store?"

"From zero to ten years of age?" Italo added.

"Scipioni is with you, right?"

"Yep."

"All right then, leave him there and let him stick to Berguet like glue. In the meantime, you follow the other guy, what was his name? Cerruti, the VP."

"In all this rain?"

"What's the matter, don't you have a car?"

"We have one car between the two of us!"

"What the fuck!" Rocco swore and swung a fist at the plastic dashboard, opening a laceration right above the car radio. "But I told you that you needed to be able to move independently!"

"The other car was out of gas, sir."

"Ain't that great. Then you can take a cab to police headquarters and get another car there. I'll pay for the taxi."

"Who ever took a taxi in Aosta?"

Rocco looked out of the window, cursing between clenched teeth. Then something in the street caught his attention. He got out of the car.

"DEPUTY CHIEF? DEPUTY CHIEF?" ITALO LOOKED over at Antonio Scipioni. "He hung up."

"I don't doubt it. You're driving him crazy with all this talk about taxis."

"What is that supposed to be my fault?"

The rear door opened without warning. "Who the . . . ?"

Rocco Schiavone had just hopped into the car and was shaking the rain out of his hair. "Deputy Chief!"

"So take my car," and he handed the keys over to Italo. "It's the Lancia parked right over there, you see it?"

"You mean, we were talking on the phone and the whole time we were . . . ?"

"Fifty feet apart. You, Antonio, stay on Berguet. So this

is the shop?" and he looked straight ahead out the windshield.

"That's right," said Scipioni.

The sign on the shop window read: "HeyDiddleLiddles! Everything you need for your HeyDiddleLiddles. From zero to ten years of age."

"Can anyone tell me what a HeyDiddleLiddle is?"

"A kid in a nursery rhyme?" Scipioni ventured.

"Good work, Antonio! How on earth did you come up with that?"

"I couldn't say, sir. I've been sitting here looking at the shop window for the past half hour puzzling it out."

"And who knows how much longer you're going to have to stay here. Okay. So get going, Italo."

"And what are you going to do, sir?" asked Pierron.

"Umbrella?"

"In the back," and Scipioni pointed to the rear compartment. Rocco turned around, grabbed it, and opened the door. "You get any news, call me," as he got out of the car.

"Hold on," Italo stopped him.

"What do you want?"

"Is there gas in the tank?" he asked, holding up the keys to the Lancia.

Rocco rolled his eyes. He reached for his wallet and pulled out fifty euros: "Here, fill up the tank, keep the change, and don't bust my chops again!" And he stepped out into the lashing May rain.

All it took was the two puddles he centered immediately and Rocco Schiavone could kiss goodbye the eleventh pair of Clarks desert boots he'd owned since he moved to Aosta.

"Fucking hell!"

To make matters worse, Scipioni's umbrella, clearly of Chinese manufacture, had already lost three of its stretchers. It was flopping in on itself like an unsuccessful omelette, letting splashes of water gush onto the deputy chief's loden overcoat and down his collar.

"May God and all the Saints curse this city, this rain, this wind, and this fucking cold!"

Police headquarters was no more than a hundred yards away. He only needed to cross the street. Cars went sailing past on Corso Battaglione Aosta, leaving wakes of frothy water like so many speedboats. There were no pedestrian crossings, but that had never presented a problem for a Roman. The natives of the Eternal City, and Rocco was one of their number, are used to crossing even very high-speed, high-traffic, seven-lane arteries right around a blind curve. Then again, it must be admitted that an unusually substantial portion of the city's health care spending is devoted to caring for people hit by reckless drivers. Reckless Roman drivers who—as has been duly noted and even mentioned in guidebooks for tourists—refuse to brake at pedestrian crossings, though they may be occupied by a ninety-year-old woman with a walker.

Without a second thought, Rocco stepped off the sidewalk. The cars honked and flashed their brights but given years of experience on Roman streets, the deputy chief was able to thread his way, as elegant as a daring toreador, and enter the office unharmed. Aside from his Clarks desert boots, of course, now basically a pair of mouldy orange peels not even worth composting, the only real victims of the rain.

"SURE, SURE, I KNOW . . . WHAT CAN YOU DO ABOUT it? Anyway. . . ." Furio was getting closer and closer to the end of his rope, after sitting for hours in the Bar Settembrini on the street of the same name, in Rome's Prati quarter, listening to Adele's relationship problems. The topic was this: things between her and Sebastiano seemed to have come to an insuperable impasse. Furio had tried without success to defuse the situation, arguing that Seba was just that way, distracted as he might seem, he still loved her every bit as much as the first day he'd fallen for her. But Adele wouldn't listen to reason. She talked and talked and talked, and by now Furio was utterly indifferent to the fate of that couple.

He kept saying, over and over again like a broken re-cord: "Sure, sure, I know . . . what can you do about it? Anyway. . . ."

It was one o'clock. Sitting at that wobbly round café table since ten in the morning, he'd completely savaged his stom-ach with three espressos, a fresh-squeezed orange juice, and an enormous chocolate muffin. Where did Adele even find the energy? He watched the young woman's lips moving, forming words, but he could no longer grasp the meaning of what she was saying, now an incessant background noise without any intrinsic logic.

"Sure, sure, I know . . . what can you do about it? Anyway. . . ."

He can just go fuck himself, thought Furio. If Adele wants to dump him, then she should just dump him. All things considered, he'd been trying to tell Seba this for some time now, he and Brizio and even Rocco: "Look, unless you shape up, she's going to dump you. You don't show her any special attention, you never make her feel special." Seba spent his time at home in a bad mood, slumped in front of the television set or else surfing the web. And Adele? He'd basically forgotten about her, Adele, who had a line of men stretching out the door, eager and willing to step into Sebastiano's shoes. "He's worse than a bear these days. And he takes no care about his diet. Have you seen how fat he's gotten lately?"

Actually, as far back as anyone could remember, Seba had always been fat, but to avoid a squabble, Furio just went on nodding.

"Sure, sure, I know . . . what can you do about it? Anyway. . . ."

"I even tried to make him jealous, by going out with Er Cravatta. That lasted two days. Then he went back to being his usual self."

Suddenly, to break that monotony, to break up the cadenced, slightly somnolent rhythm of her laments, Adele grabbed Furio by both hands. "Furio, help me!" she implored.

"Help you? How am I supposed to help you?" Furio knew that if he found the answer, he'd be free to go. What was needed was a drastic solution to the problem, something that would restore his friend's hope and get him free from that café table where he had already been gathering moss for far too long. "Why don't you leave town?" he suggested.

"Where am I supposed to go?"

"To your mother's, to your brother's place in Brescia. Just go, don't say a word to him, and power off your cell phone. If he asks me, I don't know a thing."

"My brother's not in Brescia anymore. They transferred him to Berlin. I'm not going to my mother's, not if you put a gun to my head."

"Don't you have a girlfriend?"

"In Rome."

"No, not in Rome. He'd find you if he set his mind to it." Then a crazy idea popped into his mind, but he said to himself: why not? It might even work. "Go stay with Rocco."

"In Aosta?"

"Yeah, that's right. Rocco would back your play."

"Furio, I don't know about that. I haven't talked to him in months."

"Try giving him a call. His phone number hasn't changed. Go up there and take it easy. I'll take care of Seba. And I'll let you know how he reacts, whether or not he starts tearing his hair out. At least that way you can make up your mind once and for all what you want to do."

"You know, it's not a bad idea."

"Right?"

Furio was pleased. He'd found the solution, and now

Adele had a smile on her face. Which meant he could finally leave the Bar Settembrini and, with his stomach doing flipflops, go have a bowl of spaghetti all'amatriciana at Stella and Brizio's, in honor of their second anniversary.

THE HOURS SLIPPED BY AND CHIARA BERGUET WAS IN ever greater danger. Hopefully, the demand for cash had already taken place, the agreement had been worked out, and the machinery of the ransom was already in motion. But he could no longer delay, the time had come to talk to the judge. Baldi had listened to him for a solid quarter of an hour. Never nodding, never stirring, like a mongoose observing the cobra before lunging at it, jaws snapping. Or the other way around, with Baldi the cobra and Rocco the mongoose. When Rocco was done laying out the situation, Baldi took a nice deep breath. And exhaling all at once, he spat out the words: "Why did you wait till now?"

"Because I wanted to be convinced. And now I am."

"But what if it's too late?"

"I doubt that."

"What makes you doubt it?"

"She disappeared late Sunday night. Today, maybe, they've established contact."

Baldi, hyperactive as he was, leapt to his feet, walked across the office, and without a word left Rocco sitting at his desk. But the policeman wasn't particularly surprised. He'd become used to the magistrate's surreal reactions. He noticed that, after many months, the photograph of the man's wife had reappeared, a sign that Baldi's conjugal relations had perhaps been restored to their prior state of serenity.

When Baldi came back and sat down, he had a pastry in his hand and was chomping loudly. "Want some?"

"No, thanks."

"It's disgusting. I got it from the vending machine. So what moves are you making?"

"I've got two men tailing the girl's father."

"Mm-hmmm," and the judge took another bite out of the little pie. "There's no criminal complaint. I'd have to order a wiretap without any criminal complaint."

"Would that break any laws?" asked Rocco. The judge didn't even bother to reply. He balled up the plastic wrapper from the pastry and tossed it into the trash can. The wrapper bounced off the edge and rolled across the floor.

"Plastic . . ." said Baldi. "We're all going to be suffocated by plastic until we die, you know that?"

Rocco nodded.

"Somewhere in the ocean there's an entire island made of plastic, and it's the size of Europe. And yet it would take so little."

There was not a single topic, be it political, environmental, or military in nature, for which Judge Baldi hadn't already come up with a solution. From the salaries of parliamentarians to the problems of retirement or arms trafficking, the public debt, and unemployment—as far as he was concerned, everything could be tied up in a neat and simple knot.

"Do you know how we could defeat the rising tide of

plastic on this planet? You just fire it out into deep space, far past the earth's orbit. Every continent can build rockets and, instead of sending satellites into orbit—we have more than enough of them, after all—use them to launch tons and tons of plastic into the immense void. After all, what's a continent of plastic the size of Europe if it's just drifting through the galaxy? Nothing, a drop of water in the ocean. And for us it would be a lifesaver!"

"It strikes me as a very good idea, and a very expensive one," Rocco retorted.

"Why expensive? If the government builds the rockets, it would just be the cost of the raw materials and the rocket fuel."

"What about labor costs?"

"All you need to do is draft the fuckoffs with steady government jobs who spend all day in the office without lifting a finger. Already just here in the district attorney's office, I could give you ten names."

"Wouldn't it be quicker to outlaw plastic packaging?" the deputy chief suggested.

"Let me give that some thought . . . To get back to us, I'm in agreement with your plan. Let's keep a low profile. Without kicking up a fuss. We can't run any risks."

"All I'm asking you is to authorize an investigation into the assets of Edil.ber. I don't think they're doing particularly well. Also, I want to understand exactly what relationship they have with the Vallée Savings Bank. The director is called. . . ."

"Laura Turrini. I know her very well. What do you have in mind?"

"I don't know. But if a company has been picketed by their workers and the unions for failure to meet payroll and then things suddenly all work out, well then, clearly, someone must have fronted them this money."

"And so what you want to know is whether it was the bank, logically enough."

"Logically enough."

"What makes you think it might not have been the bank?"

"Because I wasn't born yesterday, and this isn't the first time I've had to deal with this kind of a situation. You know—and I know—that businessmen often run short of cash."

"So you suspect that it wasn't the bank that got them out of their fix?"

"That's right, Dottore."

"The newspapers are full of these stories, Schiavone. But let me inform you, you're taking a wrong turn here, and you couldn't be any more wrong. Turrini is an eminently moral person, and the bank that she represents is a gleaming mirror of honesty. In all these years, I've never seen anything that would arouse even the slightest suspicion."

"Still, it's a lead, isn't it?"

The judge pulled open a drawer and extracted a plastic water bottle. He unscrewed the top and drained half of it at a single gulp. "Ahhh . . . that's disgusting . . . Now, what

I'd like to do with the bank, though, is check to see if any money has been moved around. If as you say the girl has been kidnapped from home, then Pietro Berguet is going to have to figure out some way of paying, right?" With a second gulp, he drained the water bottle and sailed it straight into the trash can, this time hitting dead center.

"I don't think they've paid already. It's too soon."

"Very true, Schiavone. You're right. And after all, people who own large companies like Edil.ber might be using foreign accounts and funds. In other words, they're not just going to the teller at the bank to withdraw two million euros."

"No. Kidnappers want cash, not a damned wire transfer."

"For real?" Baldi asked sarcastically. "It's going to take them a while to find the cash. It's not something you can do in a couple of days. And maybe they'll draw on more than one account here in Italy, and most likely outside of the country as well. All right, let me get busy and see what I can do in those areas. You keep tabs on the family."

Rocco stood up. But Baldi stopped him. "You know? Edil.ber is competing for a very big contract here with the Valle d'Aosta regional government. We're going to have to move very cautiously."

"That's why I checked things out before coming to talk to you, Dottor Baldi," the deputy chief replied.

"Smart move. Who knows about this at police headquarters?"

"Me and my most trusted men."

"Laurel and Hardy?" Baldi asked, referring to Deruta and D'Intino.

"No, not them."

"If anything leaks to the press, I'm going to hold you personally responsible."

Rocco looked the judge in the eyes. "And I could say the same thing to you. Who can guarantee me that here in the district attorney's office some dickhead doesn't decide to develop a very deep throat?"

Baldi sat there for a few seconds and stared at him. "I'm going to pretend I didn't hear that."

"No, make sure you did. If the big mouth was at my house, you'd have read all about it in the papers today." He grabbed a copy of *La Stampa*, and slapped it under Baldi's nose. "And there's not a word of it in here."

Baldi nodded. He smiled. He took the paper.

"It seems to me that you and I will go far together."

"I don't know about that, Dottore. I personally don't want to go any further than a beach on the Côte d'Azur where I can bake my bones in the hot sun till the day I die."

"Why don't you do like me. Instead of thinking about a house on the beach, why don't you concentrate on a boat, instead? With one of those, you can change the beach every day."

"I hate boats, I hate waves, and I hate the smell of seaweed. I need to be able to walk and I don't even have a boating license."

"Sooner or later I'm going to get a two-masted sailboat straight out of a dream, you'll see, and then I'll sail straight for the horizon once and for all."

"I'll leave you the address of the beach where you can

find me. But maybe you can give me a hand. I need to nose around in a shop, it's called HeyDiddleLiddles."

"What did you say it was called?"

"HeyDiddleLiddles," Rocco said again, with no change in his expression.

"What the hell kind of name is that?"

"According to one of my officers it's a combination of Hey Diddle Diddle and Liddles, as in kids."

"Then why not HeyLiddleDiddles?"

"Maybe because that sounds like a public urinal, or something worse?"

"True. Hey Diddle Diddle for Littles?"

"That's too long. And then, you've got a double-t and two double-d's, and then you've lost your pun, as well as any sense of fun."

"Deputy Chief Schiavone, don't you think that we're sinking into a logical quagmire that's pure nonsense?"

"I get the same impression."

"So, HeyDiddleLiddles. And just why do you want to know more about this shop?"

"Because our man Pietro Berguet is there. At a time like this, doesn't it strike you as odd that a businessman should be out shopping for clothing for children from ages zero to ten years old? After all, Chiara is his only daughter and she's eighteen years old. Don't you agree?"

The judge thought it over. "No more than an hour and I'll send a well-drafted fax to you at police headquarters. Right now, Judge Baldi has some work to do." He got to his feet and extended his hand toward Rocco. Who had no choice but to shake it.

"Take it from me, Schiavone, absolute radio silence. A girl's life is at stake."

"But I just told you that in the first place."

"I was only suggesting that you make use of methods more in keeping with the rank you represent."

"I've never done any different."

"That's not true and you know it perfectly well."

"May I have my hand back now?"

"Of course you may." And the judge finally released his grip.

How long has it been? How many days? Where is it that I read this, or maybe I saw it on TV. The longest you can go without water is a week. How long is it I've been here? Two days? Three? It's getting dark out again. Night is falling.

She'd spent the whole time concentrating on not feeling the itch, not feeling the pain. She was weak, and all the muscles she was able to move were hurting badly. What's more, she could feel her buttocks, her hands, and her feet all tingling as if they'd gone to sleep. Her blood wasn't circulating properly.

A week is the longest you can go without water. How long can you survive bound and hooded? Six days? Five? The orange cat. Where is that orange cat with the bell on its collar? If there's an orange cat with a bell on its collar, then there has to be another house nearby.

Sure, but they can't hear you.

She'd screamed until she'd gone completely hoarse and had spat a reddish phlegm. She'd injured her throat, and had nothing to show for it. No one had heard her at all.

It might just be a stray cat. They only have stray cats in the city. So that means I must be near a city.

Who told you such a thing? Cats are everywhere. Even in the countryside. And who says you're in Aosta? You could be anywhere.

"Where are you? Where are you? Why don't you come? Why?"

Where is whoever tied me up here? Where has he gone? Why doesn't he come back to give me something to drink? I'm thirsty. I'm thirsty and I'm hungry.

The old wooden door shivered in response to some sudden impact. Chiara's heart stopped pumping, her blood chilled and curdled, and her stomach shrank tight until it was smaller than a peanut.

There they are now. They're here!

Two more loud bangs. She expected to see the chain slide through the hole and the door swing open, and maybe a man wearing a ski mask might come in with food and water.

My God! If they come in right now they'll see me without the hood on my head! And if my kidnappers come in without ski masks, I'll see their faces, and they'll have to kill me!

"My eyes are closed! My eyes are closed!" she shouted

with what little voice remained to her. "I don't have the bag on my head anymore, but my eyes are closed. I can't see anything, I swear to you!"

She sat waiting. Her eyelids squeezed tight. She waited for the sound of the chain sliding, the door opening.

But nothing happened.

The seconds ticked past. She opened her eyes again.

"Is . . . is anyone there? Please, just answer me!"

THE JUDGE HAD MOVED VERY QUICKLY. NOT EVEN half an hour later, Rocco's fax machine had spat out a page full of information about the infants' and children's clothing shop. As Rocco was reading it, Italo Pierron sat waiting. Caterina was no longer in the room. She'd gone home early because she'd felt the fever rise throughout her body.

"The shop is named HeyDiddleLiddles. It belongs to a certain Carlo Cutrì. He's a resident of Lugano. He has a partner, from Valle d'Aosta, called Michele Diemoz." Schiavone laid the sheet of paper down on the desk. "I think we should go pay a call. What time is it?"

"Six fifteen."

"Let's get moving."

"Rocco, I'm so sleepy I'm dying on my feet. Do you remember? We've been on the go since two in the morning."

"All right then, head on home. And tell Scipioni to go home too. Is he still on Berguet's tail?"

"Yes. He called in. Berguet went home at about five

thirty and hasn't been seen since. His wife and his brother are still there too. But I was on the tail of that other guy, Cerruti. He has an Audi TT, and if you ask me, he has a second line of work picking up girls at discotheques."

"What did he do?"

"He went to see a notary, here, this is the address." He pulled out a sheet of paper and left it on the desk. "Dottor Enrico Maria Charbonnier. He's on Rue Piave, three numbers up from your place."

"Got it. Memorized. Excellent. Italo, you go ahead and get some sleep. Don't worry. I'll go ahead to the store on my own."

"Thanks. See you tomorrow?"

"Usual time."

"Nine in the morning?"

"Is there a store that sells Clarks shoes here in Aosta? The place I used to go went out of business."

"Are you out of shoes?"

Schiavone nodded.

"Eleven pairs?" Schiavone nodded again.

"But why don't you buy some other kind of shoes?"

"But why don't you mind your own fucking business? So is there or isn't there?"

"Uh uh, I don't think there is. . . ."

"If you happen to hear of one, can you buy me a pair? Men's size 10."

"Message received. . . ."

Rocco stood up from his chair. "I'd better go, or they'll close. Any news from the De Rege brothers?"

"D'Intino and Deruta?" asked Italo as he got to his feet. "Nothing so far. They're MIA."

Schiavone nodded and, saying nothing, left the office.

IT WAS ALMOST DARK OUTSIDE AND THE LAST GLOW OF the day was barely lapping at the shadows in the room.

It was just the wind that had slammed the old weather-beaten door against the jamb. Chiara started shivering with the cold. The rain hadn't stopped for an instant, and the dank chill of the cellar room was starting to creep into her bones. Soon it would be pitch dark out, and inside, too. Then her brain would start zigzagging freely, without a destination, with no landmarks to go by.

I don't like it. I don't like it. In the dark you see things that aren't there. You see the gray shadows of rats, you see giant spiders. And the darkness has a respiration all its own . . . like an enormous body, hiding and breathing. It draws near, it moves away. It squats quietly in a corner, and then, as soon as you fall asleep . . .

Twelve hours of darkness. Twelve hours of presences, shapes, nightmares, and obscurity.

I'm not going to be able to hold out. I hurt all over. My head . . . is hammering. Down below, it's like a wave. My legs. My arms. All over. Nails? Staplers? Pliers? Flames? Blades? I've got it all working on me . . .

Try smashing your head against the column. That way you could knock yourself out and at least you'd get some sleep, the little voice suggested to her.

Chiara did her best not to listen.

What would it take? One sharp bang and you're done! You get a nice long nap!

If I tug on my wrists, in the end I can get them loose. I'll cut them, but I'll get them loose. If I wait I'll just get weaker and weaker. The sooner I try it, the better for me.

Try with your legs. Your legs are stronger.

My legs?

Your legs.

This time, the little voice had a point. Your legs are always stronger. Especially *her* legs, since at age twelve she was thought to have had a future as a competitive skier. Her calves and her quadriceps were powerful. She had to give it a try. Maybe she could do it.

If only I had a drop of water.

Oh, yack and yack and yack and instead of doing you just talk and cry. You talk and you cry. Come on!

She started pushing her legs forward. They were tethered to the chair at her ankles.

If it's a chain, you can tug for the rest of your life, and it'll never break.

"If it *is* a chain, you asshole. But it doesn't make any noise, does it? So it's not a chain. It's duct tape!"

She shut her eyes and rocked forward and back, forward and back. It was no good. The grip didn't loosen, didn't yield. She reinforced each lunge by hopping a little in the chair. Her buttocks were tingling and beginning to ache. So were her quadriceps and the muscles in her arms. But Chiara wouldn't give up. She was clenching her legs, then spreading them wide, jerking them forward, yanking them back. Her ankles were fastened tight to the chair. She kicked again, once, then twice. She heard a sudden crack, the sound of rotten wood shattering, then the chair beneath her collapsed. She tipped to one side, hit the floor, smacking her head as she did so. A blazing blade of pain stabbed into her thigh.

She screamed with all the breath she had in her lungs. She stretched out her legs, now free to move. A section of chair leg was still fastened to her right ankle. Behind her left leg, a few inches below her buttocks, a wooden dagger had been driven into her flesh. The intolerable pain was paralyzing her.

What is it . . . ? What is it . . . ? A . . . piece of wood? A big splinter? It's in my leg. It's inside. God, how it hurts. It burns. God, it burns!

The shattered chair leg had plunged straight into her biceps femoris. The dark stain of the wound kept spreading.

Blood? I'm losing lots of blood.

Her muscles were trembling like jello. Chiara narrowed her eyes and got a glimpse of herself, sprawled on the floor on her side, left leg wounded and bleeding, right leg bent back, hands still strapped to the backrest of the chair, face pressed against the chilly floor. And pain amplifying by the minute.

If I stay still, it'll calm down. If I stay still, it'll calm down. I'll stay still, and I won't move, and it'll all get better.

Good girl. Stay still. That way you're bound to lose every last drop of blood in your body. Then you'll die.

● ● ●

It had stopped raining. The streets were awash, and everywhere you turned there were puddles, worse than a minefield. Rocco was careful not to step in one as he walked. His phone rang.

It was Furio, from Rome. Rocco's heart started flapping its wings.

"Hey old friend, how are you doing?"

"I'm good, Rocco, I'm good. What do you say?"

"What do I say? Same old bullshit as always."

"Listen, let me just take a minute of your time."

"Tell me all about it."

"It's about Adele."

"Has she dumped Seba again?" Rocco asked, already out of patience.

"No. But she's planning to. That guy is an asshole."

"It's what I've always said."

"So me and her came up with an idea. She drops out of circulation for a while. He gets all jealous and he comes looking for her, and then she has the proof she needs."

Rocco thought it over. "Yeah, that strikes me as a pretty good idea. But where is she going to hide out, though? Seba never has any trouble tracking her down."

"We thought it over and came up with a flash of genius."

"Let's hear it. But step it up, because I'm in the middle of a nasty case."

"Simple as could be," said Furio. "She'll come and stay with you."

Rocco stopped. "With me? What do you mean, with me?"

"It would never occur to Seba that she's staying with you."

"But . . . where would she stay?"

"At your place, no?"

"But have you ever been up to my place in Aosta? I only have one bed."

"Well, don't you have a pullout couch or something?"

"Sure, but Adele. . . ."

"Don't worry, it's just for a couple of days. Then she'd go back to Rome."

"If you ask me, you're both crazy. But still . . . okay . . . tell her to call me when she makes up her mind."

"Sure, will do. Oh, good luck on that, and I'll get off the line now."

"Look, I'm expecting you up here, you know?"

"Sure, now that it's getting warm, I'll come up. That's a promise."

"And I believe you. Take care of yourself, Furio."

Adele in his apartment. That was a strange, deranged thing. For two reasons. First of all, because it sort of seemed like he was playing an unfair trick on Seba. Even if, when you stopped to consider, he was doing it for the man's own good. The second reason was Adele. A friend, Sebastiano's woman—and to Rocco any friend's woman automatically became a man. But to have her in his home, maybe right there, first thing in the morning, as he was waking up . . . well, he'd have to use all his willpower not to behave like a complete asshole.

What about Marina? What would she have to say about it? She'd always been such an intensely private person. She wouldn't want to have Adele sharing their private space. She'd probably put up a fuss.

Maybe he needed to find her a hotel. For that matter, no one had ever set foot in his place. And no one ever should.

Rocco turned the corner. At the end of the street the signs of HeyDiddleLiddles glowed. The street was dark and deserted, and if it hadn't been for the shop's neon signs he would certainly have put his foot squarely in the stream of water running like a mountain torrent along the curb toward the center of the city. Cautiously he approached the plate-glass window. He leaned toward it and peered inside. The shop was empty of customers. The overhead spotlights turned on full inside gave the place the clinical appearance of a hospital. A sales clerk, a young woman in her early thirties, short and stout, was at the cash register. She was punching the keys, tearing off receipts, pushing the cash drawer shut, and repeating the operation. She did it at least six times. When Rocco entered the store, she was so startled she almost jumped off her chair. She stared ashen-faced at the deputy chief and said: "Good evening. May I help you?"

"Yes. I'm looking for some terrycloth onesies. Like the ones you have in the front window."

The shop was hot, like a greenhouse, and an odor of plastic reigned over all.

"That's fine!" and the young woman came out from behind the counter. "If you'd care to show me. . . ."

Rocco pointed to them. "There, those two. One's yellow, the other's green."

They were terrycloth onesies for newborns. The price was exorbitant, and nothing else had occurred to Rocco.

"Hmmm . . ." the girl was thinking. "How old is the baby? Two? Three?"

"Three? More like four months."

"Ah, right, of course . . . that's true. Those onesies, after they turn one. . . ."

". . . are useless. Unless the baby is having some serious growth issues," Rocco finished her sentence for her.

"All right, there ought to be some . . . hold on . . ." and she walked over to a shelf piled high with boxes. "There ought to be some. . . ." She studied the boxes, with the tip of her finger in her mouth. She climbed the stepladder, which creaked under her weight. Rocco got ready to launch a lunging rescue in case the ladder collapsed.

"No, they don't seem to be here. Hold on a minute," and she went over to a cabinet full of drawers. She started opening and closing them compulsively. "No good, they aren't here either. I'm really sorry. But I haven't been working here long. Maybe in the back?"

"Are you asking me?"

"No, I was just thinking that maybe they're in the back. One moment, please."

She opened a small door wedged beneath the shelves and vanished from sight. Rocco stepped closer to the cash register. The young woman had left the drawer wide open. It was empty. Not so much as a single banknote. Just a few coins and a couple of metal paperclips. The receipts the young woman had just rung up were on the counter, neatly stacked. The last one showed a total of 320 euros. He heard a commotion and quickly returned to his place at the center of the store. The young woman emerged from the doorway. She had a box in one hand. "Here, I found one. It's red. Is that okay?"

"Could you show it to me?"

The young woman brought the box to the counter. She opened it. She removed the tissue paper and showed off the onesie. There was the face of Elmo of the Muppets stitched onto it. "How much does it cost?"

"Hold on . . ." she looked on the box. No sign of the price. Then she went to the front window. She came back: "It's seventy euros!"

"Good lord!" said Rocco. "All right then, I'll take it. Even though I had planned to get two, but at these prices."

"It ought to be very good fabric, you know?"

"Really?"

"Yes, I think so."

The deputy chief pulled out his wallet and his credit card. The young woman looked at the magnetic card as if it were some exotic specimen of black widow spider. "No!" she said, clearly frightened. "No. No credit cards or debit cards, either. Only cash, please."

"I don't have cash."

"But the credit card terminal is out of order."

"Then what are we going to do?"

"I don't know," said the young woman.

"What do you say I come back tomorrow?"

"Yes, that might be good. It strikes me as a very nice idea."

"All right then, I'll come back tomorrow. So, will you set it aside for me?"

"Of course, of course." The shop clerk put the onesie back into the box.

"I'd recommend you lower the temperature a little. It's stifling in here."

"I wish I could, but I don't know how to do it."

"There must be a thermostat around here somewhere, don't you think?"

"You think so? Let me take a look."

Rocco nodded and went back to the front door of the shop, which was all fogged up now from the difference in temperature with the exterior.

"It's been a pleasure."

"Same for me. See you tomorrow."

"See you tomorrow . . . what's your name?"

"Carmelina. Melina, to my friends."

"See you tomorrow, Melina."

"I'll be expecting you."

My dear Melina, Rocco thought to himself, of course I'll come back. But not tomorrow. Much, much sooner.

HEADING HOME. DRIZZLY SKY. LOW CLOUDS, TEM-perature dropping. He felt a shiver run through him, beneath the thin cloth of his loden overcoat. It would certainly start raining again soon. The stores were closing up for the night but he was still in time to pick up dinner at the pizzeria. The wet asphalt reflected the colorful lights of the shop signs and the shadows of the passersby. The plate glass windows of the pubs and cafés were all fogged up. And so was the window of the by-the-slice pizzeria. He was just a few steps short of the pizzeria when he saw Anna. Rocco stopped in the middle of the street. He bowed his head and headed over to the sheltering shadow of the dark stretch of street at the foot of the building, far from the streetlamp. He saw Anna step down from the sidewalk and head straight for her house. She hadn't seen him, or else she'd pretended not to. For that matter, she'd made it perfectly clear when they'd talked on the phone. He waited until the woman vanished into her building, then he continued at a brisk pace toward the pizzeria. He was tired, his bones ached. All he wanted was to go home and get a few hours of sleep.

MARINA ISN'T HERE. I CAN'T FIND HER ANYWHERE. Not even in bed. I sit down at the dining room table. I unwrap the package from the pizzeria. The slices strike me as so many scabs covered with pus, the wounds of a burn victim, the lacerations of a herpes outbreak. I can't bring myself to eat these shoe soles. The supplì—rice-and-cheese fritters— are black, they must have fried them in engine coolant. And the Coke is lukewarm. Even when it's cold out, a Coke should be ice cold. Warm Coca-Cola sticks to your palate and extinguishes the will to go on living. That is, if you have it in the first place.

So sleepy. I'm dropping on my feet. It's strange. I've been thinking about that girl, Chiara, all day long, and I don't even know what she looks like. Whether she's tall, whether she's skinny. Does she resemble her mother? Her father? Tomorrow, I'm going to come get you, Chiara. Tomorrow, I'm going to come get you, for sure.

God, this sofa. You sink into the cushions. You just sink too deep.

"All right then, tell me. For 100,000 euros. She starred opposite Marilyn Monroe in Gentlemen Prefer Blondes."

He doesn't know. He's twenty years old, this young contestant. What does he know?

Jane Russell, you asshole!

"Lauren Bacall?"

You just pissed away 100,000 euros. You go on a quiz show and you lack the basic knowledge? So why are you even bothering, I say. Change channels!

"Time. Time. What is time? The Swiss manufacture it. The French hoard it. The Italians squander it. Americans say it is money. Hindus say it does not exist. You know what I say? I say time is a crook!"

No, not Beat the Devil. Now I'm going to have to watch the whole thing.

"I like an associate of mine to have a sense of humor. A good laugh does more for the stomach muscles than five minutes' setting -up exercises."

"And now that we've had our moment of fun and all the better for it, let's get back to the question."

WEDNESDAY

*Y*ou fell asleep."

"What . . . what time is it?"

"I don't know. It's late," Marina replies, brushing back her hair. How does she do it? She brushes it back, she seems to knot it, and it doesn't loosen. What does she have, glue on her hands?

It's late. It's dark out. There's a cartoon playing on the TV.

"I was watching a movie."

"I know. But it's been over for a while now." Marina smiles at me.

"Where were you, Marì?"

"Why don't you go to bed?"

"Because I can't. I just can't. It hurts all over."

My back, my neck, my shoulder blades, my pelvis, and even my legs. "Do you remember when you'd come home in the early years and you'd give me massages?"

"Of course I do. Every day that God sent us here on earth."

"Didn't you like it?"

"Not even a little."

"Why didn't you ever tell me?"

"I don't know . . . it seemed to make you happy."

"Well, now I can reveal the truth: I hated getting massages."

We both break out laughing. "There are so many things I never told you."

"Like what?"

"I didn't like you with short hair."

"What else?"

"I didn't like it when you wore ballet flats."

"Never had a pair."

"One summer you did. In Santo Stefano."

"But you gave me that pair."

"It was a mistake."

"What else didn't you ever tell me?"

"For a while I thought you had another man."

"Me? Who?"

"Prosperi."

"Giorgio? Serena's husband? The surgeon?"

"The very same."

"Sweetheart, he took out my appendix."

"So?"

"What do you mean so? He was the husband of my closest friend!"

"Exactly, that's a classic. You always invited him to dinner."

"We always invited them to dinner."

"He even rooted for S. S. Lazio. You acted the fool with him."

"Sweetheart, Giorgio and I went back thirty years. Come on, let's not talk about that nonsense anymore. What else didn't you ever tell me?"

"That I miss you, Marina, I miss you so much I can't stand it."

"That's not true. You know why you say it? Because you're scared."

And what am I supposed to be scared of? "Of what?"

"It's not me you miss. It's you."

"You're wrong. Do you remember that phrase? The desire you feel for a person is immortal."

"But if you satisfy it, it vanishes. And with it, your need for that person vanishes as well."

"How am I supposed to satisfy it?"

"Maybe you already have." She strokes my hair. I look her in the eyes. "You know something, Marina? I think my eyesight is getting worse."

"Your eyesight has nothing to do with it." And she dries one of my tears. "It's two in the morning, Rocco. Go to bed."

"I can't. I tell you, I can't."

• • •

ENZO BAIOCCHI BREATHED SLOWLY UNDER THE SHEETS as he looked up at the ceiling. Which was blue. The security lighting tinged everything blue. The ceiling, his hands, his fingernails, the metal nightstand, the empty neighboring bed, the door and the bars on the window. This was the right time. Twenty past two in the morning. The guards had made their last round ten minutes ago and the trash truck would be pulling in an hour from now. He needed to get moving. First of all, he put on his socks and his running shoes, fastening the Velcro straps. He took off the pajama top, remaining in his black T-shirt. He kissed the gold crucifix that he wore around his neck. Then he went over to the window. The courtyard was deserted. Only the trees and bushes swayed in the night breeze. A cat trotted briskly across the gravel driveway, only to vanish amidst the leaves of a small dragon tree.

In three days, they'd be taking him back to the cell, and so long to the fresh sheets and infirmary food, so long to the music that every morning the male nurses would blast at top volume, so long to the newspaper, and most important of all, so long to all the painstaking work he'd done on the third bar to the left in his window. It had taken him two weeks of effort to unseat that bar from its housing. And now it pulled out as easily as the molar of an old man with periodontitis. He'd been on a strict diet, he'd lost seven pounds, and sure enough, he fit right through the remaining bars. He didn't even have to squeeze that hard. He was already on the ground floor, and it took only a drop of a couple of feet and he was standing in the flowerbed. He looked around.

The infirmary lights were all out. Only that spectral, blue security spotlight told the world that the patients were all fast asleep. In the control room, however, the light was still on. At that time of night, the male nurse, the physician on duty, and the two guards were playing Risk, the board game of war and world conquest with little brightly colored plastic tanks, a pair of dice, and a world map. A craze imported by Frangipane, the younger nurse, and it served to combat the boredom of the graveyard shifts. In order to duck the closed-circuit security cameras, Enzo had to reach the exterior wall and creep along with his back pressed against it. He moved forward slowly, trying to stay as silent as possible while crossing the gravel. Once he reached the wall, beyond the light cast by the yellow area lights, inch by inch, creeping carefully as any sloth, Enzo made his way closer to the iron gate, which stood hermetically sealed just outside the control room.

"I attack the Middle East from Egypt with seven tanks." It was Frangipane's voice.

"I'll crush you!" That was Vito, the guard.

As Enzo approached the gate, there was only one point where he would be fully exposed to view. It was brightly lit and there was no way to hide: he'd just have to cross it quickly and pray no one was looking at the center of the courtyard at that moment. There were only two guards. Luckily, the funding cuts imposed by the last few administrations had decimated the number of correctional officers assigned to security. Which meant it would be a simpler matter. If they'd been fully staffed, Enzo could never have dreamed of trying to escape. There would have been at least four men on the guard towers and three more in the courtyard. But now, with just two guards, their attention focused on protecting the territorial integrity of China or Yakutia, the idea seemed eminently feasible. He could go.

"One, one, two, damn it, what shitty luck!" Frangipane shouted.

"Ha, ha, ha. You're not touching the Middle East, you bastard. Instead, I'm attacking you from North Africa," Vito shouted.

"What's the matter with you, Vito?" came a third voice. That had to be the doctor on duty. "If you do that, Paolo can attack you from Brazil, right?"

"Why don't you mind your own fucking business, Doc!" That had to be Paolo, the other guard, who clearly had high hopes of colonial expansion into Africa once Frangipane had been weakened in that theater of operations.

Enzo shut his eyes, took a breath, and in spite of the fact that he was all of sixty years old, he lunged like a lightning bolt straight toward the metal door. A pair of sky-blue pajama bottoms with a black T-shirt over them crossed the spotlight-illuminated yard. Quick as a dream upon waking. No one saw him. No one sounded the alarm. No one was monitoring the security cameras.

Enzo slumped at the foot of the gate. He was panting and he mopped the sweat from his forehead. Now he just had to wait. Soon the metal gate would swing open and the garbage truck would enter the courtyard to load up the infirmary's garbage. Three gray plastic sacks that were already waiting on the ground outside the control room. That would be the second-most difficult moment. He'd have to leap onto the back of the truck, get over the side of the garbage bed, and hunker down there, waiting for the garbage sacks to come sailing over the side, full of food scraps and who knows what other waste produced by seven patients, five male nurses, two physicians, and four guards standing different shifts. The important thing was not to give into the temptation of sleep. But Enzo Baiocchi wasn't worried about that. He had so much adrenaline pumping through his body that he was unlikely to sleep for days, weeks, possibly months. One thing was certain: he wouldn't rest before going to pay a call on that bastard. Something he'd been waiting to do now for five long years.

AT THREE IN THE MORNING THE LIGHTS AT POLICE headquarters were all turned off. Only on the ground floor and in the operations room was there any sign of life. At the front entrance, Officer Miniero, newly transferred north from Vomero, was trying to solve a rebus in the weekly puzzle magazine.

"*Buongiorno!*"

The deputy chief's voice brought him back to reality. He snapped to attention. "Deputy Chief. In so early?"

"Yes." Bundled in his loden overcoat he climbed up to the offices without turning on the lights. After all, he knew the way like the back of his hand. He entered his office, picked up the receiver, and dialed the phone number.

"He . . . hello?"

"Italo! It's me, Rocco."

"But. . . ."

He could just picture him, Officer Pierron, looking around wildly, trying to figure out whether that phone call belonged to reality or to the dream that he'd just left on his pillow.

"What . . . what time is it?"

"Three in the morning!"

"And what . . . what's happening?"

"What's happening is that you're going to get dressed and hurry down to police headquarters. We have a visit to pay."

"At this hour of the morning?"

"There's a girl being held prisoner somewhere not far from here, and she may already be dead. Do I have to remind you of that?"

Pierron said nothing. "Italo! Have you fallen back to sleep?"

"No, no. Give me ten minutes."

"And don't come in uniform!"

Rocco hung up and at the same time, opened the drawer of his "secular daily prayers," as he'd renamed his need for a daily dose of marijuana.

At night the temperature drops. It's a well known fact. But that May night was really overdoing it. He took the last toke. A faint smile was already starting to appear on his face. He flicked the roach out into the street and shut the window. Italo was about to come in, and Rocco decided to go meet him.

He switched off the light and left his office. In the dark

hallway the faint light of a vending machine illuminated a pair of shadows. Two figures were standing there, motionless in the middle of the hall, hands dangling at their sides, looking like something that had just stepped out of a nightmare.

"What the fuck?" exclaimed the deputy chief.

It was Deruta and D'Intino. Their wrecked appearance made them resemble a pair of homeless vagrants fished out of the waters of some foul-smelling swamp. They were no longer two police officers, but a distant memory of those public officials. Their uniforms were verging decidedly on the brown. Their pale, lunar faces were streaked with black drops of mud dripping down their cheeks, designing a spiderweb of horror. D'Intino was drenched and still wore his now-shapeless cap. Deruta was in shirt sleeves, and the front of that shirt was torn wide open, while the cuffs of his trousers were dragging under the heels of his shoes. Two survivors of some colossal defeat, like a veteran of Caporetto or a deserter from the Russian front in 1943.

"What the fuck have you two been up to?"

It was Deruta who spoke: "We've been looking for Viorelo Midea's house."

Rocco had to force his memory to try to remember who Viorelo Midea was. That uncertainty was detected by Deruta: "The Romanian, the one who was killed in the car crash."

Rocco concealed his momentary confusion. "I know that, of course. So?"

"We found it!" D'Intino said happily. Then he turned and vomited on the floor next to the coffee machine.

FIFTEEN MINUTES LATER IN POLICE HEADQUARTERS' passport office, Italo and Officer Miniero had given the two wretched men a little tea from the vending machine, while Rocco observed the scene with an air of detachment.

"It was hard, sir," said Deruta. "Very hard."

"And how did you do it?" Italo asked.

"We thought about it."

"Stop the presses, that's the biggest piece of news all day," said Rocco.

"Here's how it happened. We started at the apartment of the Abyssinians."

"Eritreans," Schiavone corrected him.

"That's right, anyway, those guys. And we searched the whole building."

"We stuck the key in every door," D'Intino continued. "And it was no good. No match."

"Just think, one old woman even hit D'Intino over the head with her purse because she hadn't seen his uniform. So we searched the whole building next door and then the building on the other side."

"Nothing, it never matched. It would drive you crazy, Dottore!"

"And that's when I had a thought!" said Deruta.

"Actually, I thought of it!" D'Intino retorted.

"What are you talking about? I told you to go to the quarter. . . ."

"No, I did, and then you up and said: no! But I managed to convince you that. . . ."

"Whatever, you came up with the idea between the two of you. Tell me the rest of the story," Rocco broke in.

"Then we thought that if this guy doesn't have money, then maybe, just maybe, he lives in a poor part of town."

"Well how about that . . ." said Italo, stifling his laughter. "Not bad."

"True, Italo, not bad at all. That is a fantastic deduction. And who would ever have thought of it?"

D'Intino smiled at the deputy chief: "Right? And so we went and walked around in the poor part of town. Though in Aosta they don't really have any!"

"No."

"Then this cretin," said Deruta, pointing at his colleague, "what do think he went and did?"

"I don't know. What did D'Intino go and do?" asked Rocco.

"He put the car in reverse as he was leaving the parking space and BAM!" He clapped his hands to emphasize the event. "He went and crashed into a cargo van."

"And the car?"

"It crumpled the fender and a little bit damaged the headlight," D'Intino replied, eyes downcast. "Now it doesn't run so good and smoke pours out of the motor."

Rocco rolled his eyes.

"All the same, even in our misfortune, we were fortunate indeed," Deruta went on.

"Shall we cut to the chase?" By now, Rocco couldn't take much more. Either they got to the point or he was going to have to throw every file box in the passport office at their heads.

"We crashed into a cargo van full of Romanians. Who were loading it full of stuff to take to Rumenìa." He mangled, as was his way, the name of the country.

"Romania, Deruta, Romania!"

"Romania, right. But listen, Dotto', don't interrupt, otherwise we'll lose the thread."

"That's right," D'Intino reiterated, backing up his colleague.

"I promise not to interrupt again."

Deruta took a deep breath. "So we fought with these Rumanians. That is, D'Intino fought with the Rumanians, it was his fault. But we asked them, as long as they were Rumanians, if they knew this Viorelo Midea. And one of them smiled and said yes!"

"And he even told us where he lived. And we went straight over!"

"Now this is the good part. We got to the place. We went up to the apartment. We put the key in the lock to see if it matched and BAM!" Deruta clapped his hands again.

"They poured out and were all over us! There were four of them, Dottore. And they were throwing punches and kicking us like nobody's business."

"And me and D'Intino were giving as good as we got. It

was total chaos. And then I threw a punch with both eyes closed. Only I hit D'Intino, right in the ribs."

"Which were already pretty sore."

"Fists were flying everywhere. I caught a punch in the face and another to the ear."

"And I got one in the ribs, but that was Deruta, and another in the head, and I mean right in the head!"

"But who was hitting you?" Rocco shouted.

"These guys in the apartment. So D'Intino and I went running out the front door into the street but those guys chased us. And D'Intino fell right into the puddle."

"Right, Dottore, you know those puddles they have at the side of the street? What's the word for them. . . ."

"Puddles," Rocco replied.

"Yeah, that's right. Well, I fell right into one."

"Instead, they threw something at me and hit me in the head and I fell in. Then, when we came to, by the light of the streetlamps, even though it was night, those guys realized we were cops, and they apologized."

"That's right, because they thought we were burglars."

"Burglars?" asked Italo.

"That's right, burglars. Because in that apartment, Viorelo lived along with four guys from Senegal, and wow, those guys from Senegal really know how to throw punches. Anyway, these four guys from Senegal with a friend of theirs from Tunisia had come home. . . ."

"A few hours earlier. . . ."

"That's right, good point D'Intino, a few hours earlier, and they found the place turned upside down."

"It's just that they can't report it to the authorities because they don't have a valid residence permit."

"And in fact, they pay their rent under the table, in cash."

"Fine. Anything else?"

"Yes. Do you want to know what the burglars stole?"

"What did the burglars steal?" asked Rocco.

"Nothing," Deruta replied.

"What do you mean, nothing?"

"Nothing, nothing at all."

"Oh, well," Italo broke in, "it's not as if there was cash or expensive jewelry in a wall safe, was there?"

"No, no. There was a television set, an iPod, and a stereo. And they were all still right there. The burglars just went through all the drawers and cabinets."

"Anyway, all they did was turn the place upside down and nothing more." Italo was smiling, but Rocco was thinking. "That's strange," he said. "A professional burglar wouldn't go to the apartment of these poverty-stricken wretches. They're as poor as he is, and it wouldn't do him any good. It's just a strange thing."

"That's the same thing we thought!" D'Intino exclaimed, bursting with pride. "I mean, I would at least have taken the iPod, right?"

"Right. Good work, men. If this were wartime, I would have nominated you for medals. But there's no war going on."

"Right, damn it," said D'Intino through clenched teeth.

"Still, the two of you have done a fantastic job. Now you can go home. And tomorrow you can come in late, too."

"How late?" asked Deruta.

"Later than usual," said Rocco.

"Listen, and what are we supposed to do about the fact that they're all living here without a residence permit?"

"What are you supposed to do? Nothing."

"We shouldn't arrest them?" asked D'Intino.

"I'd say you shouldn't," Rocco replied.

"And what about the fact they're paying their rent in cash, under the table?"

"For now, just keep cool and collected. Go home and get some rest." Rocco nodded to Italo and together they left the passport office. Deruta smiled at D'Intino.

"Nice job!" he told him, and shook his colleague's hand.

THE METAL GATE SHIVERED. ENZO SLOWLY MOVED away from the wall. An orange blinker flashed as a warning that the gate was opening. In the doorway of the control room, the figure of one of the two guards appeared: Paolo. Once the gate was fully open, the headlights of the little garbage truck appeared as the driver ground his gears and crept forward cautiously into the infirmary courtyard. Enzo went all in at that instant, that flash of light. He moved rapidly from the shadows of his hiding place to the back of the garbage truck as it crawled through the entrance at walking speed. He managed to get a foothold on the rear bumper, right above the license plate, and held tight with both hands to the big metal dump bed. Then, even though the truck was moving, he managed to climb up. He threw himself over the edge and slid like an eel down the side of the metal bin into the garbage. He landed on a pile of gray plastic bags that reeked of rot. He clamped one hand over mouth and nose and waited for the steel gate to close behind the trash truck.

Half an hour of waiting. Then the trash bags collected by the janitor came flying one after the other into the big steel bed on the back of the truck, slamming down onto Enzo's body and face. Those bags of infirmary garbage carried the stench of death. Enzo gulped a couple of times, but then lost control and vomited up his dinner. He heard the garbage truck start up again. Sprawled face-up on that horrendous mattress, his eyes turned up toward the black dome of the night sky, he saw the procession of area courtyard lights, exterior walls, and guard towers stream past. Then he felt the garbage truck speed up. Faster and faster. Faster and faster and faster. The gears ground as the driver shifted and the truck gained speed.

Enzo Baiocchi was a free man!

HE PARKED A GOOD LONG WAY FROM THE STORE. Then, Rocco and Italo walked along the sidewalk. There were just two streetlights, one at the beginning of the street, the other at the curve. They weren't enough, though. In the darkness, the air had turned chilly, Nordic, and inhospitable.

"Do you want to let me in on what you're planning to do?"

But Rocco didn't answer. When they arrived at HeyDiddleLiddles, he looked around. He walked back a few yards to a metal gate. He climbed over it easily.

"Where are you going?"

"Come on!" and the deputy chief made his way into the courtyard of a small apartment building. Italo, muttering phrases of hatred and resentment toward his boss, followed him.

PRIMO CUAZ HAD NO CHOICE BUT TO WATCH LATE-night television—not because he particularly liked it, but because ever since he was a young man he had worked only and exclusively by night and had slept during the daytime. At age eighty-four, those kind of routines were hard to break. His habits had resulted in a series of problems. His skin was pale and white, his eyesight was weak, and the schedule of his meals was deranged. He ate breakfast at two in the afternoon, lunch at nine at night, and dinner at five in the morning when truck drivers or else factory workers like his wife were just downing their first morning espresso. Often they'd sit at the table together, she with a breakfast pastry and he with a bowl of pasta with tomato sauce, respectively telling each other stories about the day they'd just finished or the one they were about to start. Since he'd retired, he'd done nothing but rattle around the apartment while Iside snored peacefully alone in their king-size bed. He'd tried to subvert that state of equilibrium with the aid of sleeping pills or by going days at a time without shutting an eye in order to shift into step with the rest of humanity. But he just couldn't seem to do it. He went to bed at six in the morning and woke up at two in the afternoon, as punctual as a German alarm clock. During one of his solitary nights, Primo had done some calculations. He slept eight hours, so did Iside. In their sixty years of marriage, it was as if they'd only spent twenty together. The other forty years? Each of them sleeping alone. In order to make love, a habit they'd only lost in the past seven years, they met in those shadow phases between the time one of them would wake up and the other would knock off work, between her return home and his leaving the house in his uniform. They were both convinced that it had been that very set of logistical difficulties that had kept their desire and lust for each other kindled over the long decades. Four children and six grandchildren had been the result, unmistakably visible to anyone who cared to look. At four a.m. on that dark May morning, as chilly as a slab of marble, Primo had turned off the television set as the closing credits of *Stagecoach* appeared on screen. He went to the window to scrutinize the sky. No stars. Clouds. In the apartment building courtyard, all the lights were out. But however weak his eyesight might be in daylight, at night it seemed to be miraculously restored. Something wasn't right down there. He straightened his eyeglasses and squinted to see more clearly. He could have sworn that there were two shadowy shapes down there in the courtyard, moving furtively. Very furtively.

Burglars, he decided. Fifty years of honorable service reawakened with a roar in his aging arteries, in his bones, and in his brain. He still had his pistol, in the chocolate box put away on the top shelf. Striding briskly now, he went to retrieve it. Some cans of tomatoes fell to the floor. He put them away, but when he turned around, there was his wife standing in the doorway, asking: "What's going on?"

"Burglars. In the apartment building."

"What do you care? You're retired!"

"Let me pass, Iside. Let me pass."

"Primo, please!"

But the elderly security guard wouldn't listen to reason. He brusquely shoved past the woman and left the apartment. Iside yawned and decided to go back to bed. "*Fè tcheuca senque te vou*," she murmured. "Do what you want." He was a grownup, with plenty of experience under his belt.

ITALO HAD CAUGHT UP WITH THE DEPUTY CHIEF OUT-side a ground floor window in the courtyard.

"Italo, if my calculations are correct, this is the back of the store."

"Maybe it is. So what?"

"So you wait and watch."

"Hands up!"

Italo and Rocco turned around. In the shadows, a figure was brandishing a revolver. "I caught you! Now I'm going to call the police."

Rocco smiled: "Actually, we *are* the police."

The man took a step forward into what little light there was. "Who are you?"

"Deputy Chief Schiavone and Officer Italo Pierron."

The old man adjusted his eyeglasses. "I don't believe you."

"Is it all right if I put my hand in my pocket?" Rocco asked. Primo nodded. The deputy chief handed over his badge to the retired security guard. But he couldn't read it. He angled the police ID to catch a little light. "I can't . . . I can't read it. . . ." He tucked the pistol under his armpit and tipped the badge with both hands until he finally found the right angle. "Ah . . . all right. Yes." He handed the badge and ID back to Rocco. "And do you mind if I ask what you're doing at the rear of the store at this time of night?"

"We need to get inside without being seen because we suspect there are illicit goods being moved through here."

"Through the children's store?" Primo asked in astonishment.

"That's right. Now, if you don't mind. . . ."

"What are you doing?"

Rocco heaved a sigh of annoyance. "I told you! I need to get inside."

He pulled his Swiss army knife out of his pocket. He chose a small file and started working on the shutters. He was scratching away chunks of wood and paint.

"What if there's an alarm?" Italo asked.

"They don't have one," said the security guard.

"Oh, right. The alarm will just summon the police. And all these guys want is to keep the Carabinieri and the police from setting foot in their shop," Schiavone added.

"But these guys who?" asked Italo.

"Wait, are you or aren't you a police officer? Don't keep pestering your superior officer with questions."

A large chunk of wood came away. At that point, Rocco folded away the file and pulled open the knife blade.

"It just takes a little patience," he said, sliding it into the opening he'd just managed to make. "No good, there's a metal reinforcement. I need a pair of pliers. Do we have a pair in the car?"

"Stay right there. I'll get one." The security guard left the two policemen alone.

"So what are we doing now?"

"Waiting for the pliers, right?"

"You want to try and give me a clearer explanation?"

"All right, so what they do in here is they issue receipts without taking in cash."

"What are they, stupid?"

"No, Italo, they're not stupid. What they're doing is laundering cash. They pretend to take in payments from customers, they even pay the taxes on them, and then they deposit clean, freshly laundered money in the bank."

"Just think about that . . . and who does this kind of thing?"

"Who do you think? The Jesuits?"

Iside could hear her husband rummaging around in the kitchen broom closet.

"Primo, what are you doing?"

"Nothing, you just keep sleeping."

It was easy for him to say that, idiot that he was, now that he'd found the Beretta and gotten it out. Iside had unloaded the gun years ago, but who knew what else he was getting up to in the kitchen. She put on her slippers and went to see. Primo had pulled out pliers, pincers, half his tool chest. "What's all this?"

"We need to break open a shutter."

Iside was baffled. "What do you mean, *we*? Didn't you go out to arrest some thieves?"

"Woman, you couldn't possibly understand!"

"Oh, I can understand, don't you worry. Would you explain what's going on?"

"All right, but don't breathe a word. There are two policemen out there who need to get into the HeyDiddle-Liddles store, because they suspect there's illicit traffic being conducted there."

Iside thought it over. "Then explain one thing to me. Why don't they do it in the light of day with a search warrant from a judge, the way the police always do on television?"

"Because that's television, Iside, not real life."

"Still, it strikes me as odd. At four in the morning, these guys need to break into a shop by forcing open the shutters. You don't think you might be going senile, do you, Primo?"

Suspicious, now, the man left his apartment.

PRIMO CUAZ CAME BACK WITH TWO PAIRS OF PLIERS, a rubber mallet, and a hand drill.

"Why are you trying to get in at four in the morning by breaking and entering instead of waiting for broad daylight and a warrant from a judge?" Primo asked.

"Because the judge knows nothing about it, because the people who own this store can't know that we went in, and because the only ones who can know about it are the three of us, and then, my good sir, because you can't stop these people even with a warrant from a judge. These are people who'll shoot you without even stopping to ask who you are."

"What kind of people are they?" the elderly security guard asked in a faint voice.

"Very nasty people," said Rocco. "You just think of the worst kind of people you can imagine. And you still haven't come close."

"Terrorists?"

"If only!"

Primo held out his arms. "There, I've brought you some tools."

"Thanks. The pliers would have been enough."

Rocco set to work. He yanked a couple of times until he heard a loud SNAP! and the shutter swung open.

Now he just had to deal with the window.

"Easy. It's wood, it's old, and it's single pane. Hand me your jacket."

Without understanding, Italo handed it over. Rocco wrapped it around his hand, and then with a short sharp blow, he shattered the glass into pieces. It made a barely audible noise.

"Are you sure you've always been a policeman, Dottore?" asked Primo.

"Maybe not in another life."

"I'd say so!" tossed in the security guard, elbowing Italo in the ribs, while the deputy chief carefully extracted the shards of broken glass from the window frame. Then Rocco handed Italo's jacket back. "Careful when you put it on. A few shards might still be stuck somewhere."

"I've never heard of such a thing. . . ."

"We need to get going now. By the way, my name's Rocco. And you are?"

"Primo."

"Thanks, Primo. You can head on home, now. I don't need to tell you that we were never here and you never saw us."

"Unnecessary."

Italo handed the tools back to Signor Cuaz who headed back to his apartment with a spring in his step. "It was a wonderful night. Thanks, Rocco."

"Thank *you*, Primo."

The deputy chief stuck his hand through the freshly broken window and turned the handle. The empty window frame swung open.

"Let's go in and take a look around."

THE STOREROOM IN THE BACK OF THE SHOP WAS roughly a thousand square feet in area and was stacked high with cardboard boxes. Most of the boxes were marked with Chinese ideograms. Using their cell phone flashlights to see their way, the policemen moved cautiously through that forest of stacked boxes. Rocco looked as comfortable as if he were strolling around his garage at home. Relaxed and untroubled, he read the labels on the boxes, squeezing them as if testing fruit for ripeness, practically whistling as he worked. Italo, on the other hand, was tense. He moved slowly, ears pricked up to capture the slightest suspicious sound, and was sweating copiously. In fact, he could already feel his armpits wetting his shirt, even though the room was quite chilly.

"What are we looking for?" Italo asked in an undertone. The deputy chief didn't answer. "Rocco, maybe we should do something in the daytime. I'm not comfortable with this," and he turned back toward the window they'd just forced open.

Beethoven's "Ode to Joy" rang out through the dark room.

"What the fuck!" Rocco snapped.

Italo's blood ran cold. "Your phone's ringing, idiot!" he said.

Rocco quickly answered the phone: "Who is it?"

"Why are you talking in a whisper?"

It was Anna.

"Anna, what do you want?"

"You haven't called me all day long. Does that strike you as normal?"

"You told me to go fuck myself yesterday. Why would I have called you?"

"I don't know. Maybe to apologize?"

Rocco spread his arms wide. Italo continued to look around wildly, like a trapped hamster.

"Anna, this isn't a good time. I'm right in the middle of a police operation."

"Of course you are. And what's this police operation called? Elisabetta? Barbara?"

"Fuck, Anna, I'll call you tomorrow. I swear."

"Save yourself the phone call. And have a nice night."

She hung up.

"Who the fuck was that?" Italo practically yelled.

"A woman I know. And by the way, I heard you, you know? You called me an idiot."

Italo looked down at his shoes. "Sorry. I was scared."

"Don't let it happen again," Rocco warned him. "I'm still your superior officer."

"All right. But you should have turned off your cell phone."

"Then how would we have been able to see?"

"I have a flashlight."

"And you think *I'm* an idiot? Turn it on!"

Italo did as ordered.

Behind a stack of cartons there was an empty space. At the center stood an old metal desk, straight out of a post office. A Naugahyde chair and a steel lamp. Schiavone went over to the desk. Which had two drawers. In the first drawer there was bric-a-brac and junk, as well as sheets of paper. In the other was a ledger. Rocco sat down, turned on the light, and began perusing that ledger as if he were a book-keeper.

"The light!" Italo called in a hoarse whisper.

"Don't worry. All right, now, what have we here?"

A sheaf of paper with a long string of names. Next to each surname was a number. Some of the names were underlined in red.

"What is it?"

"A list of some kind. Look here. Federico Biamonti . . . Gressoney. 130,000. Paride Sassuoli. Pila. 85,000."

"What's it mean, though?"

Rocco looked up from the ledger. "Debts, Italo. Debts. Are you good at taking pictures?"

"How do you mean?"

"Take your cell phone and photograph every page of this thing. It's only five pages." He got up from his chair and gave Italo his place. "And do it fast, before day dawns."

Italo pushed the button for the cell phone's camera and set to work. Rocco finished up his examination of the place. He walked over to a big carton. He pulled out a jackknife and opened it up. Inside were boxes.

Car stereos.

He opened another. Electric kettles.

"Are you done yet?"

Italo photographed the last sheet of paper and put the ledger back where it belonged. He turned off the light. At the same time, a key creaked in a lock.

"Fucking. . . ."

"Over here!" hissed Rocco. Italo hurried over to the deputy chief who was standing behind the stack of cartons. "What is it?"

"Someone's here."

They turned off flashlight and cell phones.

"Lass Crizma, I gevv yoo mi ar," someone sang, butchering a seasonal evergreen. "And de rilli good play yoo mèche it awaiiii." One after another, the overhead fluorescent lamps flickered on. The storeroom was lit up like a supermarket at rush hour. Italo blinked, wide-eyed. Rocco remained motionless. He held the pocket knife in one hand.

"Dis yeer too sevv yoo from deers . . ." A shadow moved forward into the storeroom. Rocco and Italo shrank as small as they could, pressed against the stacks of cartons like a couple of mice. "Lass Crizma, I gevv yoo mi ar . . ." the shadow took shape. It was a man. Short, with a beard. He grabbed a carton, opened it, checked the contents, then heaved it up onto his shoulder. "Too sevv yoo from deers . . ." The body dissolved back into a shadow, the fluorescent lamps switched off, the key creaked in the lock again. Rocco and Italo were plunged back into darkness.

"Jesus, that was close."

"I know, right? We can go now, Italo."

The officer mopped the sweat from his brow, then followed the deputy chief. Without turning on any light sources, they reached the window they'd forced and looked out into the courtyard. It was all dark outside. No sign of life. Rocco went through first. Italo followed him. Above them, in the second-floor window, Primo Cuaz was waving goodbye. Rocco and Italo waved back and, hugging close to the apartment building's outside wall, they made their way back to the metal gate, climbed over it, and found themselves out on the sidewalk, just in time to see a red Alfa Romeo roaring off toward the center of town.

"So where were we just now, Rocco?"

"In a very nice little place. Things look much clearer to me now. How about you?"

"They're laundering money and selling stolen merchandise!"

"That's right. That's what these people do for a living. They launder money and they loanshark. And the two activities are linked, Italo. Closely linked."

As they were heading back to the car, Italo elbowed Rocco in the ribs. "Look at that!"

Rocco looked up and stood there, enchanted, as if he'd just beheld the Madonna floating over the rooftops of Aosta.

It was snowing.

"I don't believe it. In May?"

"These things happen. Come on, Rocco, let's get going! Don't worry, with all the rain we have, it's not even likely to stick."

Sleep, wakefulness, more sleep, more wakefulness.

Even breathing seemed to be getting harder. With the hand still bound to the piece of the chair's backrest, she'd succeeded in touching the floor next to her wounded leg. There was a gooey puddle, as sticky as jam.

Blood. Blood dripping from the wound.

You need to get up.

She wasn't even bothering to answer that voice anymore. She didn't have the strength. She just answered it in her head.

There was no point trying to speak aloud now.

How am I supposed to get up? Any suggestions?

You just need to brace your knee against the floor and haul yourself to your feet. Use your injured leg for leverage.

Impossible. I already tried. It hurts too much! My head'll start spinning and down I'll go, got it? I can't do it.

Yes, you can.

No, I can't.

Yes, you can, you drooling idiot!

No.

Okay, then you can just die. You realize that you're going to die, don't you?

The night was ending. A faint, pale light was starting to tinge the darkness of that cellar. However faint the light, it helped. It strengthened her courage. It dusted off her brain a little. She looked out the little window. It was snowing.

Don't just lie there waiting for something to happen. You're burning out. You're going to burn out like a candle. Clench your teeth and try. Give it a try!

She slowly leaned her torso forward, both hands clenching the seat of the chair.

No pain.

Now she had to brace her right knee against the ground and try to bend the other one, too. Her whole body was tingling. Her chest hurt, and so did her shoulders, her pelvis, and her ankles. And her left leg, with that section of broken chair leg stabbed into it like a harpoon, was straight and rigid, as hard as a piece of ice. She tried to wiggle her numb toes. It took a few minutes to wake those tingling toes back up, but in the end, she could feel them moving inside her hiking boots. And no pain in her thigh. Then she moved on to her calf. That too was getting stiff, and she no longer felt any pain. Now the hardest thing of all, the quadriceps. She tried to tighten that muscle. Slowly, just barely contracting it. No pain. Fine. The leg was awake now, maybe the pain back there was only lurking in ambush.

Your knee. Bend your knee!

Slowly, she did it, bending her knee inch by inch, but continuously. The pain shot through her like a whiplash and froze her motionless.

Go on!

I don't think I can.

You can't stop now, unless you bend it, you won't be able to get up on your knees. Go on!

She tried again.

God God God that *hurts*!

Don't stop!

It wasn't a fair fight. She was on one side, and on the other was a monster with sharp fangs.

"Chiara, bend that knee!"

It wasn't the little voice anymore. Now it was a man's voice.

"Chiara, bend it, God damn it, bend it!"

Was that Stefano? Stefano, her ski instructor, her teacher. Was he there? Was he watching her?

"Chiara, bend your knee, for Christ's sake!"

"I'm bending it, I'm bending it!" she shouted as she pulled her foot toward her.

"Not enough, bend it more!"

"It hurts!"

"I know it does, but you have to pull on it. Come on, Chiara. Work on it, Chiara!"

She was pulling her foot back and sweating. The pain was biting into her, but she still had a duty to bend her knee. She could do it, she had to do it. Stefano wanted her to bend her knee.

"Good work, Chiara, that's it, that's it!"

One last shout. Her left leg was bent halfway.

"Good job, Chiara!" said Stefano.

Good job, Chiara, echoed the little voice.

Tongues of fire were torturing her, but they were fleeting flames, nothing in comparison with what she'd just been through. With her torso bent over the good leg, she was breathing raggedly and waiting. Now the fire just needed to quiet down, the pain lessen so she could make one last major effort and get up onto her knees.

But right there and then she decided that the best thing to do was to give in to a bout of liberatory sobbing.

At five a.m. on a gray morning with flakes of snow still dropping from the sky, with his office door shut, the deputy chief had turned up the heat. He smoked as he jotted down notes on a pad. The coffee from the vending machine had left a taste of old mud in his mouth. He was starting to miss the morning rituals of an espresso at home, breakfast at Ettore's, and a nice relaxed joint in his leather armchair before starting the day. He absolutely had to lay his hands on whoever had kidnapped Chiara and make them pay, for those sleepless nights if nothing else. The phone rang.

Who could it be at this time of day? he wondered.

"Deputy Chief Schiavone, it's me, Baldi."

"Judge Baldi, are you having trouble sleeping too?"

"That's right. The thought of Chiara Berguet is devouring every neuron in my brain."

"Any progress?"

"I'd say so. Listen. I've discovered something. Now then, a month ago Edil.ber was the subject of union complaints because of delays in payment, and it ran the risk of losing a substantial number of union employees. The three main Italian unions—CGIL, CISL, and UIL—invoked Article 18, Pietro Berguet had a narrow brush with bankruptcy, lawyers got involved, there was a considerable back and forth, and you know the routine. But now comes the interesting part. Pietro Berguet resolved his financial problems and managed to pay his back wages, and Edil.ber continued to operate and managed to take part in the competition for regional government contracts."

"So far, nothing startling. . . ."

"Except for this: neither the Vallée Savings Bank nor any other banks issued loans or lines of credit."

"Are you certain of that?"

"One hundred percent. So the question is this: where did they find the money?"

"Fucking hell . . ." Rocco murmured.

"Excuse me?"

"I said 'fucking hell,' your honor."

A silence ensued. "Right, I'm with you," said Baldi. Only now did Rocco realize that the judge's voice was weary and broken. "Fucking hell."

He hung up the phone. Just then, Italo walked into the room with printouts of the pictures of the ledger that they'd found in the shop. He tossed them onto Rocco's desk.

The deputy chief stood up from his chair. "I need to go have a chat with Berguet." He grabbed his overcoat. "Is it still snowing out?"

"No, it stopped. But don't worry. Like I said, it's not going to stick!"

But, in fact, it had stuck. Aosta had woken up blinding white, and Rocco walked out of police headquarters cursing all four seasons, the month of May, and most particularly, that sun-forsaken land.

"Crazy, isn't it?" Miniero, the officer originally from Vomero, had commented, as he looked out sad-eyed at the soft blanket that the city's snow plows were already clearing off the streets.

This just isn't right, Rocco kept repeating to himself. You don't let people get a glimpse of the colors of the flowers, the green of the meadows and lawns. You don't fill the air with sweet scents if you're just going to put the cork in the bottle again and put things back the way they were. You don't do that.

He got into his Volvo, reflecting that at least the car had

four-wheel drive, and drove away from Corso Battaglione Aosta.

ANTONIO SCIPIONI'S CAR WAS RIGHT AROUND THE curve, in front of the Berguet villa in Porossan. The officer hadn't gone to bed at all. He'd spent the whole night staked out, in spite of the fact that the deputy chief had relieved him of that duty.

"Here. It's nice and hot," Rocco said as he got into the squad car, handing a piping hot espresso to Antonio, along with a paper bag containing a cream-filled pastry and a strudel.

"Dotto', keep that up and you're going to spoil me, and I'll get the belly of a retiree."

"Why didn't you go get some sleep?"

"Because I wanted to keep an eye out and because I can't stop thinking about that poor girl." Antonio opened the tiny thermos of espresso and poured it into the cup. "Do you want a sip?"

"No, thanks, I've have already had some. Pretty, isn't it?" asked Rocco, pointing to the snow.

"I like it. You know that, I told you before. I prefer it to the beach."

Rocco looked at him without commenting.

"This cream pastry is spectacular," said the officer as he took his first bite.

"You've got sugar all over you."

Scipioni laughed and a drop of cream filling fell onto his uniform. He wiped it away and took another bite. "The lights were on all night long on the ground floor." And he tilted his head in the direction of the Berguets' lovely villa. The trees in the garden were weighed down with snow, as was the enclosure wall. On the asphalt, there were only scattered tire tracks here and there.

"Ground floor, so in the living room."

"Umbround vive vat uvver guy . . ." Antonio mumbled.

"Just swallow and then you can talk. I can't understand a fucking thing you're saying."

Antonio gulped. "Around five that other guy showed up . . . the one with the soul patch, the one who drives an Audi TT."

"Cerruti."

"That's right. He was here for an hour or so. He just left ten minutes ago with a stack of papers under one arm."

"All right. Good job, Antonio. Now get the hell home."

"What? You just brought me my morning coffee, sir! Now I'm awake." Then Antonio Scipioni, as if he'd suddenly been transformed into a bloodhound, started sniffing the air. "Listen, aside from the fact that I reek of sweat, don't you catch a smell of grass?"

"Who, me?" asked Rocco with the most innocent look imaginable.

"Yeah. How could that be?"

"Search me. It must be the snow that's burning the resin. I'm going to pay a call on the Berguets. Be well, Scipio'," and so saying he slapped him on the leg and got out of the squad car, leaving the officer to finish his breakfast.

"IT'S TIME TO GET THE HELL UP," BRAYED THE WOM-an's voice, strangled by forty cigarettes a day. The woman got no answer.

"Hey," and she delivered a kick to the mattress lying on the dusty floor.

Enzo cracked an eye open. "What time is it?" he asked.

"Time for you to wake up and get the fuck out of here."

Enzo got up. The light penetrating through the half-closed shutters barely illuminated the room. The window panes had been repaired with duct tape and the wallpaper was peeling away in various spots. "Is there any coffee?" he asked the woman.

"Go down to the café and get yourself some. I have to go out. When I get back, I want to see you gone. I don't want you around here." She turned away. Enzo could barely see the pattern of red and green flowers on her nightgown as she glided out of the room. Then he opened the other eye.

"Whoa, thanks a lot!" he shouted. But there was no response. He threw the filthy sheets aside. He swung his feet down onto the floor and rubbed his face. Getting up from the mattress was no simple matter. He found a chair nearby that was serving as a nightstand. He got a grip on it and hauled himself to a standing position. As soon as he was on his feet, his head started spinning. He took a deep breath, waited for the merry-go-round to slow down, then left the room. He stuck his head into the kitchen. The woman was at the marble sink, washing glasses made of Nutella jars and colorful glass dishes.

"Come on, Robertina, aren't you going to make a nice little cup of coffee for Enzo?"

The woman set the glass down in the plastic drying rack. "Listen up. I know how to count. I finished eighth grade. And there's another three years left to go before I had any reason to see you back out on the street. Now, I don't want to know what you're doing here at my house. I never saw you, I never talked to you. But the night is over, and you need to get out!"

Enzo smiled. "What about a cigarette? You got a cigarette?"

"I gave up smoking," the woman lied. She dried her hands on her nightgown. Then she pushed back her hair, half blond, the other half dark roots, black and gray. Enzo looked at her carefully. She looked at least fifteen years older than her age of thirty-two. "You look wrecked," he said.

"Oh, do I? You think? It must be because I bust my ass from dawn to dusk mopping apartment house stairs and wiping old ladies' asses, what do you think? It might be because I don't have money to feed the kid, and that I have Grandma to thank that I even have this rag of a home to live in."

Enzo shot a glance at the kitchen. There was a layer of soot and grime over the old Formica cabinets. There were two ramshackle chairs. There was an old television set propped up on wooden fruit crates. "You call this shithole a home?"

"It's still better than living under a bridge somewhere, no? Better than being behind bars."

"It's just that you've never had ambitions!"

"Not like yours, you mean? Have you taken a good hard look at yourself? If you ask me, you've spent more time in prison than out on the street. Or am I miscounting?"

"That's no dishonor, as far as I'm concerned."

The woman took a couple of felt tip markers and two notebooks off the kitchen table and went over to put them away in an old cabinet that had a tarnished mirror too big for the tiny front hall. "Ah, no?" she asked. "It's no dishonor? You think it's a good thing?" Then she went back to the kitchen, picked up a wet rag, and wiped off the table, which was covered by a plastic tablecloth with big blue flowers. "Well? How much is it going to take to get you out of this house and out of my life?"

Enzo nodded. "You got twenty euros you can lend me?"

Roberta scorched Enzo with a burning glance. "You want to know something? I envy my girlfriends whose fathers are dead. You want to know why? Because at least they can remember a father and maybe they have some nice things to cherish. The dead have this advantage over the living: they don't talk, they don't breathe, and they don't stink." She tossed the wet scrap of cloth into the battered marble sink, leaving her father to chew over those words.

IT WAS DOLORES, THE FILIPINA, WHO OPENED THE door. She had deep dark circles under her eyes and a dead, sleepy gaze. She looked at Rocco without recognizing him.

"Good morning, Dolores. Schiavone, from Aosta police headquarters."

The Filipina stood aside to let him in, as if she'd expected that man with the strange overcoat to come back, sooner or later.

The house was cold. The same silence and the same scent of cinnamon reigned over everything as it had yesterday. Pietro appeared from the kitchen. He was still wearing the same suit as the day before, or else another one that looked just like it. The shirt was open at the collar, no tie, and he hadn't shaved.

"Dottor . . ." he began, but he didn't remember the name.

"Deputy Chief Schiavone."

"Of course, certainly, certainly. And forgive me, these are days that seem to be a little . . . do you want an espresso? Anything else? Please, be my guest," and he waved Rocco into the living room. Rocco walked through the double doors, under the nativity that dated from the Cinquecento, and entered a room that was all gold. The walls were gold, the furniture was gold, and so were the picture and mirror frames. The valances over the windows were gold. It all looked as if it had been bombarded by bursts of sunrays. But there was no sunshine, in that apartment, or for that matter anywhere in Aosta.

"Not even a glass of water?" asked Pietro.

"Not even water."

The master of the house pointed to one of the three enormous sofas arrayed in front of a marble fireplace decorated with carved grapevines.

Rocco sank into it.

"Sorry my wife isn't here, she's still sleeping."

"Maybe what you meant to say is that she just went to bed?"

Pietro looked at Rocco with a tense, fake smile on his mouth. "I don't . . . I don't understand."

"Aren't you going to ask me why I'm here?"

"I imagine it's about that thing you were looking into yesterday? About the dead construction worker, no?"

"At twenty minutes to seven in the morning?"

Pietro looked at his watch. "True. It's not even seven o'clock yet." And he turned his gaze back to Rocco.

"Berguet, let's stop pulling each other's leg." The shift in tone hit Berguet like a punch to the gut. "All right then, did you talk to Chiara?"

At the sound of his daughter's name, Pietro turned pale. He dropped down onto the sofa and just sat there. He put both hands onto his head and burst into tears, shaking his head.

Rocco took a deep, sorrowful breath. "So you haven't spoken to her since she disappeared?"

"No."

Dolores walked in with a tray. She stopped at the door. She looked at the master of the house bent over at the waist and, light as a feather, set the coffee down on the marble tabletop. Then she vanished.

"Who was it?"

Pietro sighed. He picked up the cup of espresso. He drank it. "If you know that my daughter is missing, then you probably also know who took her."

"Let's not play children's games, Pietro. What do they want?"

"Money."

"You're lying."

"What else do you think they might want?"

"Something else," Rocco said. "I'll just summarize, and after that, shall I tell you my own best guess? I think that you and Edil.ber haven't been flourishing lately, and that you have some serious cash-flow problems. I know that for you the upcoming bid on the regional government contract is of vital importance. I also know that you normally use the Vallée Savings Bank for your lines of credit, but that they weren't the ones who covered you in your last crisis."

"Just think of all the nice things you know."

"I do, don't I? All right, then. Now you're going to tell me who Carlo Cutrì is."

Pietro's head was bobbing back and forth as he looked at the marble coffee table. Just at that moment, Giuliana Berguet entered the room. Corduroy trousers and a turtleneck sweater. Eyes that had already squeezed out all their tears, with dark circles underneath them, worse than a portrait by Munch. "Deputy Chief! Are you still looking into this thing with the car?" she asked in a tone of forced enthusiasm. Rocco got up from the sofa. Then the woman looked her husband in the face.

"Giuliana? The Commissario already knows everything."

"Deputy Chief. . . ."

"Excuse me?"

"My rank is deputy chief," Schiavone clarified.

As if a sledge hammer had taken her legs out from under her, Giuliana Berguet collapsed onto the armrest of the sofa, and she accompanied that collapse with a faint sound that came from somewhere in the back of her throat. She looked and sounded like a deflated air mattress at the end of the summer season.

"Dottor Berguet, just who is Carlo Cutrì?"

"I don't know. I've never seen him. I've always spoken to Michele."

"Then tell me all about Michele Diemoz."

"Yes. He's who I've always talked to. A man from Cuneaz. A Valdostan."

"Who gave you the money?"

"I told you already. This Michele was the intermediary, and he secured the loan for me."

"How much?"

"At first, 500,000 euros. After that, another 700,000."

"They wanted more than three million back," Giuliana broke in, her eyes welling over with tears.

"They who?" Rocco shouted.

"For fuck's sake, I don't know who they are!" Pietro exploded. "I've already told you that. People from down south I've never met!"

"Down south?"

"Cosenza," said Giuliana. And even though she was several yards away, Rocco had the impression he could hear the woman's bones shivering. Cosenza is home to the notorious organized-crime clan, the 'ndrangheta.

"So what do they want know? And don't tell me money, because I won't believe you."

"They want part ownership of Edil.ber. More than half."

Rocco nodded. "Help me understand. You're supposed to sign over part of your shares to . . . who exactly?"

"I still don't know that. Whoever comes to the notary's office so I can sign over a chunk of my company to them. The company that belonged to my father. And to my grandfather before him."

Rocco got to his feet. "And we're not going to let that happen."

"You want to tell me how the fuck I'm supposed to stop them?"

"Why didn't you call us? Why didn't you let us know what was going on?"

"What good would it have done?" It wasn't Pietro who'd asked the question. It was his brother, Marcello, who had just appeared in the doorway to the living room. "Would you explain that to me, Deputy Chief? What good would it have done? If you want to know what the result would have been, I can tell you. It would have guaranteed we'd never see Chiara again. And your presence in this apartment is certainly no testimonial to my niece's health and safety!"

"We'd have put wiretaps on the phones. We would have taken decisive action and put an end to this whole thing."

"We would have this, we would have that, we would have the other thing!" Pietro stood up and got dangerously close to the policeman. "And where were you or your colleagues when all the banks turned off the spigots? When my suppliers demanded payment? When my company was out of cash and I didn't know what saint I should pray to to get out of trouble?"

"I can't tell you where I was when all that was going on, Dottor Berguet. All I know is that you asked the wrong people for help!"

"Sure, easy to say, but now what are we supposed to do?" asked Giuliana. "At this point, they've got Chiara."

"Have you spoken to her?"

"Not yet."

"They've called," Marcello broke in, and after he spoke a graveyard silence settled over the room. "They're going to let us speak to Chiara this afternoon."

"When did they call? Where?" Rocco shouted.

"Here at home. Half an hour ago. A man's voice. With a southern accent."

"Come on, let us help you, for Christ's sake! I'm talking to you, Signora. Let us put a tap on the phone line and. . . ."

"No!" Giuliana shouted. "No! They have my little girl, do you understand that? They have her and who knows what things they might be doing to her . . ." Then she burst into tears again. Pietro walked over to his wife. "I'm begging you, Dottor Schiavone, as a father and a husband, I'm pleading with you. I've already made up my mind. I'm happy to turn over the shares in the company, to retire, to travel to the farthest corner of the globe, but I want to get Chiara back. That's all I ask."

Rocco walked over to the window. Outside it had started

snowing again. "You can't retire. These people need you. What are they going to do with a share of Edil.ber if they don't know the right people? Without your skill set? No, my friend, you're never getting out of this thing. They're like quicksand. As long as you're useful, they'll keep you alive. Piece after piece, they'll whittle away at you and only when they've decided that they're done will they let you go. But by then you'll be drained and tattered like a floor mop. Do you understand that? And you can add another factor to the mix. You'd never think it, but I have my own professional ethics. Now that I know this crime has been committed, what do you think I'm going to do? Go back to my office as if nothing had happened?"

"This is Italy, my friend!" said Marcello.

"This is Italy, my ass, Signor Marcello Berguet," Rocco shouted back.

"What's the matter, does this somehow offend your sense of justice?"

"Yes, it offends my sense of justice. My own personal sense of justice, let that be clear. And let me add that I don't like being made a fool of, having the wool pulled over my eyes. When it does happen, I turn into a wild animal. Justice, with a capital J, has little or nothing to do with all this. But being made a fool of has everything to do with it. Not here, not me, and not by people like you and this motley crew of fucked-up 'ndrangheta gangsters. I hope I've made myself clear."

And he strode briskly toward the hallway, taking long steps.

"Don't do anything reckless, Dottore. I'm begging you. My daughter's life is at stake."

"I've never done anything reckless in my life, Signora Giuliana, please believe me. There's just one thing that I ask of you. I want to know when you talk with your daughter. Don't do a thing until you've heard her voice, sounding healthy and happy. Have I made myself clear?"

Pietro Berguet nodded.

"Demand to speak with her. Otherwise, don't budge, be stubborn. Trust me, it's the only way to get her back alive."

"You know something, Deputy Chief Schiavone?" Giuliana asked, looking Rocco right in the eye. "Since the minute you entered this home, I immediately caught the whiff. The whiff of trouble and death."

"Death? What do you know about death?"

SHE'D DONE IT! SHE'D SUCCEEDED. RAVAGED WITH pain, her eyes almost blinded with her tears, Chiara was on her feet. Clinging to the wall, but on her feet.

She'd lunged at the dripping faucet. Every tiny step brought a stab of pain, but she felt as if she were getting used to that hellish suffering. She'd tried to open the faucet with her teeth, but she hadn't been able. She greedily licked at the drops as they fell, one every four seconds. It tasted of rust, but it was definitely water.

What if it isn't drinkable? the little voice had asked.

"Who the fuck cares."

The pain let her alone only when she leaned back

against the wall, with all her weight on her good leg. She managed to turn her head and glimpse the broken chair leg stabbing into her muscle like a knife in butter. The blood had run down her thigh and then her calf and into her shoe. Dark and dry. But the bleeding had stopped. Chiara looked up at the small window above her. The snow had half-covered it.

It had snowed! Very good, very good indeed. That means I'm not far from home. Only in Aosta does it snow in May. Or else on the Tofane Mountains. I'm close to home. I'm close to home. My hands. I have to get my hands free.

She looked at the clutter on the shelves. There were old newspapers of metal and wooden crates, but nothing that could help her to saw away those plastic strips that bound her wrists to the backrest of the now-broken chair. She looked at the old wooden door.

I can slam against it. Maybe one or two or three times and it'll collapse and swing open.

Maybe you'll break your neck.

That's not right. That's not right.

She looked around the room. The column they'd tied her to was shedding chunks of concrete at the base, displaying the iron framework inside. Maybe she could do something with those iron rods?

Like what? Scratch against them? Pointless.

Halfway up the column the hood still hung. It had caught on a nail. And it wasn't a hood at all. It was a burlap sack, the kind that potatoes come in. The door was about thirty feet from the sink where she had stopped to catch her breath and lick a few drops of water. The only way to safety lay through that old worm-eaten door.

I need to get to it. But I can't put any weight on my wounded leg. I'll hop over to the door. I'll hop, one step at a time. One little step at a time.

"The way you do things is by putting one foot in front of the other, right, Stefano?" she told her ski instructor, and for the first time since she'd woken up in there, she felt like smiling. She thought about Max.

Where is that dummy? At home? What's he doing? What about Mamma and Papà? Are they looking for me? Is anyone searching for me? Or have they forgotten about me?

No one's coming, haven't you figured it out yet? No one's coming.

Sure, I've figured it out, of course I know that.

She looked at the door. She bit her lip. She counted to three and moved away from the wall. A first hop on her good leg, and a blade of pain sliced into her left thigh. She clenched her fists, her teeth, and her eyes. Second leap. Second blade of pain. The pain hadn't left, it had only taken shelter in the shadows, like a wild beast lying low, still ready to lunge and sink its fangs. Third hop on the good leg and third lightning bolt. Pain piled atop pain, multiplying exponentially. Now, a yard from the wall, far from anything she could grip, Chiara had no choice but to keep moving. She was caught midway, turning back would be every bit as painful as continuing. She'd carry on.

Fourth leap on her good leg. Fourth devastating lightning bolt. It was too much: she collapsed. Too much even for Chiara Berguet, the tough girl, the one who never quits, who knows how to get herself out of dire straits, the girl all the boys are in love with, the girl with her hands bound to the backrest of a broken chair and a giant wooden splinter planted in her thigh, the one who lets herself drop to the floor because she's practically blinded by the pain, because everything's dancing and swirling around her, the girl who's now vomiting green liquid onto the cellar floor in an isolated house on a godforsaken slope more than three thousand feet above sea level while, outside, it starts to snow again.

"Ah, you came back for your onesie?" Melina asked with a smile.

Rocco didn't answer. He just kept walking straight toward the little door to the back of the shop.

"Excuse me, Signore? Where are you going? You can't go back there!"

Schiavone threw the door wide open and entered the warehouse he'd visited the night before. He made his way through the cartons. Sitting at the iron table illuminated by the steel lamp was a man with a beard. The man asked, "Who are you? What do you want?"

Rocco reached up and grabbed one of the cartons, tore the cardboard open, so that boxes containing cell phones tumbled out and onto the floor.

"Michele Diemoz?"

"That's me, but what the fuck . . . ?"

"I'm sorry." It was Melina, who had run after Rocco. "I tried to stop him, but I couldn't."

"Deputy Chief Schiavone."

"The police? What a coincidence. Do you know that last night someone broke the window and. . . ."

"Silence! You're coming with me to police headquarters."

Michele smiled at him defiantly. "Why should I?"

"Show me all the bills of purchase and lading for these cell phones. Or for those car radios that I can just glimpse around the corner over there. Or for all these electric kettles."

Michele pulled the cell phone out of his pocket. "I'm not going anywhere with you."

Rocco strode over to him. He grabbed the cell phone out of his hand.

"I want to call my lawyer and. . . ."

It was only after his head suddenly swiveled toward the wall on the far side of the room that Michele realized an express train had just slammed into his cheek. The pain arrived two seconds later. The deputy chief had moved so suddenly that Diemoz hadn't even seen the fist heading toward him. He felt the policeman's grip on his neck and an irresistible force dragging him toward the storeroom exit. His head was spinning and he could see a reddish shadow in his right eye.

"Melina, help me!" he shouted, as if the chubby young woman could actually do anything to stop that force of nature.

The young woman was standing in a corner, clearly

frightened, hands clasped over her belly. She pulled her head in like a scared turtle when Schiavone dragged Michele past her.

Outside the shop, the man partially regained consciousness. "Let go of me. Let go of me. I swear that I'm going to report you to. . . ."

Instead of replying, Rocco just smacked him hard, openhanded, on the back of his neck, the kind of whack you give a misbehaving child who's pulled some stunt or prank. "Shut your mouth and get moving!"

He shoved him into the car, in the passenger seat. Then he got behind the wheel.

"This is a kidnapping!"

"And don't bother trying to open the door. There's a security lock on it."

Michele lunged at the deputy chief's throat, scratching his face. In response, Schiavone slammed his elbow into the man's ribs, which quieted him down while he struggled to breathe. Then Schiavone grabbed him by the back of his neck and with one sharp shove slammed his face against the dashboard. Michele Diemoz lost consciousness.

"What the fuck . . ." grumbled Rocco. The face of Hey-DiddleLiddles' owner had finally cracked the plastic dashboard. Now he was going to have to take the car to a body shop.

DERUTA HAD LOCKED MICHELE DIEMOZ IN THE HOLD-ing cell. Rocco was standing outside police headquarters, waiting for Italo. The snow had already been cleared from the sidewalks and streets but the sky was threatening to spit down yet more. Officer Pierron came racing up, his car doing fifty, and he screeched to a halt just inches from the deputy chief, kicking up a wave of mud and ice that splashed all over Rocco's trousers.

"What the fuck were you thinking?"

Officer Pierron came running around to the deputy chief. "Sorry. Did I splash you? I guess so, from the look of your shoes."

"I'm not getting much sleep, my circadian rhythms are completely shot, I've got a case of jet lag that feels like I just flew in from Tokyo, so I'm just a little bit edgy," Rocco replied as he reached out a hand to take the ledger of debts from the HeyDiddleLiddles shop that Italo was handing to him.

"Here. What you asked me to bring!"

"Excellent. Who's at HeyDiddleLiddles?"

"Scipioni and Casella."

"All right then, I'll run over and see the judge. The pictures you took aren't needed anymore. We have the original." And brandishing the ledger he headed back to his Volvo. "Go see whether that idiot Deruta remembered to lock the door when he put Diemoz in the holding cell."

"Okay. And then what?"

"Wait until you hear from me. By the way, about the shoes . . . have you figured out where they sell them?"

"Not yet."

• • •

His feet soaking and a throbbing permanent pain in the middle of his temples, Rocco had been waiting outside Judge Baldi's door for ten minutes. As usual, he was trying to piece out the strange patterns that formed in the wood grain and knots, patterns which seemed to change every time. Exhaustion and lack of sleep: he couldn't see a thing. Just a bloodhound's head, or else maybe looking at it from the other side, it might also be a cannon. He clenched the ledger and nervously bounced his right leg.

"Here I am, Schiavone!" The words resonated from behind him. Baldi, followed by a male assistant, was walking toward him, signing papers as he arrived, and then handing them to the assistant who would promptly produce a new one to sign. "What's happening?"

Rocco got to his feet as Baldi was signing the last document and dismissing his assistant. "Come on in."

Schiavone handed the ledger to Judge Baldi. "Now, what I need is an arrest warrant for Michele Diemoz and a search warrant for the HeyDiddleLiddles store where I found this."

"Wait a minute, Schiavone. Let me get this straight. You want a warrant for things you've already done?"

"Exactly!"

Baldi exploded: "Fucking Christ, Schiavone!" The judge slammed the ledger down on the desk. "What did I tell you? What did I tell you? You keep doing things the way you want to, or the way we put it where I come from: You keep screwing the pooch!"

"Listen to me, just listen to me, this is important!"

"I need to be told about things before they happen! I must have told you a million times!"

With a quick glance, Rocco noted that the photo of the magistrate's wife was once again face down. No, things at the Baldi home were definitely not working out. "Please, listen to me! This shop was set up to launder money. And that ledger contains a list of everyone in this part of Italy who owes money to the organization."

The judge's mood—like a summer thunderstorm that shakes and floods everything and then, with a flick of its wings, veers away—had shifted in the course of a few seconds. "Tell me more."

"Now I've arrested the proprietor, but I arrested him for receiving stolen goods. That's the important concept. Receiving stolen goods. That ledger I'm giving you is evidence of the money laundering and the loansharking those bastards are involved in, but we're going to keep it for me and for you."

Baldi finally opened the ledger and started reading.

"But I'm going to keep this Diemoz behind bars because, aside from being a loanshark, these jerks have a storeroom full of stereos and electronics that are obviously stolen. Hence the charge for receiving stolen goods."

"Why do you want to hide the real reason for the arrest?"

"Because I need to throw a rock at the beehive to stir up the swarm. I can't let them catch on to the fact that we've caught them. But I need to make them wet their pants. And it goes without saying that wetting your pants puts you in a defensive position."

"And you smell bad, too," added the judge.

"Precisely."

"So what's the plan?"

"Find the girl before it's too late. They have an appointment with the notary to hand over the company. I need to stall them for a few days."

"How are you going to do that?"

"I've got an idea."

"If you're planning to shoot the notary, I'd recommend you find some other way."

"I wouldn't go that far, Judge Baldi."

The judge stood up and started pacing the room, taking long strides. He was hyperactive. He was unable to stand still for more than thirty seconds at a time.

"The girl still hasn't talked to her parents. They haven't heard from her. Something's not right. Do you understand?"

Baldi stopped in the middle of the room. He swept back his blond bangs and looked the deputy chief in the eye: "Do you think she's dead?"

"I don't know. But we certainly can't rule it out."

The judge went back to his desk and sat down. "All right, I'll sign your warrants. Will you talk to the chief of police?"

"Certainly. I'll convince him to hold a nice big press conference focusing entirely on the stolen goods. A successful police operation, he'll be pleased, and whoever it is we're interested in will read in the papers and online that the authorities were only interested in a ring of fences."

"Meanwhile, our sons of bitches. . . ."

". . . are going to start worrying that we've found out about a lot more than just a roomful of stolen stereos."

The judge nodded. "I don't like the way you operate, and that's no secret. But I'm going to turn a blind eye just this once. I'm doing it for Chiara."

"How old is it?"

"How would I know? Maybe thirty years old."

Enzo Baiocchi looked at the Beretta 6.35 still wrapped in plastic. The serial numbers had been filed off. "How much work has this little girl done?"

"Again, how am I supposed to know? If you want to know the truth, I don't even remember why I have it in the first place," Flavio replied, rubbing a hand over his bald head as he stood by the window.

The traffic out on Viale Marconi was hellish. Car horns, screeching brakes, ambulances—and every bus that went by made the apartment shake.

"Who wants an espresso?" Flavio's mother shouted from the living room. She was eighty-five years old and she could only see out of one eye.

Flavio looked Enzo. "I don't understand why my mother has to shout. Even if you answer, she can't hear you."

Enzo shrugged.

"Are you interested in this espresso or not?" the woman shouted again. Flavio heaved a sigh of irritation and left the bedroom. Enzo remained there with the pistol. He hefted it. It was light. And it could be easily concealed.

"You didn't want the coffee, did you?" asked Flavio, coming back into the room.

"No. But with this thing, you have to shoot from close up."

"I don't want to know what you're planning to do with it. Anyway, trust me, the 6.35 takes care of business. And you can stick it in your pocket. It's light, you can hardly see it."

"What about something bigger?"

"You want a 9 mm? That's a heavy gun, it's got a helluva kick, and you can't stick it down your pants. This one you can. Give it a try."

Enzo stuck the gun into the pocket of his jeans. It was true. It fit comfortably, and he could hardly even tell it was there. "It's certainly comfortable and convenient. When was the last time this thing fired?"

"I don't know. I've always kept it clean. Take a couple of shots with it down by the Tiber."

"Are you going to give me the slugs to go with it?"

"Of course."

"And how much do you want?"

"Let's say 200 euros and I don't want to see you again."

"Payment?"

"As soon as you can."

Enzo looked at his friend. "Flaviuccio, I just got out yesterday."

"I know." Flavio tucked his checkered shirt into his trousers. His watermelon-sized gut rolled heavily over the belt. "And they're looking for you, too, aren't they?"

Enzo nodded. "That's why I don't have the money right now."

Flavio heaved an exasperated sigh. He ran his hand once again over his bald head. A bus went by in the street below. The window panes rattled, as did two Murano glass ballerinas set on the walnut sideboard. "At the very most, in a week."

"You're a friend, Flavio."

"Come on, let's go, I'll treat you to an espresso. At the bar though, not the swill my mother makes."

THE PHONE CALL WITH THE POLICE CHIEF HAD BEEN brisk and concise. Costa had already called a press conference, not especially pleased that he'd be dealing with the detested newsvendors but—and Rocco knew this well—if there was one thing that gave meaning to the life of this particular high government functionary, it was the opportunity to dominate the scriveners of the printed page. And he never missed a chance to confront them when he was playing from a position of unmistakable superiority. Costa loved to see them hanging from his lips, so to speak, and this latest exploit by his deputy chief, rapid, efficient, and with a handsome outcome, was something about which he alone had intimate and detailed knowledge—knowledge that none other than Schiavone had supplied to him. None of those wretched newsvendors knew anything about this vast fencing ring. They'd learn all about it from him, then they'd rush to their newsrooms and their computers to quote the police chief's exact words. This, for him, was a gratifying taste of revenge upon those ghastly creatures, people that Costa placed only one step on the evolutionary ladder above the lowly amoeba. His wife had left him years ago for a journalist at *La Stampa*. And since that day, the chief of police had transferred his hatred for one individual to the entire professional category, without distinction of gender or creed.

"I'M PERFECTLY IN AGREEMENT WITH YOU, DOTTOR Schiavone, we need to keep it quiet, but do you realize what you're asking me to do?"

"I just want you to delay for a couple of days, Dottor Charbonnier, just for a couple of days."

The notary scratched his right earlobe and went on puffing at his now-cold pipe. "I don't know. What could I say to convince them?"

"For instance, that you're dealing with a routine tax audit?"

"That's not very believable. But are you certain?"

"That girl was kidnapped, Dottore. And they're not going to let her go until Pietro Berguet hands over his shares in Edil.ber."

The notary nodded. He put down the pipe. He pushed the button on the intercom: "Graziella, if you would, bring me the Edil.ber documents."

"Right away, Dottore," the secretary replied over the intercom.

"You know something, Dottor Schiavone? I'm almost seventy years old, and nothing like this has ever happened to me. I just figured I'd work away quietly until retirement, but instead. . . ."

"But instead. . . ."

"I know about you. I read the newspapers, and I know you're a responsible policeman. But you understand, don't you? I'm going to have to talk to the chief of police and. . . ."

"Wait. I'm going to beg you not to do that. If word got around, the only one who's at risk is the girl. She's only eighteen."

Graziella entered with a file folder. She laid it down on the desk in front of the notary and vanished like a flash of lightning. Enrico Maria Charbonnier opened the folder. "Now then, the beneficiary of this transaction is Dottor Ugo Montefoschi, who is the president of a company called Calcestruzzi Varese. They make reinforced concrete."

"That's nothing but a front, guaranteed. I already told you who's behind this filth."

"You know, this whole thing struck me as fishy right from the start, you realize that, Schiavone? Anyway, Edil. ber isn't exactly thriving, but now, with this new competition for the regional government contract . . . well, earnings ought to double. What's the point of signing away shares? But I do my professional duty, even when things don't really add up. I don't know this Pietro Berguet. On this piece of business, that other man always came in, the one with the very well-trimmed beard."

"Cristiano Cerruti?"

"Exactly. Who seems to be some sort of right-hand man to Dottor Berguet."

"What else do you remember?"

"He was in a hurry. He was always in a tremendous rush, as if some great danger were snapping at his heels. I never liked him, you know? Arrogant, dismissive, and any time he talked to me, he was also talking to who the hell else on his cell phone. He always had that earpiece working."

"All right, then, Dottore, are you going to help me out?"

Enrico Maria Charbonnier took a deep breath. "You're asking me something that goes against my professional ethics."

"All I'm asking you to do is trust me and give me a little time."

The notary picked up his pipe again. "I don't know. A routine tax audit, you say?"

"If you want, I can arrange to get some genuine officers from the tax office to come by and do an audit." The notary's eyes widened. "A pretend audit, obviously."

"Do you have children, Schiavone?"

"No."

"I do. Three of them. And two grandchildren into the bargain. One of them is the age of this Chiara. Let's do this: there's no official investigation, but I do need a document." And without hesitation he picked up the phone.

"Hello, this is the notary Charbonnier. Could you put my brother on? Thanks, of course I'll wait."

He loaded his pipe with tobacco. Rocco couldn't wait for the notary to light his pipe so that he, too, without having to ask, could light a Camel of his own.

"Ciao Alfredo. It's me, Enrico. I need a favor. Have you

seen my latest blood tests? You have? Is there anything that looks out of line?" Enrico Maria Charbonnier nodded his head.

"Mmmhmmm . . . but don't you think an urgent hospital stay might not be advisable, for further testing? That's right, I need it desperately. You think so? Today, immediately? That strikes me as prudent. And, technically speaking, what is it I've had? An atrial fibrillation . . . excellent, very good. Perfect, then, see you later."

He hung up the phone and finally lit his pipe. It wasn't until his third puff that he looked over at the deputy chief who had in the meantime stuck his cigarette in his mouth. With a wave of the hand, the notary gave him permission to light up. "You know what? This morning I found blood in my stool."

"Really?"

"Yep. And I also had a ventricular fibrillation. And even though I take a Tambocor every morning, I still think that the wisest thing would be to have myself admitted for at least three days at the clinic where my brother works. Urgently. He's a first-rate cardiologist. You know, at my age, the risk of a heart attack is always just around the corner."

"Heaven forbid, Dottore. Let's not joke about these things."

"All right, then, let me finish this pipe, and then I'll have Graziella drive me over."

"If you like I'd be glad to take you."

"Don't worry about it. In fact, the less we're seen together in public, the better. I'll tell you, this is the last thing

I needed." The plumes of smoke from his pipe filled the room, along with the smell of wood and moss. When the cloud of smoke disintegrated, the notary's face re-emerged.

"Dottor Schiavone. Make sure you get Chiara back home. Safe and, if possible, sound."

Rocco nodded. He shook the notary's hand and left the office.

THE VIA TIBURTINA WAS AN ANCIENT ROMAN CON-sular road that led to the spa town of Tivoli, where the patrician nobility of long ago had their villas. From Tivoli it led on to Ostia Aterni—the city we now call Pescara. It's no longer called a consular road, merely an Italian state highway—the route hasn't changed much, and it's not clear how much of the pavement dates all the way back to the origins. The Via Tiburtina runs through Rome from the Termini train station and then on through the outlying suburbs. It's a pipe clogged with traffic at every hour of the day and night, at least until you get well outside Rome's beltway, the Grande Raccordo Anulare. Unlike most Romans, who preferred to take the A24 superhighway to reach the region of Abruzzo, Enzo Baiocchi was driving along the Via Tiburtina in an old Ford he'd stolen an hour ago. Less traffic, less risk of running into the police, and so he felt more at ease. Still, the car was a complete jalopy. It was low on gas, and the engine struggled and shrilled every time the tachometer on the dashboard reached 3,000 RPM. Windows wide open, he'd already left far behind him both the city and the outlying neighborhoods. The chaos and the countless tall apartment buildings of Italy's capital were nothing but a memory now. He was starting to glimpse the countryside. And cars were few and far between.

The reserve fuel light had been on for ten minutes now. He needed a gas station, he couldn't put it off any longer. On the right, a sign informed him that there would be one in 300 yards. The escapee smiled, put on a filthy baseball hat that he'd found in the back seat, and lit a cigarette. He turned on his blinker and pulled into the gas station. It was perfect. No houses nearby, just farmland and the occasional desolate ruin on the horizon. Cars were few and far between and, most important of all, none were lined up for fuel. He parked the car at the pump. A man in his early seventies, with a slow, weary step, walked toward him. "How much you need?"

"Fill it up."

The man took the hose from the pump and started filling the tank. Enzo got out of the car. He looked around. He peered into the glass-and-aluminum-frame booth full of automotive products. Deserted. So the gas station attendant was all alone.

"Hot out, isn't it?" he said. The attendant said nothing. He put the pump back and walked over to Enzo.

"That'll be fifty euros."

Enzo put his hand in his pocket. He pulled out the pistol and slammed the handle sharply against the old man's temple. The attendant collapsed to the ground without a sound. Enzo leaned over the body and unzipped the fanny pack. He looked inside. It was stuffed with banknotes. Cheerfully, he climbed back into his car, and took the Via Tiburtina toward the mountains.

A little mutt without a collar emerged from the glass-and-aluminum booth and lay down whimpering next to its master. It licked the man's face, but he gave no sign of life.

"I WANT TO KNOW IF THEY'VE GOTTEN IN TOUCH. IF you've talked with your daughter," Rocco said, clutching the receiver tight, as if he were afraid it might fall out of his hand.

On the other end of the line, Pietro Berguet was breathing deeply. "Only for a few seconds. They talked to my brother. All she said was: I'm fine. Then someone else took the phone back. And hung up."

"Well, at least we know that. That she's alive."

"Commissario, I'm going to say it again. . . ."

"And I'm going to say it again to *you*, I'm not a Commissario, I'm a deputy chief."

"Deputy Chief, I'm going to say it again. It no longer matters. Let's do this thing, I'll get my daughter back home, and then we can act, if the law can still help me."

"So that's what you want?"

"That's what my wife and I both want. I'm begging you, for now just stay out of it. I'm down on my knees, begging you."

"All right, Dottor Berguet. All right. In that case . . . I'll just wait for a word from you, and I'll unleash police headquarters on the case." He hung up the phone. He looked at Italo. "They talked to her. Apparently, she's okay. How is that piece of shit Diemoz?"

"He just keeps hollering that he's an innocent man. It doesn't matter, though. We're transferring him to the maximum-security prison today."

"Excellent."

"So what are we doing, Rocco?"

"We're going to just keep going. What is Caterina up to? Is she coming in?"

"Yes, she's on her way to the office," Italo replied. "Her temperature has dropped."

"Well, set her loose on this Calcestruzzi Varese and this alleged Ugo Montefoschi." As he talked, Italo was taking notes. "Right now, the kidnappers think that tomorrow, at the very latest, they're going to the notary's office for the transfer of ownership. We have three days to figure out something more. Antonio?"

"He brought in that poor girl, Melina, the shop clerk. All she does is cry and says she doesn't know a thing."

"Let her go, she knows less about it than D'Intino."

He hadn't finished mentioning the officer's name when none other than D'Intino himself stuck his face in the office door. "Dotto', may I?"

"What is it, D'Intino? This isn't the time! Do you want to go home? Then go home!"

"It's a bad thing. A very bad thing."

Rocco rolled his eyes. "Will you tell me *what* very bad thing?"

"They found a dead corpse."

Rocco stared at Italo. "Did I understand him correctly? Did he just say a dead corpse?"

"I think he did, Dottore. His exact words were: 'a dead corpse'. But by that, I think he just meant a dead man," Italo clarified.

"Who?"

IT WAS ROSA THE CONCIERGE WHO HAD CALLED THE police. When she entered the apartment to do her routine housekeeping, she'd found Cristiano Cerruti's dead body sprawled face-down on the floor in the dining room. There was an enormous red stain on the carpet and the glass side table was shattered into a thousand pieces. Cerruti's neatly trimmed, sparse little beard was smeared with blood and spattered with bits of brain. Rosa was sitting on the apartment house staircase, pale as a Christ on the cross, dabbing at her eyes, which were red with weeping. After dismissing Casella—who had an unfortunate reputation for contaminating crime scenes with his own DNA in various formats, ranging from urine to saliva, with a sideline in fingerprints—Rocco wandered the room while waiting for his frenemy Alberto Fumagalli. There were also blood sprays on the living room wall and even on an oil painting by Schifano. It struck him as novel and intriguing that the red bloom of blood actually seemed to improve the painting. The apartment was small and furnished in Japanese style. Only a few very fine pieces of furniture, a lovely clean and tidy kitchen, no bric-a-brac in sight, not even a book. It felt more like a residential hotel than someone's home. The bedroom was enormous. Clearly, Cristiano hadn't slept alone in the king-size bed. Both pillows were crumpled, the blankets tossed aside, and the sheets bore the impressions of bodies on both sides. On a nightstand lay a pair of glasses and a book by Jon Krakauer; on the other side, on the bedside rug, a tray with two cups and some cookies with bites taken out of them. In the bathroom, too, which seemed like something out of a resort hotel, there reigned a maniacal neatness—if you overlooked the toothbrush on the edge of the sink and a razor still encrusted with shaving foam.

The only certainty was that *that* murder—whatever the burden of violence and stupidity which it had brought with it, rocketing heedlessly into Rocco's life—at least formed part of the same story, the same thread, and was not simply some unlooked-for addition to the mess he was already dealing with. He heard a commotion in the living room. Fumagalli had arrived. As usual, the two men exchanged no greetings. The medical examiner, squatting down next to the corpse, was putting on a pair of latex gloves.

"Nice hard smack," he said, sticking his fingers into the wound that had opened up right at the back of the skull, producing a sound of floppy flesh. Rocco's stomach gripped tight. "Really a good hard smack."

"Can't you just try to avoid sticking your fingers in the wound, making these disgusting noises, and for once behave like a normal human being?"

"Listen to who's asking what. All right, so, do you know who this poor soul is, or was?"

"Cristiano Cerruti, right-hand man to Pietro Berguet, president of Edil.ber."

"And do you know why someone did this to him?"

"Just a notion."

"Okay, now I'm going to stick a thermometer in him and we'll try and figure out what time he was killed."

Rocco made a point of paying no attention to the operation and went on looking around the room. There was the video intercom, a device he was determined to have installed in his own apartment one of these days, and a door so heavily armored and reinforced that it looked like it belonged in a bank. Everything was in perfect order. He opened a few cabinet doors in the living room and found stacks of dishes, glasses, napkins, and utensils, all neatly arranged by shape and color. When he turned to look at Fumagalli, he noticed he was busying himself curiously around a fire engine-red Chinese cupboard. He was fiddling around with a long metallic object.

"What is it?"

"Here, Rocco, let me give you a hand. You can use it." Alberto was carefully observing the golf bag leaning against the wall. "I've figured out the murder weapon."

"What makes you think that?"

"This set of golf clubs is missing the driver. That's the club you use to take your first shot. No golf player can do without a driver."

"What's one look like?"

Alberto pulled out a club. "Here, at the end, it has an enormous head, big but not really all that heavy." Then as if he'd lost his mind, he took a swing in the air. "A blow with this thing to the back of the skull will send you straight to your maker, even if you're wearing a helmet."

"How would you know?"

"Listen, sweetheart, you're talking to a second-category handicap who's won at Villa Olona and La Pinetina, you know that?"

"Wouldn't it have been quicker to just say: I play golf? What the hell do you think I care about your trophy cabinet?"

"I know, but I like to make you eat your heart out."

"I'm not eating my heart out, I don't give a damn about golf. It's not a sport."

"What do you mean it's not a sport?" the doctor asked indignantly.

"A short walk over the fields dressed like a clown and swinging a club at a little white ball? You call that a sport?"

"So what would you call it, instead?"

"A short walk over the fields dressed like a clown and swinging a club at a little white ball."

"In 2016, they're bringing it back as an Olympic sport."

"Along with bocce ball?"

"You're not right in the head, Rocco."

"Ah, speaking of which, what's the name of the missing golf club again?"

"The driver."

"The driver. Which is now lying at the bottom of the River Dora."

"Or else in a dump somewhere, or buried, how am I supposed to know?" Fumagalli said and then went back to the corpse. "Yes, the wound could match. Well, I'll take this young man to the hospital. If he tells me anything more, I'll get in touch."

"If he tells you anything? Oh, right, of course, sorry." Rocco had forgotten that Alberto Fumagalli, in the long hours he spent alone with his corpses, tended to talk to them and to consider them living, animate beings.

As always, Italo had steered clear of the actual scene of the crime, but now he timidly stuck his head in the front door: "Deputy Chief? Rosa here has something she wants to tell you. . . ."

"Who?"

"The concierge."

THE WOMAN, STILL SITTING ON THE STAIRS, WIPED her nose with the handkerchief that she clutched in her hand, by now a shapeless mass, streaked and damp.

"Come on, Rosa, tell the deputy chief what you told me," Italo encouraged her.

At last, the woman seemed to have run out of mucus, and she looked up at Rocco. "I saw someone leaving Dottor Cerruti's apartment."

"Excellent. And . . . what else?"

"He went right past my apartment. I live on the ground floor, and the place is tiny, because I'm the concierge, plus I clean house for a few of the tenants. For instance, I cleaned

Dottor Cerruti's apartment. That's why I went in this morning, and in fact, I was the one who found the body. I was in my apartment when someone went by, I wasn't alone because my nephew is staying with me, actually, he's here from Civita because he's taking a civil service exam for the regional government, and let's just hope that the Madonna grants us the grace to get him a good job. I put him in my room to sleep, even though he told me over and over he'd be glad to sleep on the couch, poor thing, but I said no, I'm fine on the couch . . . and so. . . ."

"Signora, you're putting me to sleep here!" the deputy chief blurted. "Why don't you tell me about this guy that you saw."

Rosa blew her nose, then went on: "You know, Dotto'? I knew that Cerruti had a lover. And I know that she never came in through the front entrance. He always had her come in through the garage, downstairs. Then she'd ride up in the elevator, and afterward she'd ride back down and leave through the garage. But I never once saw her."

Rocco nodded. "He was a very private individual, wasn't he?"

"It strikes me. But maybe it was important to know this thing, right?"

"Yes, it was important . . . so what can you tell me about this guy you saw?"

"I only saw his back. He was big, fat, I mean to say. But you know what? He definitely wasn't a tenant—that much is certain."

"Long hair? Or short? Blonde, brunette?"

"I don't know. He was wearing a woolen watch cap and a black jacket. I don't remember anything else. Could he have been the murderer?" asked Rosa in a faint voice.

"Yes, or he could have been a plumber. I don't know, Signora, maybe you should explain what you meant about the garage."

"You can enter the building from the garage, but you either need to have a special key or else someone has to open the gate for you from inside the apartment."

"And do all the tenants use it?"

"Not at all. There are only three parking spots. One belongs to the general who's been too old to drive for years, the other belongs to the architectural design firm on the second floor, but they use it to park a cargo van, and then there's the spot that belonged to the late lamented Cerruti. He used it, like I told you. To let his lover come upstairs."

Rocco gestured to Italo. "Come on, Italo, let's go down to the garage. We take the elevator to get down there, right, Signora?"

"Yes. Push the letter B."

The two policemen boarded the elevator. "Do you suspect this woman? Do you think she killed him?"

"I think *he* killed him, Italo. The lover was a *he*."

"A . . . a man?"

"Do you know many women who shave first thing in the morning?"

● ● ●

229

SHE HADN'T MOVED IN HOURS. EVERY SO OFTEN SHE opened her eyes, then she'd close them again.

I'm falling slowly, gently, from some very high story. Extremely high. My heart is in my ears. And it's beating slowly, just a beat every now and then. How cold it is. It's cold in here. But it's strange. Now I'm going to pull the comforter over me . . . it's at the foot of the bed. Didn't I put it on the bed? Didn't I put the down comforter on the bed? Dolores, where is the down comforter? Do you think I went and fell asleep with all the windows open? What a dope. I'll get up and open them. I can't hear a thing. Is it still snowing, or did it stop? Snow eliminates all noises. Even the air becomes silent when it snows. You can't hear footsteps. Only the tree branches, when the wind blows . . . and the gusts toss the pine needles. I can hear the wind, and the footsteps on the snow. That's why it's so cold. I've fallen. I've fallen into the snow. Where was I? Stefano . . . was I skiing? I think I must have fallen while skiing. My leg hurts so much. I must have broken it. Stefano, I broke my leg, didn't I? Why aren't you coming to get me, Stefano? Help me! Where are you? Aren't you going to talk to me anymore? Have you left? Have you all vanished, all of you, just like that? Into thin air? I'm so tired. Now I'm going to get some sleep. Five minutes. Just five minutes, then I'll wake up and get back on my feet. I'll get up and go home. Go home. Go home . . .

ROCCO AND ITALO WERE LOOKING AROUND. THE GA-rage was small, and it was mostly used by the tenants for storage. As the concierge had told them, there was a cargo van parked there. On the side was written, "Architecture and Interior Decorating," and then there were two other empty parking spots.

"What are we looking for?" asked Italo, his eyes focused on the pavement.

"Nothing. I just want a stroke of luck. Every so often one might come in handy. You see? The murderer came through here. That means he parked, took the elevator upstairs, did what he came here to do, and then came back down to get his car. . . ."

"Or his motorcycle. . . ."

"Or his fucking bicycle, how would I know?"

Rocco went over to the metal gate that led directly onto the street.

"But, just one thing . . ." and he shook the gate. "Listen. If the way he got in is that Cristiano opened the gate from upstairs, how did he get out?"

"He must have taken Cerruti's keys?"

"It doesn't take a key. You see?" and he pointed to a strange little pentagonal socket. "You have to insert a plug of some kind that closes the circuit and opens the gate."

"All right," Italo corrected himself, "then he must have taken Cristiano's plug."

Rocco heaved a sigh of annoyance.

"What's the matter?"

"I'm going to have go back upstairs again."

"So what? You just need to ride up to the fourth floor."

"Right, and when I get there I'm going to find that ballbuster Ernesto Farinelli from Turin. Who's sure to read me the riot act."

"How do you know that he's here?"

"I can sense it!"

Italo shrugged his shoulders. They started walking toward the elevator when Italo stepped on something. The two policemen froze in place and looked down at the floor. There was a fragment of transparent plastic.

"What's that?"

Rocco picked it up. "Take a look at it. I'd say it's plastic, not glass."

"This is polycarbonate."

"Translate, Italo."

"They use it to make automobile headlights."

"Do you think this is the stroke of luck?"

"Maybe so."

"Who can give us a hand identifying it?"

"Umberto. My friend from the highway patrol. He used to be a mechanic. He certainly would know someone."

"Then go, and don't waste any time!"

"Until the elevator gets here, I'm not going anywhere, Rocco."

THERE WERE ALREADY TWO OFFICERS FROM THE FO-rensic squad in Cerruti's apartment. They were already at work in their white jackets. The poor victim's body had been covered with a tarp.

"Ciao, Schiavone." The unmistakable voice of the deputy director of the forensic squad took Rocco by surprise, from right behind him.

"Come on, Farinè, tell me how we fucked up this time."

"Nothing I know of so far. But how come today you aren't asking me how my wife is?"

"Are you two still together?"

"Yes," the policeman answered with some satisfaction. Today, for who knows what reason, he seemed to be in an excellent mood.

The age-old mystery. Signora Farinelli, a woman of such stunning beauty that in Turin she stopped traffic, continued to share her life with Farinelli, who to Rocco Schiavone's eyes was the quintessential paragon of earthly squalor. Average height, no hair, the kind of face you forget as soon as you turn the corner and, even worse, devoid of the slightest hint of a sense of humor.

"Yes, we're still together. Does the fact upset you?"

"Not me, no. What I don't understand is why it doesn't disturb her."

"Were you looking for something?"

"Yes. The keys to the apartment. Did you find them?"

Farinelli nodded. "Cerruti, was that his name? He was a very tidy fellow. I love tidy victims. They make my job so much easier. Two bunches of keys, in the top drawer by the front door, you see? That Chinese cabinet?"

"It's not Chinese, it's Tibetan," Rocco retorted.

"What do you know about it?"

"Forget about it, Farinelli. Just let these things slide. And if you piss me off, I'll even tell you how much it costs. So, in these bunches of keys, were there any plastic plugs?"

"Yes, there is one. I already asked the concierge about it. They're used for. . . ."

"Opening the metal gate down in the garage," Rocco finished his sentence for him.

"I see that you know all about it. She told me that every tenant has two of them."

"Two of them? Then where's the other one? This Cerruti really didn't keep track of his things, did he!" He smiled at his colleague. "But, unlike you, I know where it is."

Farinelli cocked his head slightly to one side: "So where is it?"

"If the murderer is smart, he tossed it out, along with the murder weapon. If he's a moron, he's still carrying it in his pocket."

"Too bad."

"What's too bad?" asked Rocco.

"That painting by Schifano. Blood spattered it."

The two men stepped closer to the framed canvas. "If you ask me, it looks good on it," said Rocco.

"I'm going to have to take it in to get the blood analyzed. It might not be the victim's blood. My motto is: Leave no stone unturned!" said Farinelli, and after slipping on a pair of latex gloves, he pulled the painting off the wall.

Behind it was a safe, with a keyhole, not a combination dial.

"Good work. Bravo, Farinelli!"

"You see? What happens when you're a stickler? Shall

we open it?" and he started over, sorting through the bunch of keys.

When they got the safe open, they found nothing of value. Just a sheaf of papers. Rocco grabbed them, beating the deputy director of the forensic squad to the punch. "Lemme just take a quick glance. . . ."

They were account statements from a bank, with balances, transactions, and debits. "Axion Bank, in Lugano. A Swiss bank."

"Well, how about that . . . and what does it say?"

"It says that our friend," Rocco muttered as he quickly shuffled through the papers, "has an account balance of three million euros."

"Nice going, Cerruti."

"But you want to know the most curious detail about it? Of the three million, two million nine hundred thousand was deposited less than a week ago."

Farinelli looked at Rocco. "What do you mean?"

"A wire transfer. From another bank in Lugano. That gives us something to think about, doesn't it?"

"Quite a bit."

Rocco handed the whole sheaf of documents to his colleague who began reading.

"What should we do about informing the judge?"

"You take care of it, Farinelli. You're well behaved and organized, and the judge likes neat and tidy types." Rocco turned to leave. Then he stopped in the door. "Would you explain one thing to me? Why do you seem to be in such a good mood? You usually never are!"

"Because if there's one thing I love, it's snow in May. It's so strange, so fluffy. It takes me back to my childhood."

"You're not trying to tell me you had a childhood, are you?"

"I'M HORRIFIED. I'M A WRECK, I'M SPEECHLESS. WHAT on earth is going on?" shouted Pietro Berguet. Someone had called from the office to tell him about the murder. Giuliana was overwhelmed, sprawled like a wet rag on one of the gilt sofas.

"And now what? Who did it? How could this have happened?" The president of Edil.ber was pacing back and forth in the large living room. "What should I be thinking? I've lost a friend, and now the police are going to come camp out in my offices. And those guys? They haven't freed Chiara. What's more, the notary Charbonnier . . . has been admitted to the hospital." He looked at his wife. "What are we going to do?"

When Pietro Berguet finally sat down, Rocco took the floor. "Can I have Cristiano's cell phone number? Cerruti's account might have phone calls between him and the murderer. I need to get it and I need to try to track down the phone calls he made."

"Of course, of course." Pietro got up and went to the front hall.

"Do you think it was them?" Giuliana asked in a faint voice.

"I don't know. Anymore than I know why Cerruti had a Swiss bank account in Lugano with a balance of no less than three million euros."

Giuliana's jaw dropped. "Three . . . three million?"

"Did he earn that kind of money at Edil.ber?"

Pietro, who had just walked back into the living room with a sheet of paper in one hand, answered the question: "He earned very good money . . . but three million!"

"As far as you know, had he come into an inheritance? Or had he won money? Anything that might justify such a huge sum of cash?"

"No, absolutely not. Dottor Cerruti was single and had no real family. An aunt, down in the Marche, but I don't think that . . . no, I'd rule that out entirely."

"In that case, the matter becomes shrouded in mystery, don't you think? Dottor Berguet, I'm going to ask you with all the willingness to listen and indulgence that I possess. Who suggested you turn to those people for the money? Who told you about Michele Diemoz?"

Pietro chewed his lip. "At first it was the bank itself that told me to try to find someone who could help me out. But the actual suggestion . . . I'm not sure. One night, we were in the office. . . ."

"We who?"

"Cristiano and I. And this Diemoz came in and introduced himself. I tried to understand who he was, and it was Cristiano who took down all his details. He seemed like a respectable person, someone who knew all the right people in Switzerland. That's right, it was Cristiano who checked Diemoz out, and determined he was a solid person. But so, you're telling me that. . . ."

"That you were nurturing a viper and it turned on you, Dottor Berguet."

Pietro raised his hands to his face. Giuliana, on the other hand, narrowed her eyes, which had turned deep and mean. "So if that bastard, God rest his soul, was working with them, then why did they kill him?"

Rocco heaved a sigh. "That's something I still can't say. I have no idea of the motive. Who knows, maybe he'd had enough, and was planning to come and tell you about it. Or else. . . ."

"Or else?" Giuliana asked, practically shouting.

"Or else, things went another way. And the people from down south had nothing to do with it. But then it's a different kind of murder. A private matter. In other words, let's say that whoever killed Cristiano might be someone who's very close to him, and that he had some urgent, thorny matter, still unresolved. Now, about the people from down south, here's what I want to know: have you heard from them again?"

Giuliana and Pietro exchanged a glance. "No," said Pietro. "Not since last time."

"They'll call to make arrangements about the notary. But we're going to have to start over from scratch now that Charbonnier has checked into a clinic."

"And Chiara? Out there somewhere, all alone, in the hands of . . ." Giuliana burst into tears. Pietro walked over to her, giving her a handkerchief. Then he turned to Schiavone.

"Here's the number," he said, handing him the sheet of paper. "That's the number Cristiano used for office business."

"Thank you." Rocco put the slip of paper in his pocket. "What do you intend to do now?"

The two Berguets, husband and wife, ashen-faced, wrapped in a helpless embrace, gazed back at the deputy chief. It was Pietro who finally answered: "We have no idea. We'll wait for instructions. It was Cristiano who made arrangements with the notary. I . . . we don't know what to do."

"What about Chiara?"

"Like we told you. Marcello only heard her voice for a second. But it sounded as if she was alright. I wouldn't worry about that."

"I would, and very much so," Rocco replied. "What assurances do you have that it was really her on the phone? None at all."

"Then what are we supposed to wait for before we can be sure? An earlobe in the mail?" Giuliana snapped.

Just then, the home phone rang, and it was worse than an icy dagger in the hearts of the Berguets. Rocco raised a hand: "Calm down. Answer the phone. And try to act normal. Is there a second line?"

Pietro nodded and pointed to a phone sitting on a Louis something-or-other side table.

"Good. You take the cordless. If we pick up at the same time, they won't notice."

Pietro went over to the wireless phone. The sound of the ringing continued to echo through the apartment. Pietro went back to the living room. They all looked each other in the eye, their eyes dark with despair, eyes that hadn't had a wink of sleep in days, eyes as deep and hopeless as artesian wells.

"When I count to three," said Rocco. "One, two, three!" Pietro and Rocco picked up the receiver simultaneously.

"Hello? Who is this?" Pietro asked.

"What the fuck is happening?" replied a distant, cavernous voice.

"Is that you?"

"What are the police doing at the office?"

"Someone . . . someone killed Dottor Cerruti."

Giuliana went over to Pietro.

"I want to hear my daughter's voice."

"Don't fucking bust my balls!"

Rocco recognized the accent. Calabria, without the shadow of a doubt.

"You talked to her before. The notary is in the hospital. Now we're going to change things . . . we'll let you know the name of the notary we're going to now."

"Why did you do this to Cristiano. . . ."

"Quit talking bullshit, who ever touched that faggot? I'll call you back. Tomorrow, not later. Berguet, do your best not to pull any crap. Speak a word to the police and your daughter dies!"

Click.

"Hello? Hello?"

Rocco hung up the phone. Pietro pulled the receiver away from his ear. Giuliana was there, waiting for news like a dog waiting for a biscuit. "He says they'll call back to tell me the name of the new notary. Tomorrow."

Giuliana went back to the sofa. Pietro slumped against the wall.

Without saying a word of farewell, the deputy chief left the Berguet home.

"What is all this?" Costa shouted into the phone as Schiavone was driving back to police headquarters.

"Sir, we arrived on the scene and found Cristiano Cerruti's corpse."

"I've summoned a press conference about that fencing ring and all the stolen merchandise. Now the reporters are going to ask me about this murder and I don't know a thing!"

"No, Chief, believe me, for now there's not much anybody knows. All you need to tell them is that your investigators are at work on this, and after all, the investigators in question would be me."

"I want more information, I can't let those newsvendors in my underwear without ammunition!"

"Let me send Officer Pierron over to you right now. He'll brief you fully, and give you a nice snug pair of trousers. He's been working with me on the investigation, every step of the way."

"I need you to come, too."

Fuck no, thought Rocco. Not the press conference. In the general hierarchy of pains in the ass, press conferences were the ninth degree. "Chief, I can't."

"So let's hear why not? And don't try to feed me some bullshit this time. I want the truth."

Maybe the time had come to level with the police chief. Hiding the facts was no longer a good idea. "Dottore, I'm on my way in to police headquarters right now. In ten minutes, I'll be in your office."

"But you won't find me there, I'm out of the office. Come on, tell me what you've got!"

Rocco told him everything, without skipping a single detail. That is, if you leave out his agreement with Judge Baldi, his agreement with the notary Charbonnier, his agreement with the Berguet family, and the unauthorized search of the HeyDiddleLiddles store.

"Holy crap . . . this is an unholy mess!" the police chief exclaimed when he was done.

"Yes, sir, it is. But I'm begging you, not a word to the press. The life of an eighteen-year-old girl hangs in the balance."

"Who the hell have you taken me for, Schiavone? One of your Laurel-and-Hardy cops? Let me remind you that I'm your superior officer and you were obligated, let me repeat, obligated to brief me on the whole matter."

"Dottor Costa, I haven't slept a wink in the past two days. I've done nothing but drill down on this thing. I assure you I had no intention of keeping you out of the loop."

"Are you playing on my side or are you playing against me?"

"Always on your side, Dottore. It hardly seemed appropriate to alarm you needlessly, putting pressure on you before matters had become clear."

"Don't forget that I root for Genoa C.F.C. So I'm well accustomed to living in a state of constant pressure. Spare the coaxing and simpering and save it for one of your lovers. . . ." Then he suddenly changed tone: "By the way, did I congratulate you on that notch in your belt?"

"Yes, Dottore, you certainly did. And I also know that you found out about it from your baker."

"Good. Now, as I was saying, spare me the coaxing and simpering and save it for women like Anna. I want everything to be transparent and crytal clear. I never want anything of the sort to happen again, do you understand me?"

"It won't happen again, Dottore."

"And look, just to be clear, if a nice big ass-fucking comes down the pike, we're going to share it fifty-fifty, is that clear?"

"The metaphor is a hundred percent clear."

"And now it's your fault that I'm going to have to go out in front of the newsvendors in this tense state of mental turmoil!"

"Don't let it get to you. And don't forget that you root for Genoa. You'll see, you'll get through it."

"Are you trying to be funny?"

"I'd never dream of it."

"But in fact you are. I don't know what's keeping me from transferring you out of here."

"Now it's you, sir, who's trying to be funny. Because you know there's nothing that would make me happier!"

"Get to work, Schiavone."

He'd arrived at police headquarters. The sky was black and the occasional snowflake was falling slowly over the city. He looked at the sidewalk that would soon turn back into a dish of creamy vanilla ice cream.

BUT NO SIGNATURE. CATERINA RISPOLI AND ANTONIO Scipioni were in his office.

"Caterina, how are you feeling?"

A red, chapped nose, dark circles under her eyes, the face of someone who'd slept little or not at all: "Well, what can I say, sir? Every time I go out, I just get worse."

"How do you like it in my office?"

"Very nice indeed. It's comfortable and it's warm."

"Is there anything I can get for you?"

"No, thanks. I even got a cup of tea."

"Antonio . . ." said Rocco, as he handed Scipioni a slip of paper. "This is the victim's cell phone number. See if you can get a printout of the last several phone calls received on this line."

Antonio nodded. "We don't have the cell phone? By which I mean the physical object?"

"If we did, I could find the numbers myself, right?"

"Sure. But sir, the thing is? It's no easy matter, I can tell you that right away. Usually they give us a CSV format file or maybe an XSL, then we have to get to work ourselves bit by bit, pulling useful files out of it by working in SQL or else using a converter. Let's just hope that they have at least an ATPS2000."

Rocco looked at him with a blank expression: "I didn't understand a damned word you just said."

"Let me put it in simple terms. The phone companies send us digital files that are a complete mess, and finding the numbers is no joke. The kind of thing that's going to take us days."

"Days? I don't have days."

"Let me see what I can figure out."

"How do you happen to know these things?"

"I used to work at the phone company." And with an innocent smile he left the office.

"Meanwhile, I've done some digging of my own," said Caterina. "Calcestruzzi Varese is a tiny company that hasn't invoiced anyone for months. Ugo Montefoschi is an eighty-four-year-old man, and he lives in . . ." she paused and picked up a sheet of paper, then continued: "Villa Sant'Agnese, in Brembate."

Rocco nodded. "So he's just a front. Our man is this Carlo Cutrì."

"That's right, and you know what? He's a resident of Lugano. Switzerland. And apparently he owns a hardware store."

"Son of a bitch," Rocco murmured under his breath, looking out the window. "You see what he's up to?"

"No."

"He puts his share of Edil.ber in this Montefoschi's name. Then, with a second property transfer, he moves it to his company in Switzerland. He's never going to set foot here at all. Or if he does, he'll only come when all is said and done."

"But he has an accomplice here."

"Certainly, whoever it is that took Chiara and are phoning our man, Pietro Berguet. And if you ask me, the intermediary on all this filth was Cristiano Cerruti."

"Cerruti?"

"I'm sure of it. Just as I'm sure that he was probably ready to talk, but someone sealed his lips for good."

"But who?" asked Caterina. Then she closed her eyes.

"Go on home, Caterì, and maybe stop by the pharmacy on your way. I don't want to have you on my conscience."

The inspector smiled and stood up. "Thanks, Dottore, I really can't take it much longer." She started to sway. Rocco hurried over and held her up. "Should I see you downstairs?"

"If you stand so close to me, you run the risk of catching the flu yourself, sir."

They looked each other in the eyes. For a long while, too long, so that it turned slightly awkward. "All right then, see you later, Caterina."

"See you later, Dottore."

The inspector left the deputy chief's office. Meanwhile, Rocco felt his exhaustion drop onto him like a sledgehammer, crushing spine and shoulders. In the last two days, he hadn't gotten more than seven hours of sleep, total. The dark corners of that case resisted even the brightest beams of light, and he hardly felt like his brain was prompt or alert. What he needed was a good long nap. The sun must have set by now. Outside it was already dark, though at least the snow had stopped falling. Sidewalks and trees were still as white as a Christmas.

He was about to switch off the office light when the phone rang. Heaving a sigh of annoyance, he went to pick up.

"It's me, your favorite anatomical pathologist."

"Should I be sitting down?"

"No, this'll just take a second. All right now, our golf player told me what time he was killed."

"Let's hear it."

"No later than eight thirty in the morning. Not a minute later. Do you want me to explain how he told me?"

"Forget about that, you'll start by telling me what the body temperature was, I'll get lost in these details and I'm not interested. I trust in your expertise."

"It's not just the temperature. It's also the breakfast. He hadn't even started to digest. Do you want to know what he had in his stomach?"

"No. Eight thirty, is that what you said?"

"At the very latest."

"You're invaluable, Alberto. Thanks and good night."

"I'm not going to sleep at six thirty in the evening. I've got things to do tonight."

"And just what are you going to do that's fun?"

"Yoga."

"That stuff where you tie yourself up in knots and then to get yourself untangled you have to call the forensic squad?"

"Just wait till we're old men, and I'm all lithe, with my joints well oiled, and you can't even bend over to pick up your house keys. Then we can talk it over."

"Don't worry, Alberto. I'm not planning to get old."

"Grouchy and solitary. Just like any genuine policeman."

"Go fuck yourself."

"Same to you, Rocco."

It was only as he put down the receiver that he realized that there was a cardboard box on the chair.

Clarks.

Desert boots. Size 10. And a note. "I hope I got the right size."

HE WAS HEADING STRAIGHT FOR THE PIZZERIA WHERE he could order by the slice, ready for his usual gourmet repast, when he saw Anna leave the perfume shop and cross the street. Rocco in his turn crossed the street to the opposite sidewalk. Hands in the pockets of his loden overcoat, a rapid, silent stride, eyes focused on the slabs of stone beneath his feet.

"Well? Are you pretending you don't know me?" Anna's voice carried loudly across the street. Rocco slowed to a halt. "I thought you'd made yourself pretty clear on the matter."

"Do you really believe everything a woman tells you?"

"Shouldn't I?"

"You should never answer a question with another question," said Anna.

"You should never stop a gentleman in the street who's minding his own business."

"Shall we go get a glass of white?"

"All right, let's get this glass of white."

● ● ●

THE WHOLE CAFÉ WAS MADE OF WOOD. TABLES, WAIN-
scoting, chairs, bar—even the suntanned bartender looked
like he was made of sandalwood.

"To your health!" said Anna, raising her glass.

"And here's to yours!" Rocco replied. Their glasses
clinked and the clear cool nectar slid down their throats.

"Pain in the neck, all this snow, eh?"

"Yeah," said Rocco. "But by now I'm getting used to it."

"Liar." Anna laughed and swallowed another gulp of
wine. "Your face looks tired."

"Yep, I'm a wreck."

"What were you doing at the bank?"

"When? I'm starting to lose all sense of time."

"Yesterday. The day after the night that you were at my
house. After which I called you on the phone and. . . ."

"Right, right, that part I still remember."

"I talked to Nora. Look, it turns out that things aren't
so bad after all."

"What do you mean?"

"Just think, she actually thanked me. Because I managed to open her eyes, after all, to just what kind of a person
you are."

"She needed help seeing that?"

"She needed a little shove to get out of that relationship,
is what I think."

"So, let me see if I've got this straight. You took me to
bed to rescue your girlfriend. Is that right?"

Anna smiled. "Intentions and outcomes sometimes min-
gle and merge into an indecipherable fog. The important

thing is that we all obtained something positive out of it. She got rid of you, you got rid of her. . . ."

"And you?"

"I satisfied my curiosity."

Rocco poured himself another glass of white wine.

"Have I wounded your pride?"

"I don't have any, Anna. You're quite a character, you know? Cynical, cagey, world-weary, a little tormented, waging a never-ending battle against life. You designed it beautifully. But let me tell you two things: you're a single woman, ridden with complexes, and if one day you were to look at yourself in the mirror with any real honesty, you'd fall apart."

"And just what makes you say that?"

"You're forty-two years old, but you claim to be thirty-eight. You've had work done on your breasts and a light touchup on your upper lip because you smoke, so you were starting to get wrinkles. You've been married twice and you couldn't make either marriage work. You let the architect Pietro Bucci-Something-or-Other keep you in the style you enjoy. You wanted to make your mark on the world. You paint in your room at home but your paintings have never been seen by anyone—except by the wallpaper in your apartment, and let me tell you, it's hard to tell the paintings and the wallpaper apart. You attack preemptively, and then you curl up like a hedgehog. You betray a close friend and then you find a cheap life-hack to keep yourself from feeling like a shit toward her. You issue ultimatums that you fail to respect. And you cry when you make love."

Anna clapped her hands. "Good job, Signor Commissario."

"Deputy Chief."

"So, did you find out all these lovely things by rooting around in my house?"

"A few questions here, another few there, and just by taking a quick look around."

"Do you know why I was crying while I was making love with you?"

"Because of my prowess in bed?"

"No. Because I'm in love, you fucking asshole!"

The Blanc de Morgex sailed straight out of Anna's glass and onto his shirt, seeping all the way down into his trousers. Anna snapped to her feet and left the bar. Rocco sat there and watched as the liquid darkened his light-colored corduroy trousers. "This is starting to become a habit," he said. Now he reeked like a wino.

"YOU REEK LIKE A WINO."

"I know, Marina, I know."

She laughs.

"Who did you piss off this time?"

I don't answer. It hardly seems advisable.

"A woman, for sure."

I continue to say nothing.

"Will you look at me?"

I look at her.

"Rocco, why won't you leave me in peace?"

A hand clutches at my stomach and, worse than a lemon could do, it squeezes out a sulphuric acid that, hot and stabbing, rises up my throat and burns it, like a blazing match.

"No," I barely manage to cough out. "I'm not going to leave you in peace."

"I'm not upset, Rocco. You are. You're very upset. Have you taken a look around at this place?"

"What's wrong with it?"

"Nothing. Nothing is what it's got. There's not a painting, not a book, not a CD. There's just a television set, a couple of sofas, a clothes cupboard, a bed, and a kitchen you never use. What's that in your hand?"

I lift the plastic bag. "A slice of margherita pizza, and a slice with potato and onions."

"Then your breath will stink."

"I do it on purpose."

I set the pizza down on the table. I unwrap it. Actually, it smells great. And today, it doesn't look like a wound oozing pus. It looks like a well-made pizza with tomato sauce and mozzarella. And it tastes good, too.

"That's just because you're hungry," says Marina.

"Maybe so."

"So do you want to hear today's word of the day?"

"You've started that up again? What's the word of the day?"

"Fanleaf."

"What's that mean?"

"Go look it up for yourself in the dictionary. You can't always have everything served to you on a silver platter, you know," and she leaves, heading for the bedroom. Or the

bathroom. Bedroom, actually, because I don't hear the sound of water running or locks being snapped shut.

AS HE TOOK THE THIRD BITE OF PIZZA HIS CELL PHONE rang. Rocco stood up. The phone was in the pocket of his loden overcoat.

"Hello?"

"Rocco? It's me, Adele!"

For a moment Rocco wondered: Adele who?

"It's me, Adele! That dumb-ass Seba's girlfriend. How are you doing?"

Adele from Rome!

"Of course, sure, Adele. And how are you doing?"

"Terrible, I'm a mess. Listen, did Furio talk to you?"

"Huh?" He'd already forgotten. Then, "Yes."

"So it's all right with you? Have you found me a place to stay?"

"What the . . . no, Adè, I haven't found a place. I just haven't had the time. Work is killing me."

"In Aosta?"

"In Aosta. Who'd have ever thought it?"

Adele laughed briefly. "Oh well, I'll be there tomorrow."

Rocco searched desperately for a solution. Tomorrow was going to be a horrorshow of a day, he knew that already. "Let's do this. Tomorrow, you arrive in Aosta, you go to police headquarters, I'll text you the address . . . and I'll leave my housekeys for you there. Tomorrow night, you can sleep here. Then we'll see, okay?"

"Okay. Corso Battaglione Aosta."

"How do you know that?"

"Google. What about your place?"

"What? That's not on Google?"

Adele laughed again. "No. It's not."

"Rue Piave. When you get here, curl up and make your-self comfortable. Oh, right, one other thing, Adele, or really, two things. Do a little grocery shopping because my fridge is so empty there's an echo. Second thing, I don't know any-thing about this. If Seba finds out I've been hiding you, he'll kill me."

"Don't worry, Rocco, it's for a couple of days, at the very most. You're a friend."

"Don't mention it."

"See you tomorrow, Rocco."

"See you tomorrow."

NOW WHAT AM I GOING TO DO? SHOULD I TELL MARINA that Adele is coming?

I read. Fanleaf: grapevine virus spread by nematodes which breed in the vine; can lead to deformity, yellowing of the leaves, and smaller crop yields.

"Are you saying that's me, Marina?" No answer. "Are you saying that's me?"

THE WIND WAS TOSSING THE FRONDS OF THE PALM trees along the waterfront. It was a cold east wind, sweeping in from the Balkans. Corrado Pizzuti, bundled in his heavy jacket, tugged his woolen cap down over his ears. The sea was back and nothing could be seen but the white crests of the breakers. In the distance, the occasional riding lights dotting that dark watery chalkboard. Some fisherman out on the open waters. The little town was deserted. It wouldn't be crowded again until the months of July and August. So all the buildings, vacation houses and apartments, had their shutters fastened tight. In the yards, plastic sheeting covered the pedalboats, the lounge chairs, and the beach swings, reposing in their winter rest. Weeds had gained the upper hand. The seafront huts that served drinks during the holiday season were shuttered, their roll-down metal blinds padlocked, and the wind-driven sand had by now invaded the embarcadero along the beach, drifting deep from the long winter months. But it was May now, and the hard months were ending. Corrado knew it. The winter months, the time when his homesickness for Rome really pounded the bass drum of heartache. More than once, he'd been on the verge of giving in, grabbing his car, and going back to Fidene, his part of the city. Nothing much to speak, on the outskirts of the city, a former *borgata*, or farming town, now absorbed—just barely—into the city, but it was all still Rome. In the past four years, in that little provincial seaside town, he'd made three friends, and if he was looking for sex, he'd have to climb in his car and drive to Pescara, and once there, pull out his wallet. At least he had plenty of money. The bar was doing great and during the summer months he earned enough to rest easy for the months still to come. But Rome . . . now

Rome was another matter. Rome was where he'd been born, fifty-four years ago, and he'd always felt right at home in the midst of that bedlam, all that infernal stench. Going back there, though, was out of the question. If anything, he felt he'd been lucky. In four long years, no one had come to pay a call on him, to throw a monkey wrench into his business or to back him up against a wall.

He turned down the little street he lived on. It was a funny thing, but even after four years, he still could never remember what it was called. That night he looked up and read the street sign: "Via Treviso." Okay, he said to himself. So I live on Via Treviso. In little towns, no one ever says the name of the street. They say, I live by the gelato place, or right after the bank, or maybe next to Mimì. It's not like Rome, where you tell someone: I live at number 15, Via Treviso. In part because no one in this town, except for the fire department, even knows where Via Treviso is. Everyone thinks of it as the street that runs down to the Bagni di Eraldo, the beach establishment. And that's that. End of story.

He walked into the courtyard. His apartment was on the staircase marked A. It was a tiny studio, 650 square feet, and it was on the second floor. He put his key into the anodized aluminum door.

"Ciao, Corrà!"

He leapt like a firecracker. He turned around. At the far corner of the courtyard, the flame of a cigarette lighter lit up the face of Enzo Baiocchi, who was surfacing from the darkness of his memories like the worst imaginable nightmare.

"How's it going?"

"Enzo! Fi . . . fine. How are you?"

Enzo put out the flame. The darkness swallowed his face. Then Enzo took a drag on his cigarette and the red ember colored his eyes. He walked toward Corrado, taking the apartment house street lamp full in the face.

"So you . . . you got out?"

Enzo smiled. "The fact that I'm here."

"Can I get you something at the bar?"

"No." Enzo stuck a hand in the pocket of his jeans and left it there. "Let me ask you a question, Corrado. And before answering it, I want you to think it over carefully. Are you coming with me or staying here?"

"Me? I'll come . . . I'll come with you."

"Good boy." Enzo pulled the hand out of his jeans pocket. Empty. Corrado heaved a sigh of relief.

"So where are we going?"

"I'll tell you once we're on the road. Tomorrow."

"Do you have a car?"

"No. We'll take yours."

"It's got some engine knock and the tires are old. How far do we need to go?"

"We'll take yours," Enzo insisted. "Okay, now do you have a place for me to sleep?"

"Y . . . yes. I've got a pullout sofa."

"Then let's get inside. It's cold out here." He flicked the cigarette away and followed Corrado through the front entrance to the apartment building.

THURSDAY

It must have snowed for a few hours during the night, even though the sky was clearer since day had dawned over Aosta. The air remained thin and icy cold, and the city still seemed to be locked in a deep slumber. The streets had already been plowed and only a light dusting, like confectioner's sugar, still encumbered the sidewalks. It was six thirty. Too early to go over to Ettore's; he'd get breakfast later on. He had to hurry over to the office, instead. The hours of sleep had done him a world of good and he had the sensation that he'd swept the cobwebs out of his brain. He took advantage of the open newsstand. The front page carried the news of Cristiano Cerruti's murder. As he read the article, he could see that Costa had carried it off brilliantly. Just a few solemn words, boilerplate suited to the occasion, the usual clichés and phrases of reassurance. There was his own name, as the chief investigator. Surely, he'd soon receive a phone call from Judge Baldi. The day before, he'd forgotten to inform him of that minor detail.

And, just as expected, the call came in.

"Dottore?"

"So I have to read about it in the newspapers?"

"I'm so sorry, didn't Farinelli call you?"

"Farinelli never called me."

Piece of shit, Rocco thought to himself.

"But you were the one who owed me the phone call, Schiavone!"

"You're perfectly right."

"You know what you can do with your 'perfectly right'? But listen, tell me, have you got a theory of what happened?"

"More or less. I think that Cerruti was deep inside this plot, with both feet. It's very likely that they decided to shut him up."

"Do we have any evidence?"

"We're trying to figure out from the cell phone whether he made any calls, and to whom. It's just that we were unable to find Cerruti's cell phone. And knowing only the number, it seems that the matter is somewhat complex."

"So it is. Just think, two years ago a defense lawyer brought in as evidence an incomprehensible graph to prove his client's innocence. He wanted to show that on that day at that hour the accused was sixty miles from the scene of the murder."

"But instead?"

"But instead a technician who read that tangle of lines and diagrams revealed the exact opposite. In other words, the lawyer nailed his own client for the crime because he hadn't known how to read that confusing document."

"That kind of thing happens."

"Now prepare to be amazed at my generosity. Do you remember that ledger you brought me? The one you found at that shop, HeyDoodleDiddles?"

"HeyDiddleLiddles."

"Whatever it is."

"Of course I remember it."

"Good. So it contains the names of twenty-five debtors. And I've discovered that twelve of them have one thing in common."

"Which would be what?"

"They all have accounts at the Vallée Savings Bank. Maybe it's just a coincidence."

"Maybe it is. Still, good to know. Thanks, Dottore. I've got that locked away."

"I'm hoping to know things early this time, Schiavone. You and I have an agreement, remember?"

"Certainly."

"And just to let you know, if a nice big ass-fucking comes down the pike. . . ."

"You'll do the generous thing and split it with me?"

"No. I'll leave it all for you. Have a good day."

HE COULDN'T RESIST NOW. HE PULLED OPEN THE drawer and picked up a joint. He lit it, sat down, and gathered his thoughts.

On the messy desk, there were dozens of sheets of paper. No messages, no new developments. He stretched his neck. He stubbed out the roach in the ashtray and, as always, opened the window to let in some fresh air. Caterina walked in without knocking.

"Excuse me! I never thought that. . . ."

Rocco, caught red-handed, was left speechless.

"Why do you have the window wide open? Have you lost your mind?"

The deputy chief shut the window.

"I didn't knock because it didn't even occur to me that you might be here," said Caterina as she went to take a seat. The odor of cannabis was overpowering. Could Caterina seriously not even notice?

When the inspector loudly blew her nose, the reason dawned on Rocco.

"Wait, weren't you supposed to stay home?"

"I couldn't take it any longer. Italo snores like a couple of lumberjacks," and she smiled with her red nose and blue eyes, large and sincere.

"A couple of lumberjacks sounds like more company than you'd care for?" Rocco commented, in some amusement.

"Well, you know what they say!" she replied.

"No, what do they say?" Rocco asked, playing along.

"Laugh and the world laughs with you, snore and you sleep alone!" she trotted out the punch line and laughed at her own joke. Then: "Listen, deputy chief, maybe this isn't important. But yesterday I went by the pharmacy."

"Good for you."

"That's right, because if I don't take my antibiotics this cold could easily turn into a sinus infection. And that would be a serious problem."

"I know. It hurts so much you can't think straight."

"Right? Anyway, I was saying that I'd been to the pharmacy. You remember that slip of paper that you gave me? Green paper? With the mysterious phrase we'd been able to bring out by doing a pencil rubbing?"

"Of course. I took it from a note pad at the Berguet home. I was hoping for something better. What was written on it?"

"I thought it said Deflan, which is a medicine. So I took it to the pharmacist. He read it, too, and he told me that what's written there isn't Deflan, but Deflamon."

"So is that important?"

"Ummm, I don't really know. But Deflamon is a medicine, too."

"And what's it good for?"

"Hold on, I've got it written down right here." She opened her purse. She pulled out her wallet, a makeup kit, a dark-blue paperback, and the bag from the pharmacy. She reached in and found the note. "All right, then, Deflamon . . . is used to treat a vaginal infection."

Rocco squinted. "A vaginal infection?" but it wasn't a question, he was just thinking aloud. Caterina looked at him. "Yes . . . a disease that. . . ."

Rocco lunged at his phone. "Please put me through to Dr. Fumagalli. Schiavone, police headquarters, Aosta." He held the line while nervously drumming his fingers on the desktop.

"Hey there! Seven thirty in the morning and you're already on the job?"

"Do you remember when you let me look in the microscope? That stuff you found on Carlo Figus's body?"

"Not on his body, on his penis. Yes, of course."

"What did you call that virus you showed me?"

"Oh my God, Rocco, it's not a virus. It's a bacterium. *Gardnerella vaginalis.*"

"Can it be treated with Deflamon?"

"Certainly, it's a metronidazole. But why do you ask?"

"Because it's a first step, my friend."

"I told you that you needed to get a steady girlfriend. Did you catch it?"

"Not me."

"Then who did?"

"I'll tell you later!"

"Listen, it's a pretty common ailment. . . ."

Rocco hung up the phone. "It's a clue, Caterina. A small one, but it's still a clue!"

He picked up the phone again: "Oh, who's at the front desk?"

"It's me, Casella, Dottore."

"Call up the highway patrol. I need to talk to Officer Umberto."

"Last name?"

Rocco spoke to Inspector Rispoli: "Do you know Umberto? From the highway patrol, Italo's friend?"

"Certainly, he was over at my house for dinner last night. Lasagna. Umberto Lasagna."

"Casella, Lasagna."

"Gladly, thanks."

"Gladly, thanks, what?"

"Thanks for the offer."

"What offer, Casella?"

"The offer of lasagna. I'd gladly eat some."

"Lasagna is Umberto's surname, you fucking moron!"

"It was a joke. I realized that, sir!"

"I'll come down there and chew your liver out of your gut, you fool. Get moving!" He waiting with the receiver still in his hand. "Where do they put wrecked cars?"

"Usually down at the tow yard. In Villair. . . ."

"Call Italo. Tell him to come straight over to police headquarters. And get me copies of the photographs of Figus and Midea, the two men who were killed in that cargo van. Take the ones from their IDs. They ought to be in the files, but there I'm just guessing." And he hung up the phone, cutting off the call with the front desk, and shot out of the office at top speed.

"I could ask Casella where they keep them. He's in charge of the filing."

"If you're willing to talk to Casella. . . ."

CASELLA SAW THE DEPUTY CHIEF GO RACING PAST THE front entrance. "Dottore? They're connecting me now with Umbe. . . ."

"Fuck off, Casella, it's too late! Go up and report to Rispoli and obey her orders. Get moving!"

Casella hung up, abandoned the front desk, and ran as fast as he could, one hand clapped to the top of his hat, toward the deputy chief's office. At the same time, the deputy chief himself came dangerously close to slipping and falling on a step as he went out the entrance to police headquarters. He managed to stay on his feet, though, and stepped into the squad car. On the third attempt, the engine turned over.

"This piece of shit!" He shifted into gear and, tires skidding on the icy asphalt, roared away from police headquarters.

"COME ALONG, DOTTORE, THIS WAY." THE CUSTODIAN of the tow yard, a short, bald man, was escorting him past dozens of wrecked cars, all without license plates, an automobile graveyard that the snow had tried in vain to cover up.

"By any chance do you have a replacement dashboard for a 4WD Volvo XC60?"

"I can ask, but I don't think so. Why?"

ANTONIO MANZINI

"Mine's broken."

"Here you are, Dottore, the cargo van involved in that fatal crash is right here!"

Rocco tried to open the driver's side door.

"No, that one's damaged, you can't get it open. Try on the other side."

The other door was practically ripped from its hinges. Running down the side of the door was a succession of oil-change decals that made it look like part of a Christmas display. Rocco pushed it open and climbed inside. There were still dark blood stains on the dashboard and the upholstery. He looked at the floor. There was a cigarette lighter, some mud, a length of rope. He opened the glove compartment. Documents, a screwdriver, an old rag, and a brand-new box of Stilnox, missing two pills. Rocco pocketed the box and smiled.

"Does it open in the back?"

The man threw open the two rear hatches.

There was a spare tire, there was a tool chest. Hammers, trowels, a paint brush, and a bag full of black plastic strip fasteners.

"You've been immensely helpful, maestro!" Rocco practically shouted.

He ran back to get the squad car.

"How do I look?"

Enzo Baiocchi had just stepped out of the bathroom.

266

He'd turned blond. Corrado looked at him without changing expression. "You look like a German." And he drank the last of his espresso. Enzo sat down. "Did you get any sleep?"

"Not much. Are you going to tell me where we need to go?"

"All you're going to have to do is drive. Never accelerating, just nice and steady, a light foot, and straight ahead. I'll tell you when to turn."

Corrado Pizzuti put down the coffee cup. "Listen, about your brother, I didn't. . . ."

Enzo grabbed him by the front of his shirt, knocking the metal cover of the sugar bowl to the floor along with a couple of cookies. "Don't you even mention Luigi's name. Never again, understood? Never again!" He released his grip. "How long have you been living here?"

"Three years, almost four."

"You're set up nicely." Enzo drained the last of his coffee and looked out the window. "Look at that, you can even see the water from your house. And you own a bar. How's business, pretty good?"

"In the summer, yes. But it's slow in the winter. How did you find me?"

"Rats like you leave their little turds behind them."

"You didn't hurt my mother, did you?"

Enzo burst out laughing. "Do I strike you as the kind of guy who hurts a ninety-year-old woman? All I had to do was ask a couple of questions. Like I told you, you leave a stench."

"But then, when we get where we're going, are you going to let me go?"

Enzo glared at him. "If I wanted to hurt you, you'd already know about it."

"But why me?"

"Well, you see, Corrado, I don't have a lot of friends. And I need you to drive. I don't have to explain to you that, someone like me, the less I'm seen in public, the better, right? Now, quit asking so many questions cause I'm fucking sick of it. Hurry up and get ready to go." He kissed the gold-and-coral crucifix he wore around his neck.

"Do I have time to call Tatiana and tell her I'm not coming in today?"

"No."

HE SCREECHED TO A HALT IN FRONT OF POLICE HEADquarters. Italo was standing there, with a sheet of paper in his hand. "Here you are, Rocco. These are the Xeroxes of the pictures of those two and. . . ."

"Give it here!" The deputy chief didn't even get out of the car. He tore the sheet of paper from the officer's hand, threw the car into reverse, and then roared away in the direction of Via Cretier.

Italo stood there watching the car as it swerved dangerously close to a camper. "What did he smoke this morning?" he asked himself. Then a chilly shiver drove him back up to the warmth of the office.

• • •

HE'D PARKED THREE HUNDRED YARDS FROM THE school. He went the rest of the way on foot.

The kids were outside the front entrance. Among the dresses, backpacks, and hats, he spotted the blond head of Max Turrini. Sitting on a low wall, Max had his arm around a young woman's shoulders. He was craning his neck to whisper something in her ear. Something that made her laugh. As he passed by, Rocco murmured: "Oh, ciao, Max. So you've already found a replacement, I see!"

Max looked at him as if he'd just taken a punch to the jaw, but said nothing. He had neither the wit nor the time, since the deputy chief had already plunged through the front gate of the school.

HE DIDN'T BOTHER TO KNOCK. HE WALKED STRAIGHT into the office of the shrew, better known as Principal Bianchini, like a torrent of wind. The school principal jerked in startlement when he saw Rocco appear before him. Hair wildly askew, jacket unbuttoned, trousers rumpled, one shoe unlaced, and two buttons missing from his shirt.

"Dottor . . . Schiavone? What's this about?"

"Giovanna Bucci-Something-or-Other." It was no good, he couldn't get the architect's double-barreled last name into his head.

"Bucci Rivolta?" Bianchini asked shyly.

"Exactly. Where is she?"

Just then the bell rang. Looking out the window, Rocco saw the kids entering the school like a family of sloths.

"Class Five B, but. . . ."

"Take me to Class Five B. Quick!"

Bianchini put on his jacket and grabbed a bunch of keys. "Let's go. It's on the third floor."

ROCCO AND THE PRINCIPAL WERE STANDING AT THE head of the classroom. The kids came in shouting, but at the sight of the shrew, they lowered the volume of their voices. They were afraid of him. Rocco watched him out of the corner of his eye. On the principal's face there now appeared, almost involuntarily, a complacent smile. That little half-man was happy to exert his smidgen of power. And the treacherous gleam in his eyes made it clear just how vindictive he could be.

A venomous shrew.

The faces of young women and young men passed by them, nondescript, handsome and homely, pimply and unkempt. Then in the midst of those anonymous masks, like a poppy flower in a field of wheat, Giovanna's face stood out. A whole other category, a whole other gait. And the minute she saw the deputy chief she froze in the middle of the hall. Rocco smiled and went over to reassure her.

"Something's happened to Chiara, hasn't it?" she asked.

"Everything's okay, Giovanna," and he locked arms with her and led her to the window in the hallway.

"Have you found her?" asked the architect's daughter.

"Not yet. But we're getting close. Now, listen closely . . ." Something caught Rocco's eyes. Down below, at the entrance, Max Turrini and his mother were talking to Pietro Berguet's brother, Marcello, the math teacher. Laura was nodding while Marcello talked and Max kept his eyes on the ground. The bank director had come by for a conference with her son's teacher and from the grim look on her face, the news couldn't be good. But Rocco already knew that: math was one of those subjects that the young man would be retaking come September. In the end, Laura shook hands with Marcello while Max hurried back into the school. And that was when Marcello—perhaps because he felt someone watching him, or else just by chance—looked up and saw the deputy chief gazing down through the window pane. Laura, too, looked up. Marcello shyly raised a hand and waved to the deputy chief. Rocco waved back. So did Laura.

"Look, there's no two ways about it, his mother is wasting her time going around trying to make the teachers feel sorry for her. You know what? That's Chiara's uncle."

"Of course, I know that."

"Luckily, he teaches in the A Section, and I'm in the B Section."

"Why luckily?"

"Because he's super-strict and he flunks everybody."

"But you're good at math, aren't you? Your Papà can help you!"

"I'm a disaster. But my teacher is nice. He takes pity on me."

Of course he does, Rocco thought to himself, how could he be cruel to a statuesque beauty like that one?

"He always lets me off easy."

"The day he tries to put his hands where they don't belong, give me a call, Giovanna. I have a sideline in beating down guys who don't know how to stay in their place."

The girl laughed. "Don't worry. I know how to take care of myself."

"I don't doubt it for a second. All right, let's get back to us, Giovanna. Try to focus. Sunday evening. You were at Sphere."

"Yes."

"I'd have to guess there were a lot of people."

"Really a lot."

"You said that at a certain point Max started talking to a couple of *tamarri*. Which down in Rome we would call *coatti*. In any case, hicks."

"Yes, those guys were ridiculous. And they were probably in their thirties."

"I'm going to show you a picture now. I want you to concentrate and see if you recognize them."

"I don't know, Dottore. It was dark. Still, let me take a look."

Rocco pulled out the sheet of paper with the photocopies of the IDs of Viorelo Midea and Carlo Figus. "Here they are. What do you think?"

Giovanna studied the pictures attentively. "This guy with the earring, I'm not quite sure. The photocopy is too dark. But this one . . ." and she pointed to Carlo Figus ". . . definitely."

"Are you certain?"

"One hundred percent."

Rocco nodded. "You can go back to your class. We're done here."

"No, take me to police headquarters!"

Rocco looked at her, baffled.

"In first period, there's an exam in philosophy. I haven't even opened the book! If he tests me, I'm done for!"

Rocco thought it over. "Come with me!"

Giovanna grabbed her bag and followed Schiavone. Together, they encountered Bianchini, who was waiting for them on the stairs. "Everything worked out, Dottor Schiavone?"

"Things are much more complicated than I thought. I need Giovanna to come with me to police headquarters."

"But. . . ."

"No ifs, ands, or buts, Dottor Bianchini. I've already told you the way matters stand. Try to cooperate."

"Certainly, certainly," said the principal as he looked at Giovanna. The girl was playing her part quite well. If she played her cards right, with her figure and those eyes, she probably could count on a bright future in the most prestigious Italian television series.

HE'D LEFT GIOVANNA IN THE PASSPORT OFFICE WITH a book and orders not to say a word to any of the officers, except for him and Inspector Caterina Rispoli. Giovanna started reading and asked if she was allowed to smoke. "Only if you go over to the window. And with the window open, just to be clear."

Scipioni, Italo, and Inspector Rispoli were all in Rocco's office. "So, we have a new twist," said Rocco, slamming the box of Stilnox he'd found in the cargo van down on the desk. "Stilnox. It's a benzodiazepine. It's used to treat insomnia. It was in the cargo van. Benzodiazepines are also known as rape drugs. They're tasteless, they put the person into a trance, and they create a blank slate of amnesia. Often the victim doesn't even remember what happened the night before. They might just think they were drunk, but actually. . . ."

Antonio grabbed the box: "Fuck. . . ."

"What's more, we also found these in the cargo van," and he pulled the plastic strip fasteners out of his pocket. "There were dozens of them. All right, I know that construction workers use them too, but . . . Giovanna recognized Carlo Figus. He was at the discotheque the night of the kidnapping."

"So you think they were the ones who kidnapped the girl?"

"I believe so. And then there's the question of the vaginal infection. Figus had *Gardnerella*, Fumagalli found it on his penis, and someone is suffering from the same ailment at the Berguet home."

"You're saying that those bastards raped Chiara Berguet?"

"Very likely, Caterina. Now that I think about it. . . ."

"The burglary!" said Scipioni. "The faked burglary at Viorelo's place."

"Good job! It wasn't a burglary at all. They were looking for something in particular."

"What?" asked Italo.

Rocco went to his desk. He pulled open the left-hand drawer. "I say they were looking for this!" and he pulled out Viorelo's cell phone. "Italo, where are the numbers he called?"

"I put them on your desk the other day, but only the first three. It looks like the Romanian deleted them and it's taking the technician a while to put together the whole list. Then there are the numbers in the directory, but those are all Romanian numbers," and he started rummaging through Rocco's notes and documents.

"Fuck, we had the solution right in front of us for days! Who gives a damn about the Romanian numbers? I want the last three numbers he called!" the deputy chief swore.

"Certainly, if you kept things a little tidier in here, Rocco."

Antonio's eyes opened wide. "Did you just call him Rocco?"

Italo bit his lip.

"That's right, Antonio, Italo calls me by my first name. And has for a long time. Starting today, both you and Caterina are authorized to do the same."

"I don't think I could," said Caterina.

"Give it a try."

"Here it is!" Italo pulled out a sheet of paper. "These are the last three phone numbers dialed."

Antonio grabbed the piece of paper. "I'll see if I can find out who they belong to. It should just take a minute!" And he vanished from the office.

"Let me see if I understand this, Rocco," said Caterina. "The two men kidnapped Chiara and now they're dead?"

"So you see how easy it is to be on a first-name basis with me?"

Caterina blushed.

"Anyway, that's right, Caterina. Now what we need to figure out is whether they were aware of where she was being kept, or not."

"No. Given the fact that the parents talked to Chiara. Clearly, there's someone else."

"True." Rocco started to pace the room. "What do we know? That they were driving from the direction of Saint-Vincent. We ought to be able to figure out how many miles they'd driven."

"Maybe we might have a stroke of luck," said Italo. "Like, I don't know. A traffic ticket they got that day."

"No, we've run checks on all the speed-trap cameras. Nothing turns up for that license plate. And we don't have time to check through all the surveillance camera footage in the area."

"Well, we have their cell phone. We can trace back the cell tower they were connected to and we'll know where they were."

"Well, that's certainly the first thing we should do."

"Even though . . ." Italo said, "the cell or the tower doesn't pin it down that much. It can be a very approximate range. Even thirty miles, you know that? Antonio told me so."

"But there's something else you can't possibly know.

Because you didn't come with me to the judicial tow yard!"
The deputy chief rushed away, leaving Rispoli and Italo
exchanging glances.

In the hallway, they ran into the two officers. D'Intino
had a tray wrapped in paper and Deruta had a thermos.
"What is this stuff, D'Intino?"

"Pastries. I'm taking them to the young lady, your friend
in the passport office."

"What about you, Deruta?"

"Tea. Hot tea. She was thirsty."

"All right then, listen carefully. At noon on the dot, I
want you both to get the squad car and drive Giovanna back
to school. Do I make myself clear?"

"Yessir. Who's driving?" asked Deruta.

"You are. D'Intino is a disaster behind the wheel. And
don't turn on the siren. Even if the girl asks you to. Understood?"

They both nodded their heads in unison and hurried off
to the passport office. Giovanna had turned them into two
tail-wagging lapdogs.

"BUT WHAT'S SO INTERESTING ABOUT THIS CARGO
van?" asked the custodian of the tow yard.

Rocco went back to the passenger-side door. He bent
over and started reading the oil change stickers. The most
recent one was from an Agip station, and it showed Sunday's
date. And the mileage. Rocco clambered over to the driver's
side seat. He wiped the dust off the glass over the speed-

ometer and read the cargo van's final mileage. They'd only driven eighty-one miles since the oil change.

"What's your name?"

"Lucianino!"

"Lucianino, do you have a map of Aosta?"

"We have internet in the office."

LOOKING AT THE MAP, ROCCO LIT A CIGARETTE.

"Can I smoke, too?"

"Certainly, Lucianino. Now then, follow me on this. What time do gas stations close for the night?"

"Seven o'clock?"

"Excellent. Let's say that the first thing the two men do is go to Sphere, where they arrive at approximately eleven o'clock. Sphere is on the road to Cervinia."

"Right, I know that disco, my son goes there, too. It's in Saint-André. So from Aosta that's more or less . . . twenty miles. I say more or less because I have no idea of what service station we're starting from."

"Agip."

"And there are lots of those."

"This one was open on Sunday!"

Lucianino focused. "Then for sure it's the one on Via Luigi Vaccari! From Via Vaccari . . . to there is twenty miles, that's correct."

"Good. So from there, the two of them go back to the Berguet home. That's where they kidnapped Chiara."

"Who's Chiara?"

"Don't worry about that. Okay, so how far to the Berguet's place?"

"Okay, but I don't know where they live."

"In Porossan. Aosta."

Lucianino typed into the map. "And that's another twenty-three miles."

"Which means we're talking about . . ." Rocco did a quick mental calculation, ". . . forty-three miles. Now the two of them have to get back to the area around Saint-Vincent, because we're already running out of mileage."

"Back to Saint-Vincent is . . . twenty-four miles."

"And now we're at sixty-seven miles. Then on the way back to Aosta they have the crash. So for us to get to eighty-one miles, we just need another fourteen miles. Fourteen miles to figure out where the fuck they went. About fourteen miles from Saint-Vincent. Round trip, more or less."

"But who are *they*?"

"Don't worry, Lucianino. I'm just thinking aloud. Where can you go with fourteen miles from Saint-Vincent?"

"Hmmm . . . well, either you head up to Salirod. . . ."

"Or else?"

"Or else here, you see? Toward Promiod . . . or toward Closel and from there you head uphill for another ten miles."

"Any number of places."

"I'd say so."

"But am I going to give up, Lucianì?"

"I don't know. Are you going to give up?"

"Not on your fucking life. Thanks, Lucianino!"

"You're quite welcome, Dottore."

THE DEPUTY CHIEF WAS ON HIS WAY BACK TO THE OF-
fice when a police squad car, sirens blaring, cut him off
right in the middle of an intersection, blocking traffic in
all directions. Italo Pierron got out with Antonio and they
rushed straight over to Rocco's Fiat Croma. The thing that
most amazed Schiavone wasn't his officers' behavior—they
seemed to be in the throes of a bout of schizophrenia, no
doubt infected by Rocco himself—but the fact that the
cars of the Aostan motorists, blocked by that absurd and
unexpected maneuver, were perfectly silent—not even a
horn beep of protest. Such a thing in Rome would have
prompted a veritable concert, an explosion of sounds and
drivers shouting out their car windows. Instead, given the
civility of that populace, an almost surreal silence reigned
over the street.

"Rocco, we couldn't wait!" said Italo, breathing heavily.

"So, we checked the three numbers that Viorelo Midea
called," Antonio Scipioni went on. "The last three calls were
to the Posillipo Pizzeria, and to a number in Romania, but
the last one, the very last one, was to another number."

"Well, do you want to tell me which number it was or am
I supposed to sit here. . . ."

"Marcello Berguet's phone," said Italo. At that point, a
shy solitary car horn piped up from the line that had formed
behind Rocco's car.

"Marcello Berguet . . ." Rocco repeated.

"Shall we go pick him up?"

"Hold on. We have an advantage. Let's exploit it . . . What do we know? That Marcello is the one who claims to have spoken to her. But maybe he never did. Or else, maybe he did, actually. Anyway, he knows where his niece is now, that much is clear!"

The solitary horn honked again.

"What should we do?"

"Turn around and follow me to the Agnus Dei Clinic."

The officers went back to their cars, apologizing with vague gestures to the motorists still waiting patiently, while Rocco took off at top speed toward the center of Aosta.

ENRICO MARIA CHARBONNIER WAS SITTING VERY comfortably on a couch in front of the window, reading the newspaper. He had a piping hot cup of tea on the side table next to him and a panoramic view of the snow-covered Alps spread out before him.

"Wait, let me get this straight. First you send me to the clinic and now you want me to go back to my office?"

"I have to figure out whether Carlo Figus owns any property up in the direction of Saint-Vincent."

"Why, Dottor Schiavone?"

"Because he and some miserable homeless bum kidnapped Chiara, and I don't think they took her to any of the properties owned by the Berguet family."

"But who's telling you that there's no one else involved?"

"Because Marcello Berguet is the mastermind behind those two!"

The newspaper fell out of the notary's hands. "Marcello? The math teacher?"

"Exactly. Now I know that Chiara has been held prisoner since Sunday night, or if you prefer, since early Monday morning. And God only knows if she's still alive."

"Why don't you do this, you and your officers go on over to Piazza della Repubblica, to the land office. I'm going to make a call to a friend of mine who works there. You'll see, he won't take a minute."

"Thanks, Dottor Charbonnier."

"Do you need me to do anything else?"

"Nothing," Rocco replied. "Just keep reading your newspaper and take advantage of the opportunity to get some rest and have your tests done. If nothing else, I've noticed that some of the nurses here are pretty easy to look at."

The notary smiled. "At my age, in fact, I can only contemplate them, like the Alps." And with a theatrical sweep of the arm he indicated the peaks that could be seen in the distance, out the window.

NOT EVEN HALF AN HOUR LATER, THE DEPUTY CHIEF and his officers left the land office, bitterly disappointed. They hadn't found anything in the name of either Carlo Figus or his mother. Marcello Berguet, on the other hand, had a studio apartment in the center of town and a small villa over near Alagna. Rocco had discarded that. Too far away, at least based on his hunch about the mileage chalked up by the kidnappers' cargo van.

They were back where they'd started.

"Let's call the police chief," suggested Antonio.

"What for?"

"Let's have him assemble an insane group. Everyone: firemen, Carabinieri, finance police, forest rangers, alpine guides. Everyone. We need to explore an area spanning many square miles and how are we going to do that by ourselves?"

"In order to put together anything of the sort, we'd need time, hours and hours, and we don't have it. What's more it would mean making the matter public. And that could play quite a nasty trick on us, too."

"Such as?" Italo asked.

"Such as it turns out that, besides Marcello Berguet, there's someone else tangled up in this story. And that someone else could take off. I heard one of the kidnappers on the phone, and he had a Calabrian accent."

"Maybe it could have been that guy Cutrì who lives in Lugano."

"Sure, it could have been. But it also could have been someone who lives here in Aosta. We still don't really know anything about this organization. Only the tip of the iceberg. Or actually, two tips of the iceberg."

"Which ones? Marcello Berguet and then who else?"

"Chiara's young boyfriend. Max. He's involved somehow."

"Why?"

"Because he knew the kidnappers. At least Carlo Figus. And if he's involved, then so is his mother. We have nothing left but to go catch the wolf."

ANTONIO AND CASELLA, AS PER INSTRUCTIONS ISSUED by the deputy chief, had gone to pick up Marcello Berguet. Rocco had also cautioned them not to make the arrest in a classroom, to do it far from the eyes of the students, and to avoid involving school personnel if at all possible. But those instructions proved unnecessary. When Rocco returned to his office, there was Marcello Berguet in person waiting for him, sitting as stiff as a stick, impeccably dressed in suit and tie, his hair slicked back and his face still wafting the scent of morning aftershave.

"I'm happy to see you here, Signor Berguet. I'd sent my men to get you at school."

"You and I need to talk."

"I know. And in fact, I'd sent two of my officers to pick you up at the high school."

"Why would you do that?"

"Let's just say . . . kidnapping, Signor Berguet. Kidnapping and murder!" Rocco Schiavone picked up a sheet of paper.

"Kidnapping? Murder? What the hell do you think you're talking about?"

"Do you see this piece of paper? I just received it from an auto dealership. We found a fragment of a broken headlight downstairs in Cerruti's garage. Too bad for you, it happened to be a shard with the serial number on it. They traced it back to the manufacturer, and guess what they found out? These headlights are made for the Suzuki Jimny. Unless I'm mistaken, your sister-in-law Giuliana has a Suzuki Jimny, and again if I'm not misinformed, you're the one who uses that car. That's what she told us when we paid a call at the house, the same day we found it abandoned on the road with its headlights broken. Did you use the car to go see Cristiano?"

"Listen, let me just say one thing. . . ."

"No, let me talk. What possible reason could there be for Viorelo Midea, who is one of the men who kidnapped your niece, to have called your number on his cell phone?"

Berguet looked at Rocco. "My number?"

"That's right. The night of the kidnapping. Did he call you? Was he asking for instructions? Did he want to tell you that they'd taken the girl? Is that it?"

"I don't even know who this Viorelo Midea is!" Marcello yelled.

"Where did they put your niece? That's something you know!"

"If I knew, I'd go get her, for fuck's sake!" Marcello's nerves were starting to give.

"Calm down, Signor Berguet. You're the only one who spoke to Chiara."

"Certainly. I did talk to her."

"And are we supposed to take you at your word?"

"Of course. I heard Chiara saying: I'm fine. But that's all I heard."

"And you're certain that it was Chiara? After all, she only said: I'm fine. That's not much of a basis to be certain."

Marcello thought it over for a few seconds. "Well, you might be right. I don't know. I said: Chiara, it's me, your uncle. And she replied: I'm fine, Uncle Marcello. And that was it. Maybe she was upset, she was clearly very scared. But I'm sure of one thing. And it only occurs to me now. She's never called me Uncle Marcello in her life. To Chiara, I've always been Uncle Ninni. Never Uncle Marcello. Never. Why is that only occurring to me now?"

Rocco took a deep breath. "Can I have your cell phone?"

Marcello stuck his hand in his pocket. He handed his cell phone to Rocco, who immediately checked the incoming calls. "Look right here. At three fifteen Monday morning. You received a call from Viorelo Midea's cell phone. And we have that call listed in the records. The call lasted for . . . three seconds?" Rocco narrowed his eyes. "Wait, what, three seconds?"

"At that time of the night, I'm asleep, usually, Dottor Schiavone," said Marcello, "I certainly don't have phone conversations." And he ran his hand over his face.

"This cell phone, the number's only six digits long. Why is that?"

"It's an arrangement Pietro made with the cell phone provider. He wanted sequential phone numbers for everyone in the company, even though I'm only nominally an employee. My number ends in 04, Pietro's in 01, and I think Giuliana's ends in 03, Cerruti's was 07, and so on for other employees. With different last numbers, of course."

Rocco fell silent. He could feel the earth shake beneath his feet, about to open up in a yawning abyss and swallow him like a piece of candy. He turned around and stared into Marcello's face. Who in turn felt extremely awkward. "What . . . what's wrong? Why are you staring at me?"

"Did you shave this morning?"

Marcello seriously started to wonder whether the deputy chief was suffering from some mental illness. "I shave every morning. I can't stand not to."

"Fucking hell!" the deputy chief blurted out loudly, and the math teacher lost his composure and practically jumped out of his chair. "I'm an idiot!" He picked up the phone, as Marcello Berguet looked on in astonishment. "Hello, Farinelli? Are you still in Aosta?"

"No, Schiavone, but my men are there. If you want, I can put you in contact with them."

"Listen. Maybe you'll remember. On the site of the Cerruti murder. . . ."

"Yes."

"Do you remember at the exit of the apartment building? There's a common area, a garden."

"Right, covered with snow. Spider flower and firethorn bushes. Why?"

"Did you check there?"

"Certainly. Next to a shrub we found some footprints. Someone walked up to it, rummaged around, and then left."

"And what do you think they were looking for?"

"At first I thought it might have been someone with a dog. But there were no traces of animals on the snow. If it had been summertime, I would have guessed that some tenant who lived directly upstairs dropped an article of clothing from the clothesline and had come down to get it. But it's not summer."

"I'd certainly say it's not. Thanks, Ernesto."

"Don't mention it."

"Ah, thanks for reporting to Baldi. You certainly made me look like a complete asshole."

"This certainly wasn't the first time, nor will it be the last."

"I'm going to have to agree with you on that point," he said, and glanced in Marcello Berguet's direction. Then the deputy chief braced both elbows on the desk and hid his face in his hands for a period of time that seemed to Marcello to stretch out endlessly. He rubbed his weary eyes and finally looked up at the math teacher. "Do you know why certain things happen? Because you take your eye off the ball."

"I know, Dottore. The slightest distraction, a tiny error in calculation, and you can no longer solve for X."

"Right. I didn't think about the razor. The razor with the shaving foam in Cerruti's bathroom. He didn't shave."

Marcello lowered his eyes.

"Why didn't you tell me right away that you were Cristiano's lover?"

"You never asked me. And most important of all, in the time I've been in this office, you never once let me speak. If you'd listened to me instead of attacking me, we could have avoided wasting valuable time."

Rocco shook his head. "In that case, go right ahead. Have your say."

"My relationship with Cristiano was—and I hope it can continue to be—a secret matter. You understand, I'm a teacher, Aosta is a town of 40,000, and you can suddenly find yourself ostracized and mocked in the blink of an eye. We're not in Rome, you know!"

"I owe you an apology."

"Forget about it. Things weren't going at all well between me and Cristiano. He was a wreck, on edge, I don't know why, but I got the feeling he was hiding something. We're talking about the morning of the murder. I left early, it couldn't have been eight o'clock yet. I had to get over to school early. Cristiano was expecting someone at eight fifteen."

"Who?"

"He wouldn't tell me. Like I said. He was on edge, he'd snap at nothing, we'd been fighting for days."

"Maybe your brother or Giuliana had already told him. But Cristiano was somehow involved in the kidnapping of your niece."

"I know that. That's why you won't see me shed a single tear over his death. We saw each other, we talked to each other, but who Cristiano Cerruti really was, I had no idea. I thought he was . . . how could he?" Marcello looked Rocco right in the eyes. "How could he have gotten involved in such a thing?"

"Does three million euros sound like an acceptable answer?"

Marcello rubbed his hands together. "Do you have a cigarette?"

Rocco's mind shot straight to the drawer with the marijuana, but it struck him as a reckless move. "Italo!" he called out loudly. "You understand, I've finished my usual brand. Just a moment, the officer is coming. His cigarettes are disgusting, but still better than nothing."

Italo walked in. He looked at Marcello Berguet, and then at the deputy chief. "Yes sir. . . ."

"Spot us a couple of cigarettes, and smoke one yourself. . . ."

Italo threw his arms wide in surrender, offered the first cigarettes to Marcello, put one in his mouth, and then tossed the pack to Rocco. "That gives you two, sir. So you'll be all set for later," he said with feigned courtesy. "Well, did he sing?" asked the officer, who had no idea of the latest developments.

"What do you think this is, the Sanremo music festival, Pierron? Who did you think was going to sing? Sit down, listen, and be well aware that with this gentleman we've got a vast amount of mud on our face for the umpteenth time."

They lit their cigarettes and immediately a blanket of smoke filled the office. Rocco picked up a sheet of paper. "Cristiano's phone number ends in 07. Signor Berguet's, here, ends in 04. Take a look at a keypad and you can see how easy it would be for Viorelo to have misdialed. In the middle of the night, for someone nodding off in a moving van, it could certainly happen."

"What's more," Italo added, "we've cross-referenced it.

The phone call to Signor Berguet went out two minutes before the cargo van slammed into the trees. We know that because the dashboard clock stopped at that exact time."

"Outstanding work, Italo. So Viorelo wanted to call Cristiano to tell him that everything was set. The girl had been taken, etc., etc. Is that right?"

"Yes."

Rocco got to his feet and went over to the window. "Now you, Marcello, left Cerruti's apartment a little before eight."

"Exactly."

Italo's jaw dropped. He had just realized the reason that the math teacher was in Cerruti's apartment.

"Tell me all about it."

"Certainly. I shaved, got dressed, took the elevator, and got off in the basement garage. I got in my car and left. You see?" and he put his hand in his pocket and pulled out a bunch of keys. A key ring with a silver M. "This plug opens the metal garage gate."

"That's right," said Rocco, "a bunch of keys that I saw on the first day I went to the Berguet home. I should have remembered. . . ."

"And that's all. I went to school. . . ."

"While someone else entered the apartment and murdered Cristiano Cerruti," Rocco concluded. "Presumably whoever it was that the concierge saw leaving the building." The deputy chief turned to look at Marcello. "Tell me, seeing that you knew Cristiano so well. Did he own any property here in Aosta? A house in the mountain, a garage, even a barn?"

Marcello thought it over for a moment. "No. Cristiano wasn't even from here. He was from the Marche. He'd been living in Aosta for three years . . . the only thing he owned was the car and the apartment where he lived."

"And we didn't find anything interesting in his car, did we, Italo?"

"No. Nothing to speak of. . . ."

"Thanks, Signor Berguet. You're free to go about your business."

"What about Chiara?"

"We'll find her, you can count on that. And if you happen to remember anything that might be of use to us. . . ."

"Believe me, Deputy Chief Schiavone, I've been racking my brains for days."

HE HAD THE SENSATION HE WAS STANDING IN A TRAIN station where all the tracks are unused sidings. In silence, both elbows braced against the desk, both eyes shut, Rocco Schiavone was reviewing all the things he'd seen and heard in the past few days. His mind sailed along untethered, ranging from the face of Cristiano Cerruti to the faces of his friends in Rome. Furio, skinny and bald, with those Greek eyes that always seemed to be wearing dark makeup. Sebastiano, the bear, who instead had too much hair and looked as if he'd combed it with strings of firecrackers. Brizio, the handsome one, who they all called Tom Selleck, with chestnut hair and a handlebar mustache. Then he glimpsed the face of Pietro Berguet,

Giuliana's face turning into his own mother's face and then transforming into Adele who might already be aboard a train on her way north to come hide in his apartment, as part of a little game between two people in love, as hopeless as it was anachronistic. No, this isn't working, he told himself. He opened his eyes. Italo had been sitting there the whole time, still and silent.

"I thought you'd fallen asleep."

"No. I was just thinking," Rocco replied. "But I keep smacking up against the panes of glass and I can't seem to get out of the room."

"Can I help?"

"What did I miss? What am I overlooking? Whose voice was the Calabrian on the phone? When are Viorelo's other numbers going to come in?"

"Later. They say, sometime this evening."

"For now all we know is that he was calling Cristiano Cerruti."

"Then he made some international call, and the country code was for Romania. . . ."

"Some relative."

"And the Posillipo Pizzeria."

"Where he worked three days a week. The place belonged to that guy, Domenico Cuntrera. . . ."

"Known to his friends as Mimmo."

How do hunches hit you? Most of the time, all at once. Often, they're things we know already but that suddenly pop up before our eyes, like lightning bugs in June. Sometimes, they might seem to be lightbulbs that you thought were burned out but which instead, thanks to some ghost in the wiring, flicker on without warning.

"The Posillipo Pizzeria! Do you remember what that fake Neapolitan cook told us? That he had no idea who Figus was."

"But instead?"

"But instead Figus's mother, the old lady with diabetes, had a fistful of coupons in her hand, good for meals at the pizzeria. Which Mimmo, she said, had given to her."

"Do you think that's him?"

"The fake Neapolitan? He told us that he was from Soverato, you remember?"

"I don't know where Soverato is."

"Well, I do! It's not all that far from Cosenza."

"WHAT DAY IS TODAY?"

"Thursday, Rocco."

"It says here that the place is closed on Wednesday. Then why isn't anyone here?" and he peered inside the Posillipo Pizzeria. The lights were all off. "I'll tell you why. Because our fake Neapolitan has left town."

"So you're saying it's him?"

"I'm one hundred percent certain that it is."

"What now?"

"I'm fucking sick and tired of waiting." Rocco grabbed a brick from the sidewalk, brushed the snow off it, and then hurled it through the pizzeria's plate glass window. "Be my guest!" he said to Italo, who was the first to step through the now-gaping window frame.

The tables were set. The lights all switched off. The only light came from a faint blue fluorescent glow above the mirrors. Rocco and Italo walked into the kitchen. They turned on the light. If the front dining room had been a textbook example of good interior decoration, the kitchen was a stomach-turning pigsty. Greasy, dirty, black. Cracked floor tiles were smeared with grease and dark with mold. Aside from the mold, there was no other sign of life in that grimy cavern that the health inspectors ought to have shut down long ago. Aside from the red lights indicating the oversized refrigerator was running, everything else was desolate and dead. On the kitchen work counters, there were balls of pizza dough. An acrid odor of curdled milk tweaked at their nostrils. They opened the door to the office and went through. There, too, everything was neat and orderly, with the exception of a steel cabinet. Doors thrown open, it had been ransacked recklessly and in haste. Two of the six shelves in the cabinet stood empty.

"Someone was in a hurry . . . let's move on . . ." said Rocco.

They went back through the kitchen and made their way through a metal door that led into the storeroom in the back. The metal roller gate that opened onto a secondary parking spot was wide open. Tire tracks through the snow. Inside the small storeroom were stacks of wooden crates, bottled water, and two enormous tables piled high with mason jars full of whole preserved tomatoes, and a large commercial walk-in refrigerator. The door swung open. Rocco stuck his head in. The pantry shelves were lined with enough foodstuffs to hold out against a months-long siege. Cans and jars, bags of flour, salt, and sugar, enormous cans of tuna. But the thing that immediately caught Rocco's attention was a metal pail. A mop protruded from the pail, but there was no water in it.

Bank notes. In denominations of 5, 10, 20, and 50 euros. Crumpled, wrinkled, old and worn.

"Fucking . . ." said Italo.

". . . hell," Rocco concluded. "You feel like counting it up?"

"What the hell is this? Who owns this place?" Italo bent over and started counting the cash.

"You still haven't figured it out?"

"No."

"'Ndrangheta."

"The 'ndrangheta is in Aosta?"

"And why shouldn't it be? What's wrong with Aosta?" the deputy chief retorted ironically. "We need to call Baldi. We need an arrest warrant for Domenico Cuntrera. Known to his friends as Mimmo. And let's call headquarters while we're at it. Let's get some people over here. Costa will have plenty to tell the journalists."

Rocco started making calls on his cell phone. Italo continued counting the cash.

"Dottor Costa? This is Schiavone. I'm calling the officers over to the Posillipo Pizzeria. It was the headquarters of an 'ndrangheta family. They were responsible for the disappearance of Chiara Berguet. . . ." Rocco watched as Italo stacked up the banknotes, doing his best to smooth them as he went. "Yes, sir. You probably ought to put a call in to Rome. Loansharking, extortion, the usual things." He covered the receiver and asked Italo: "How much?"

"There's 37,000 euros here."

"That's right, and we've found some cash here, too. It's 20,000 euros . . . all in small bills. . . ."

Italo looked at Rocco, who winked back at him. "Certainly, sir. I'll alert headquarters."

The deputy chief ended the call. "Now, take the 17,000 euros that are left over. And hurry up, before the others get here. . . ."

"For real, Rocco?"

"Do I look like I'm joking? A little bit of funding for a worthy cause."

"Which worthy cause?" Italo asked, as he hurried to hide the bundles of cash in his pockets and his jacket.

"Let's not forget that Chiara is waiting for us. Come on, get moving."

ROCCO AND ITALO HAD LEFT THE OFFICERS FROM headquarters to take care of the Posillipo Pizzeria and had gone back to Via Chateland 92, the address of the late Carlo Figus.

"Rocco, do you mind if I don't come up? When I'm inside that place, I start to feel a little queasy."

"Here, chew this." And he handed him a gummy fruit candy.

"Will it make me feel better?"

"I couldn't say. But at least it will leave you with a good taste in your mouth."

Carlo Figus's mother answered the door. She didn't smile. She reversed her wheelchair out of the way to allow the policemen to enter. "You came back to see me . . ." she said. She was wearing the same cardigan with Mickey Mouse stitched over the heart.

"This isn't a visit of pleasure, Signora." In the meantime, Italo gazed in horror at the garbage that filled the apartment. He was nervously chewing his candy, but the smell of age and mold was too powerful and penetrating to be stopped by a mere gummy candy.

"Why? What have I done?" and the woman's eyes grew enormous behind her lenses.

"You? Nothing. But I need you to tell me the truth."

"Do you want an espresso?"

"No, thanks. It's about Domenico Cuntrera, a.k.a. Mimmo. Did he come here?"

"I don't know him."

The woman wasn't much of a liar. She'd dropped her gaze and was scratching her shoulder.

"Signora, let me ask you a second time: Where is Mimmo Cuntrera?"

"I told you I don't know him," she said, her voice quavering and both hands clutching the wheels at her side. "What would I know about it? Why are you asking me these questions? Why are you treating me like this? Weren't we friends, you and me? Weren't we friends?"

"We're friends, Signora, and if you'll answer my question and tell me the truth, we'll be even better friends."

She turned her chair. "How am I supposed to know? What do I know about it? I don't know him."

"The coupons from the pizzeria, Signora. You showed them to me the last time I was here. Who gave them to you?"

"I don't have coupons from any pizzeria. I don't have them. I don't know . . ." and then she came suddenly to a stop.

At the center of the path carved out through the mountain of objects the skeletal figure of Adelmo had appeared. Carlo's grandfather. Weary, leaning against the door frame, he looked out at the policemen confined in that garbage dump, arguing with his daughter. He had raised one hand. He wished to speak. He slowly pulled out his handkerchief, wiped his mouth, looked at Rocco, and then said: "He came here. More than once. Starting the day Carlo died. Yesterday, too. He came here."

"What did he want, Signor Adelmo?"

"I don't know. He kept asking: where is she? Where did Carlo put her? He even started searching for her here, under all this . . . all this filth . . ." and Rocco thought he saw the old man smile. "Under all this garbage, anything could be hidden, even a corpse, and no one would ever know."

"But what was Cuntrera looking for?" the deputy chief insisted in a gentle voice.

"He just kept saying the same thing: where did Carlo hide her? Where did he take her? But I swear to you, Dottore, I don't know what he was looking for. When he left, he said: Idiots! That's what he called us. Idiots!"

"Aren't you afraid?"

"What have I got to lose?" and with a sweep of his arm he took in the dump he lived in, his daughter in a wheelchair, and himself. "You tell me."

The deputy chief turned toward Italo. He reached out for a bag that the officer pulled out of his trousers. "Here, Signor Adelmo. This will help."

The old man maintained his composure. He looked at the bag without touching it. "What is it?"

"A reimbursement for your grandson's stupidity. Go on, take it, it's important."

Adelmo reached out a trembling hand. He took the bag, which crinkled in the old man's arthritic fingers. "We need to get going. So long, Signora Figus. So long, Adelmo."

Rocco executed a smart about-face and, followed by Italo, retraced his steps to the front door of the apartment.

"How much did you give him, Rocco?"

"I gave him 11,000 euros. You and me are going to have to make do with six thousand. For our living expenses."

"Excellent!" said Italo.

"Now let's get busy."

"Why?"

"Because now there's no doubt about it. Chiara has been left all alone!"

• • •

ROCCO'S OFFICE LOOKED LIKE A METRO STATION AT rush hour. Summoned urgently to attend, all the surviving officers of police headquarters had gathered there. Rocco looked at them. Aside from Italo, Antonio, and Inspector Rispoli, the rest of the landscape was dispiriting. D'Intino, with his tiny eyes, like a boiled fish, Deruta and his enormous hulk, Casella, the young man from Vomero whose name he couldn't remember, and another couple of officers old enough to retire soon.

What am I going to do with this motley crew? the deputy chief wondered as he laid the map out on the table and explained the daunting task that lay before them. "We need to find a house, probably isolated. So we're going to avoid population centers. And we need to look for it in this triangle that extends from Salirod to Promiod and Saint-Vincent."

"Fuck," someone murmured.

"But there's one thing that helps us. The snow. It started snowing Tuesday night and I believe that—seeing that the kidnappers died early Monday morning—no one's gone back to the hiding place. So we need to look for a place where there are no tire tracks, footprints, and most important of all, where no one's shoveled the snow."

"All right. Well, that's something, anyway," said Casella.

"So now, how many are we?"

Inspector Caterina Rispoli counted. "Ten counting you, Deputy Chief. A couple of us will need to stay behind at police headquarters, right?"

"Caterina, what are you going to do? Are you coming or staying put?"

"Certainly, I'm coming. Who gives a damn about a fever?"

"Excellent. How many cars do we have?"

"Six. But one has to stay here, in case of emergencies," said Italo.

"So, five?" asked Rocco.

The Neapolitan officer hesitantly spoke up. "Actually, one of them has had the engine flooded for the past three days."

"Then, four?"

"And D'Intino wrecked another one."

"You're saying we have three cars?" Rocco asked. "Just three cars?"

"Yeah, but with three cars we can fit fifteen people!" said Deruta, trying to instill a note of optimism in the proceedings.

"Deruta, we need to split up into groups of two. We need at least five vehicles. All right, I'll take my own car, and that way at least we have four."

"I have a motorcycle," said the young officer from Vomero.

"In this cold?"

"If all you've got is lemons. . . ."

"Do you have two helmets?" asked the deputy chief.

"Certainly. I've got two."

"All right then, Deruta and D'Intino in the first squad car. You're a well-established pair."

"Yessir."

"Italo and Inspector Rispoli in the second car."

"Very good."

"You, young man, you ride on your motorcycle and you'll take Casella with you."

"But why me?" the other officer objected immediately.

"Because that's the way it is. Bundle up warm, take a couple of aspirins, and climb on. You two!" and he pointed at two older officers Rocco had never seen in all his time in Aosta. "What are your names?"

"Officer Curcio," said the one with the beard.

"Officer Penzo," said the bald one. Rocco smiled. Curcio and Penzo were a pair of soccer players on A. S. Roma that he never could find to complete his soccer card collection. "All right then, Curcio and Penzo, you take the third squad car, and Antonio and I will take mine. We'll all meet downstairs in ten minutes."

"Ahem, Dottore?" Italo grabbed him by the elbow.

"What is it?"

"Car number two is out of gas."

"Well, fucking hell. . . ." Rocco pulled out his wallet and gave Italo fifty euros. "There. And that makes a hundred."

THE SHIP OF FOOLS HAD SET SAIL, AND NOW THEY truly were on a war footing. The officers watched Rocco reviewing the line of vehicles. He'd given each team a radio.

"Now listen up," he shouted, holding the walkie-talkie up high so they all could see. "Channel 2. Is that clear? Channel 2. Come on now, let's get moving!"

He hopped into his own car and waved for them to pull out. The column roared into action. Leading the line was Rocco's Volvo. The young Neapolitan's motorcycle brought up the rear. Casella's teeth were already chattering with the cold.

Hopes were slim. Rocco knew that. But he needed to act fast, his only priority was to save Chiara Berguet's life. The rest would shake out later.

"How's it look to you, Antonio?"

"Bad, Rocco. It looks bad. Unless we have a stroke of dumb luck, here. . . ."

"On our drive up, let's give it some thought. Is there something we've missed?"

"I don't know. I just don't know."

WHEN THEY REACHED SAINT-VINCENT THEY WENT their separate ways. Schiavone and Antonio Scipioni took the road toward Closel. They climbed uphill, one hairpin turn after another. Woods, boulders, everything was covered in a blanket of snow. As soon as they left the inhabited area, Rocco, with one eye on the odometer, slowed down. He started observing the houses.

"All right, Antonio, we can start scoping out the situation from here."

"Which ones should we search first?"

"The isolated houses, and then let's check out the dirt roads running off into the woods. They might lead to mountain huts."

"Well, I'd start from that one," and he pointed to a house with the shutters fastened tight. A handsome two-story villa. It looked uninhabited. In the garden, there was no sign of any human presence. The snow had covered the firewood, and there was a swing hanging from a tree branch. "That reeks of vacation home. Still, okay, let's give it a try." He stopped the car and they got out. The gate was made of wood and they had only to push to get in. Antonio looked down at Rocco's shoes: "Certainly, wearing those. . . ."

"I know!" Schiavone interrupted him, "I know! I'm used to it."

They walked into the garden. The vases on the little balcony were empty and only a few snippets of old carnations could still be seen. The snow all around the little villa was pristine. Rocco went up to the door. It was shut, locked tight. He tried to peer inside the house through the little heart carved into the wood. At last he made up his mind. He pulled out his Swiss army knife and went over to the keyhole.

"What are you doing?" Antonio asked.

"We need to get in, don't we?"

He fiddled around with the lock for a few seconds. Then it opened.

"Huh, not bad. Is that something they teach you at the police academy down in Rome?" asked Antonio.

They stepped into the little house.

It was dark. The electricity had been switched off. They pulled out their cell phones and switched on the flashlight apps. It reeked of stale air, and the furniture was all covered with dusty plastic sheeting.

"Head down into the cellar."

Antonio descended the stairs that led into the basement. Rocco climbed up to the bedrooms.

Of which there were two. One with wallpaper covered

with Smurfs and two brightly colored single beds, the other with a king-sized bed.

Nothing. He went back downstairs. He ran into Antonio.

"Well?"

"Nothing."

"One down."

"At this rate, though, you know how long it's going to take us?"

"All night long, if necessary, Antonio. All night long."

As soon as he got back in the car, the radio crackled to life: "Rocco? It's Italo."

"What's up, Italo."

"We went into a house. It looked abandoned. Instead, it had been burgled. What should I do?"

"Call in a report and keep going. We can circle back later on. Get going!"

With a sputter of static, the radio fell silent.

"While we're searching, would you tell me something?"

"If I can. . . ."

"Why were you transferred to Aosta?"

Rocco gazed attentively at the houses. "Punishment."

"For what?"

"I tend to apply the law with a less than judicious emphasis."

"Which means what?"

"Let's just say that I got a little overenthusiastic."

"Can I ask what exactly happened?"

"No. I don't feel like talking about it. And anyway, Italo knows. Have him tell you all about it."

Rocco on the left, Antonio on the right, they were gazing intently out at fields and forests. The white of the snow glared back on their weary faces, blinding their eyes.

"What about those?"

"Too close. There's a car parked outside. Lights turned on. No, we're going to skip the ones that aren't isolated."

They wended their way through two hairpin curves without finding traces of houses or side roads, aside from the hiking paths that climbed steeply up the mountainsides. "How many hours of light do we still have?"

Antonio glanced at his watch. "Not many."

"Look here!" A side road that led off into the woods. "Could that be it?"

"No one's been down there. Let's go."

Rocco turned around and veered down the side road, confronting the snow decisively. The excellent Swedish handling and the four-wheel drive propelled the car till they pulled up in front of a tumbledown shack.

"This looks like a hayloft to me," said the Sicilian officer.

"Well, let's go take a look."

In the cool air, the odor of burnt wood and resin. No sounds. Only the faint noise of snow falling from tree branches now and again.

"I say there's no one here."

The roof was old and it had collapsed in several places. The upper story had been picked clean like a carcass in the desert. The lower story, in contrast, was still intact. The door swung wide open. There were only a few bales of hay and the wheels of an old tractor inside. Nothing else. "A complete dud. Let's go back to the car!"

Then, as if an enormous hammer had struck him at the top of his cranium, Rocco Schiavone came to a halt in the middle of the snow. Antonio watched as he stared at a fixed point in the distance, glimmering vaguely.

"Are you all right? Sir, are you all right?" Antonio ran toward the deputy chief. The first thing he did was to look at his feet. He was afraid Schiavone might have frostbite. "Rocco? Rocco, can you hear me?"

"Carlo's last name was Figus, right?"

"Right."

"So was that his mother's last name? I don't think a Valdostan would have a Sardinian last name."

"Maybe that was her husband's last name."

"Then what was Carlo's grandfather's name? The one you accompanied to the hospital?" Antonio put his hand to his chin and stood there, thinking.

"Hold on. Hold on. Adelmo . . . Adelmo. . . ."

"Rosset!" Rocco exploded. "Adelmo Rosset!"

"Yes. But why?"

Rocco pulled out his cell phone. "Because maybe we have a prayer of a chance."

ITALO AND CATERINA HAD IDENTIFIED A HOUSE THAT matched the description. In the middle of the snow, isolated if you overlooked a small chalet about half a mile away. It looked abandoned. They left the car on the road and climbed up to that alpine hut high among the trees. "Can you do it, sweetheart?" Italo asked.

"Don't worry. Either I get pneumonia or I'll get better."

After making their way through a tumbledown iron gate, they reached the house. Just one story. The walls were lined with logs. It seemed to have come out of a Nordic fable. Two old stairs led up to the main door. Italo knocked. No answer. The door swung open. The place was empty. Not a single stick of furniture, bare walls.

"There's nothing here."

Caterina walked back down the steps and made her way around the house. She bent down to look through a broken window down into the cellar.

"Italo! I saw something in here!"

Italo came running. He almost tripped over a rock buried in the snow. "Where?"

"Here, down in there. I saw something move."

They walked around the main wall and found a wooden door leading into the room underneath the house. Italo tried to open it: "Chiara? Chiara, can you hear me? Chiara?"

The door wouldn't give. Italo started slamming his shoulder against it, but it resisted the impact.

"Let's shoot the lock!"

"That won't work, Cate, it doesn't work," said Italo, and he resumed pounding at the door, which started to give. He gave one last vigorous blow and the door flew open. Something shot out from behind it at the speed of light. "What the fuck?"

A piercing yelp and a little creature with dirty white fur was lying on its back with all four legs in the air at Caterina's feet, wagging its tail and barking in a cheerful, strident voice. "Little one!" Caterina bent over. "He fell inside! Poor little thing!" and she began stroking the little dog's belly. Happily, the puppy licked her hand, bundled up in the glove.

"Look out, it could have rabies," said Italo. He'd never much liked dogs.

"What are you talking about? What rabies? Look how skinny he is." Then she spoke to the dog in a different tone of voice, as if by speaking two notches higher it could understand her: "Have you not been eating? How long has it been since you had anything to eat?"

"Come on, Cate. Pretty soon, it's going to be dark."

"Come here, boy!" she said, and picked up the little dog. He was a puppy. A setter/shepherd mix, along with twenty-seven other strains. "Come here. Oh, you're shivering!"

"You can't seriously be thinking about taking it away with us."

"Oh, no? Am I supposed to leave him here!"

"You want to take this stray mutt that smells bad and probably has fleas in the car?"

"You can always just stay here and walk back to Aosta, if you want."

"The rules don't. . . ."

"Officer Pierron! You're speaking to an inspector of superior rank to your own, and she hereby orders you to stop being a pain in the ass and march straight back to the squad car."

"Unbelievable!" muttered Italo under his breath.

"Pay no attention to that mean old man. You come here to mamma . . ." and clutching the puppy to her breast, the inspector headed back toward the car.

The sun was setting. And the chances of finding Chiara were dropping with it.

"CERTAINLY, I'M GLAD TO STAY ON THE LINE, OF course. Thank you."

"What do they say?" asked Antonio. Rocco gestured that he still didn't know. Antonio grabbed a pack of cigarettes and lit one. Rocco yanked the lit cigarette out of his hand and stuck it between his lips. Antonio threw both arms wide in exasperation and repeated the process.

"Chesterfields? Not you, too?" Rocco cried with a disgusted look. "Why have you all started buying this disgusting brand of cigarettes?"

Antonio shook his head and lit his cigarette.

"Yes, I'm still on the line. Tell me." Rocco listened. Antonio had pulled out his pen and was ready to take down any information on a business card.

"Yes? Yesssssss!" Rocco jumped for joy. "All right, then, we head up toward the village of Closel . . . two-and-a-half miles after the intersection, we continue straight. . . ."

Antonio was writing. The scrap of paper was already practically full. He went on writing on the palm of his hand. "Yes. Two more miles, and then on the right, just before the fork in the road. Thank you, thank you!" Rocco ended the call. "Adelmo Rosset has a piece of property, a half-falling down bunker . . . a shepherd's hut, a little farther up." And he took off for the car. Antonio followed him, smiling.

"I'll drive, Antonio. You get on the radio and call everyone in. Tell them to come here!"

At high speed, Rocco was driving up through a series of hairpin curves toward the village of Closel. His cell phone rang.

"No. Please," he said, grabbing his phone. "Don't tell me that the land office clerk was wrong!" He answered: "Schiavone!"

"Rocco, it's me, Adele!"

"Adele. This isn't a good time."

"I'm here, in Aosta."

"How nice. Listen, the keys are at the police station. Go and get comfortable at my place. We'll see you tonight."

"But where are you?"

"You don't want to know. We'll talk later."

And he hung up the phone.

"Should you really be thinking about women at a time like this?"

"Antonio, I told you you could use my first name, but now you're pushing your luck."

"Sorry. . . ."

"All right, now, the fork in the road is down there . . . There's supposed to be a dirt road running uphill on the right. . . ."

In the summer, these mountains had to be full of beautiful emerald-green meadows with placid grazing cows ruminating in the bright sunshine or resting in the shade of the fir trees. Now, however, there was only the occasional tiny black dot of a crow here and there, hopping along in search of something to eat, and rivulets of water running under the blanket of snow down onto the road, muddying the edges. There were rocks dotted with white, up high, covering up the sky, like so many giant Christmas candies.

"There it is!"

Two straight tree branches with the bark skinned off, set upright in the middle of the snow, indicated the presence of a track running up into the mountains. Directly on their left there was a house. But it was inhabited. Rocco discarded it. "It must be on this rough dirt road." Rocco accelerated. The wheels had a good grip and the vehicle zipped along confidently, bouncing on the bumps of the mountain track. They rounded a curve and in the distance spotted a roof hidden in the midst of the fir branches.

"Is that it?" asked Antonio.

"Maybe so."

As they gradually drew closer, the roof turned into a small, one-story house. It was made entirely of stone and it was planted on a steep slope, surrounded by boulders and trees. All around it, the snow was untouched. Only the two black eyes of the windows of that mountain hut seemed to stare aghast at the approaching car. Suddenly, out of the underbrush, an orange cat crossed the road and the deputy chief only narrowly avoided hitting it.

"Fuck!"

"That's good," said Antonio. "Orange cats are lucky. If it was black, that would have meant trouble."

They reached the isolated house. Only Rocco got out of the car, moving fast. Antonio was on the radio, trying to explain to all the other officers exactly where they were.

Getting inside on the ground floor was easy. Only a few old boards nailed up over the doorway blocked their way, and they were quickly removed. Aside from a rusty old gas stove and a ramshackle wooden staircase leading up to a cobweb-covered attic, the place was empty. Ancient streaks of birdshit covered the walls. Looking up, they could see the sky through the few surviving terracotta roof tiles. Rocco turned around in the narrow hallway. There was a half-shut door in one of the larger rooms. It opened onto a stone staircase leading down to the floor below. Taking care not to slip and fall, the deputy chief descended the steps and came to an old wooden door locked with a chain that ran through a hole in the wall to the other side. The chain, like the padlock, was gleaming new. Rocco tried to push the door open: "Chiara? Chiara Berguet? Chiara, are you here?"

"ANTONIO! HURRY!"

The Sicilian policeman got out of the car. "Did you find her?" he shouted as he came running toward the house.

"Get over here!"

He led him down and showed him the wooden door. "This chain is brand new."

"Chiara?" shouted Scipioni.

"She doesn't answer. But I know she's here."

"What do you want me to do?"

"Break down this fucking door!"

There wasn't much room to get a running start. Antonio hit the door lightly a couple of times to test its resistance, then he slammed all of his muscular six-foot-four frame and two hundred pounds of mass against the old wooden planks. The door was rendered asunder like a flimsy spider web. Carried forward by the inertia of the impact, Antonio hurtled into the room.

Lying on the floor, her hands tied to a broken section of a chair, in the middle of a puddle of blood, was Chiara Berguet!

THE DOCTOR HAD BEEN BRISK AND PITILESS, AS ONLY doctors know how to be. Chiara had lost a lot of blood, her pressure was dizzyingly low; in short, it was just a miracle that she was still alive. Dehydrated to the verge of survivability, it was only thanks to her youth and a strong, stubborn makeup that she could still be counted among the living. A vicious wound in her left thigh, caused by a snapping chair leg that had then stabbed her directly in the biceps femoris. What's more, there was clear evidence of rape. Now she was in intensive care and no one could even approach the door to her room. Rocco had walked away, making phone calls to deliver the good news to Judge Baldi and to the chief of police, who had immediately called a press conference, which Rocco had sidestepped by the simple expedient of turning off his cell phone and pretending that the call had been cut off.

As he left the hospital he had glanced out the window and glimpsed Pietro and Giuliana Berguet arriving. Thanks to the kind assistance of a male nurse, he'd managed to scamper out via a side exit—a tradesman's entrance—thus managing to fend off the scenes of tearful gratitude and extended hugs. Just let them be happy to get their daughter back: so long and farewell.

In spite of the fact that night had fallen over Aosta, his day still wasn't over.

"Let's go, Italo. And give me a cigarette!"

Smiling, Italo started the engine. "Well, we did it, right?"

"Until we get there, please give me some silence. I'm a wreck."

Italo obeyed and continued driving.

The sledgehammer had come down. He understood it now. Every time that Rocco got to the end of a case, he found himself shrouded in a dark mist, like a mountain enveloped by a cloud. Italo had often wondered why it was, but he just couldn't figure it out. Italo felt happy, sometimes he even got goose bumps. In short, they'd worked together and they'd finally broken the puzzle, solved the case. Instead Rocco seemed miserable. A wreck.

"Why do you do this?" By now, the close terms they were on allowed him to ask such a personal question.

"Why do I do what, Italo?"

"Why do you get so grim? I mean, fuck, we won, didn't we?"

"What did we win? Can't you see? Don't you feel it? Every time you have anything to do with these people, with this shit, a little bit of you turns to shit as well. Don't doubt it. Little by little, more and more, and then the day comes when you look at yourself in the mirror and you ask yourself: who is this man I'm looking at? And old age has nothing to do with it, Italo, I'm talking about something I have deep inside me. It dies every day from this filth. From this mud. I can't take it any more, I can't stand to go on diving into this sewer. Getting dirty, turning into some kind of rat from putting my hands onto these people. I can't stand it anymore. Look at my shoes. You see them?" and he raised his right foot. It looked like an old tire abandoned on the side of the highway. "That's the way I am now."

"THE ORGANIZATION HAD ITS BASE IN THE POSILLIPO Pizzeria and the HeyDiddleLiddles shop. They'd dragged a lot of people into their web by the loans they made. They must have infiltrated Edil.ber through the good offices of Cristiano Cerruti. They were probably only doing it for the money. Then Cristiano must have started having troubles with his conscience, he must have stumbled and made it clear that he was starting to repent. Who knows, maybe he was thinking of going to the police. But it was too late. Domenico Cuntrera murdered him and took off. Now he's probably holed up with Cutrì in Lugano or who knows where else. They're not going to loosen their grip though, sir. These aren't people who leave the job half finished."

"But at least Edil.ber is safe?" asked the chief of police. "It's safe."

"So explain about that Max, the boyfriend. Why was he talking to those two guys in the discotheque?"

"Because Max's father is a doctor. And Max gets busy at the high school pushing psychopharmaceuticals. He was the source of the Stilnox, the rape drug, for Carlo Figus. They used it to put Chiara to sleep."

"Does the poor girl know she was raped?"

"No, sir. I didn't tell her. Probably, if she survives, she won't remember a thing. There's just one thing that needs to be done, but I have neither the power nor the proof. I'm sure that the Vallée Savings Bank is behind this whole story somehow. They were the ones who directed people in need of loans to these 'ndrangheta mobsters, probably presenting them as reliable, respectable businessmen."

"Do you plan to investigate?"

"Why not? I've talked about it with Judge Baldi. He's already working on it."

"Who's at the pizzeria now?"

"The judge, a few officers. More or less, the whole gang is there."

"And where are you?"

"In my office. It's really late and I'm a wreck."

"I talked to the DIA. This falls under their jurisdiction as an organized crime operation. Will you come to the press conference? It's important. A Mafia-style crime organization operating unhindered in Aosta is the kind of news that will make the news anchors of half the country jump out of their chairs!"

"Have mercy, Chief Costa. Just let me sleep in tomorrow."

"At least give me a brief report."

"I'll have one of my men do it. Good night."

"Good night, Schiavone."

He put down the receiver and wiped his ear. Everyone in the office was staring at him. "People, we've done an outstanding job."

Casella's teeth were chattering from the cold. Antonio and Italo were dropping on their feet. Curcio and Penzo were sprawled on the office couch, practically snoring as they nodded off. The young Neapolitan, on the other hand, seemed to have just stepped out of a refreshing shower.

"What's your name?"

The young man replied: "Pietro Miniero."

"Pietro Miniero, you've officially drawn the winning straw. It's your job to write up the report for the chief of police. Leave it on my desk tomorrow morning."

"Yessir," and Pietro Miniero was the first to leave the room.

"Casella, you go home, you definitely have a fever. I told you to bundle up. And you two can go too." Curcio and Penzo left the room, trailing after Casella.

A yelp, faint but perceptible, pierced the air. "Who's got a stomachache?"

Italo, Antonio, and Caterina exchanged glances. "I don't know," said Antonio. Rocco looked at Caterina. "What do you have under your jacket?"

Caterina opened the jacket and the little dog could be seen. The puppy was asleep, and had yelped in some puppy dream. "We found him in a house up in the mountains. I didn't have the heart to leave him there."

"I tried to tell her, Rocco, that she shouldn't have, but she insisted."

Rocco got up from his chair. He walked over to Caterina. "It smells."

"He was filthy, wet, and starving."

"*She* was filthy, wet, and starving. Can't you see that it's a female?" said Rocco. Then he reached out and took the puppy in his arms. She barely woke up, opened her eyes, and with a tongue that darted out fast as an arrow, licked the tip of the deputy chief's nose. "Are you going to keep her?" Rocco asked.

Caterina replied, "I don't know. I can't keep her at home. I thought there might be some association. . . ."

"Well, you were wrong. Do you know what her name is?"

"No," said Caterina. "It's an abandoned dog, how could I know?"

"Her name is Lupa. She-Wolf. A good Roman name. Ciao, Lupa. How are you? Welcome!" said Rocco. The puppy, as if she'd understood every word, licked his nose again. "Do you all like my new dog?" asked the deputy chief.

Caterina smiled. "So you're taking it, sir?"

"Of course, who could resist? Come on, time for you all to go home. Italo, I expect you to take Caterina out to celebrate in a real restaurant, and not some filthy dive like the Posillipo Pizzeria!" Italo smiled. Then the three officers turned to go. "Hold on a second," Rocco called after them. "Where are Deruta and D'Intino?"

"We don't know. We haven't heard from them since this afternoon. They haven't been answering their phones or the radio, either," said Caterina. "What should we do?"

"Alert the forest rangers and the mountain guides. Maybe they'll find them tomorrow morning frozen solid," and with his new companion snug in his arms, Rocco left the office with only one objective in mind: to go home and get some sleep.

BY THE LIGHT OF A BONFIRE, CLUTCHING EACH OTHER close to ward off the biting cold in a ruined mountain hut, at an elevation of roughly 5,250 feet, D'Intino and Deruta were shivering and praying through chattering teeth that day would dawn soon. Their car, half buried in a snow-covered ditch, rested in the gleaming light of the moon.

"This is the last time I'm going to let you drive, D'Intino."

"Don't you have anything to eat?"

But Deruta didn't answer. He walked over to the fire and rubbed his hands together.

ROCCO WAS STRIDING THROUGH THE STREETS OF THE center of Aosta at a brisk pace, eager to get home as quickly as possible. Lupa had fallen asleep and was breathing deeply. Tomorrow he'd take her to the veterinarian and get her dewormed, microchipped, and thoroughly vaccinated.

A few yards from his building, a shadow stepped away from the wall. The figure carried a cardboard box in one hand. By the light of the streetlamp, the shadow revealed its identity: it was Anna. Rocco looked at her.

"What do you have there?" he asked.

"I could ask you the same thing," Anna replied.

"I have a dog. Her name is Lupa."

Anna took a few steps forward. The heels of her boots echoed in the deserted Rue Piave. "I got you this. Since the ones you're wearing look pretty well shot!"

A new pair of shoes. "You're starting to cost me, Schiavone. Two pairs in two days is a little lavish, don't you think?"

Rocco smiled. "So it was you . . . thanks."

"Don't you want to try them on?"

"Here in the middle of the street?"

"Come on upstairs. I have a mirror that reaches all the way to the floor."

"What about Lupa?"

"Lupa? Huh?"

"Her name is Lupa."

"I have some very nice cushions for Lupa, too."

"I'm not going to sleep over, though."

"Who even invited you?"

Rocco looked at her. He sensed that, for this one time at least, it would be so nice to just give in, let go, not overthink it, not put up resistance, without feeling obliged to ruin anything that happened to him. He'd saved one life, he had another one in his arms. Just once, every now and then, he could try smiling. And life might even smile back. So Rocco did, he smiled as he turned his face up to the sky. And a solitary star winked down at him from above the clouds.

SOFTLY, SLOWLY, ONE STEP AFTER THE OTHER, ONE foot in front of the other. Without making noises, without any sudden movements. Tense and silent, quieter than a shadow and lighter than an insect's wings. He could hear snoring from the other room. He went on walking, outside all was silence and darkness. Only a yellowish streetlamp tinged the sofa and the living room floor. Another step. And then one more . . .

This was the moment. He threw open the bedroom door. He held the 6.35 straight out in front of him.

"Take this and die, Schiavone! This is for my brother."

And he emptied the entire magazine of the pistol into the body wrapped in blankets that spat out feathers and shreds of cloth.

Enzo Baiocchi put the gun back into his pants pocket and strode rapidly out of Deputy Chief Schiavone's apartment.

THAT WAS WHEN LUPA JUMPED UP ONTO THE BED. SHE crept close to Rocco and started licking his ears. It was only on the third lick that Rocco startled awake. It took him three seconds to realize where he was. Three seconds, an eternity.

Lupa, next to his pillow, looked at him, cocking her head to one side. It was dark outside. He was in Anna's apartment. Once again, he'd fallen asleep in Anna's apartment.

"What the fuck . . ." he muttered under his breath. This wasn't right. This wasn't the way things were supposed to go. He looked at the hour. It was four thirty. He needed to get dressed. Quietly, without making noise, without waking the woman who slept on in spite of the dog's low growl. The minute Rocco put his feet down on the floor, Lupa started wagging her tail. "Come on, let's go home . . ." he said. He slowly crept over to get his clothes from the armchair. "Be a good girl and don't bark." As he laced his shoes, he remembered about Adele. He just hoped she'd gotten in his bed and not on the sofa. It was uncomfortable having to sleep on the sofa. She wouldn't get a wink all night.

But Lupa refused to move. She stayed there, curled up in the blankets, with no intention of leaving the bed.

"Let's go, Lupa."

The puppy was whining and wagging her tail, with her nose buried next to Anna's feet.

"Come on, Lupa."

Lupa barked.

"No, Lupa, no barking. . . ."

"Are you leaving?" asked the voice deep in the pillow.

"Ah, so you're awake?"

"Are you uncomfortable here?"

"A little."

"I'm sure I don't need to tell you that I'll be sorry to wake up without you beside me."

"But just waking up is already a minor achievement, don't you think?"

A thunderclap echoed in the distance.

"It's starting to rain again. Why don't you stay here?"

Rocco thought it over. He took a quick glance out the window. The clouds had gathered over the city once again. Maybe it was safer to stay here, at least until tomorrow morning. If nothing else, it would be warmer. And the bed was cozy. Lupa had been trying to tell him that for hours now. The dog's round, watery eyes extinguished his last shred of doubt. He undressed again and got back under the covers.

"Put your arms around me, please."

Anna's feet were icy cold. She slid them between his legs. Rocco wrapped his arms around her and three minutes later he was fast asleep, with Lupa braced against his back.

Outside the rain started pounding down on the asphalt. At least it would melt the snow.

FRIDAY

Freude, schöner Götterfunken
Tochter aus Elysium,
Wir betreten feuertrunken,
Himmlische, dein Heiligtum!

Yes . . . hello? Hello?"

"Schiavone, it's me, Baldi. Where are you?"

"I'm asleep. . . ."

"It's nine thirty in the morning!" Baldi's voice was quavering with excitement.

Rocco sat up, his back resting against the headrest of the bed. He rubbed his face. Lupa was asleep. So was Anna.

"Just a second . . . let me get up."

"I don't have time. I just want to give you a piece of good news. Last night we arrested Domenico Cuntrera at the border. He tried to make a break for it, but the Carabinieri nailed him. With a bag of documents that . . . well, to put it briefly, we're going to see some fireworks. The idiot hadn't thought to get rid of them."

"I'm delighted, Dottore."

"All credit due to you and to me. It's a gratifying thing. Now here's the bad news."

"Go ahead."

"There's a joint press conference at ten thirty. The chief of police, me, the Carabinieri General Tosti of the Carabinieri, and of course, you."

His brain was still stalled. The only thing that came to mind was: "I have the flu!" but the judge merely laughed a hearty laugh. "And bring your men. It's time that their unsung exploits are brought to the light of the television cameras and immortalized in the pages of the daily press which, tomorrow, we'll promptly use to wrap fish! We'll see you at the district attorney's office in an hour."

One hour. Just enough time to go and take a shower, get changed, grab a quick breakfast at Ettore's, swing by the office for a second, say his daily secular morning prayer, and then rush over to the district attorney's office to answer questions from the press. He decided that there was no good reason to wake up Anna. Lupa instead looked up at him, wagging her tail. "We need to go, little one."

● ● ●

THE SNOW WAS GONE. THERE WAS WATER IN ITS PLACE. Lots of water. Schiavone walked ahead, Lupa walked behind, and they came around the corner of Rue Piave and reached the street door of his building.

"Now you're going to meet Marina," he told the little puppy as she drank from a puddle at the edge of the sidewalk. "Just wait, you'll like her."

He put the key in the lock. He opened the door.

There was something wrong. He realized it immediately. Something about the air. Or maybe a smell. An odor he hadn't smelled in a long time but which stagnated like some sinister early morning fog in the apartment.

"Adele? Adele, are you here?"

She was. But she couldn't answer. Wrapped in the bullet-riddled blankets, only a single pale arm protruded from the down quilt. A rivulet of blood oozed from the mattress, forming a puddle on the parquet floor.

Rocco shut his eyes. He fell back into the armchair.

He burst into tears.

THE FIRST TO ARRIVE WERE ITALO AND CATERINA. Then came Fumagalli, Casella, and Scipioni. The apartment, where no outsider had set foot in the past nine months, was suddenly full of police officers. Soon, the officers from Turin would be there too.

Rocco, sitting on the sofa, still hadn't found the strength to call Sebastiano.

Fumagalli had come over and sat down next to him.

"Eight shots, all eight hit her. Three shots fatal. Fired from very close range. If it's any consolation, she died in her sleep."

Rocco didn't even look at him. "Shots to the head?"

"No. All to the body. Six to the back, one to the right leg, and one more to the left forearm."

Rocco nodded.

"Of course, you know who she is."

"Adele Talamonti. An old friend of mine from Rome."

Schiavone was holding his arms between his legs. He looked like a bundle of dirty clothes.

"Where are you going to sleep tonight?"

"That's the last of my problems."

"Mi casa es tu casa," said the medical examiner.

"What time do you think she was killed?"

"I'll be able to tell you with precision in an hour or so. There is a detail that can help us. Her watch stopped at four thirty. It might have just stopped independently, but maybe not, in any case, it's a big help." Then Alberto gave the deputy chief a pat on the knee and went back to his work.

"Alberto?"

"Yes."

"Treat her kindly. I've known her since we were born."

Alberto nodded. And went back to the cadaver.

Rocco wouldn't be able to put it off any longer. The time had come to tell Sebastiano. But he wanted to do it without witnesses. He stood up, grabbed his cell phone, and left the apartment under Italo's saddened gaze and Caterina's worried eyes. Scipioni on the other hand seemed to be concerned chiefly with restraining Casella who was nosing around the apartment.

"SEBA? IT'S ME, ROCCO."

"I know that! I can read it on my display!" His friend's voice was hoarse, distant, and gloomy.

"I've got some news, and it isn't good."

"What's going on?"

"Have you already spoken to Furio?"

"Yes. Why do you ask? Did he tell you that Adele has gone missing?"

"She isn't missing."

"Do you know where she is?"

"Yes, I do. She had come up to stay with me."

Seba said nothing.

"Seba? Did you hear me?"

"Had come? Why had? Where is she now?"

"Last night. Someone shot her. She's dead, Seba."

"What the fuck are you trying to say? If this is a joke, Rocco, it's not making me laugh."

The call ended. Rocco tried to call back. The cold robotic voice of the phone company informed him that the party he was trying to reach was unavailable for the moment.

He called Furio.

"Rocco? Did Adele get up there? Listen, Seba. . . ."

"Listen, Furio. Something awful's happened. Call Seba right away, go straight over to his house."

"But why? What the fuck's going on?"

"Somebody shot Adele. Here at my place."

"Oh fucking. . . ."

"Hurry, Furio. Hurry, because Seba's not well at all."

THE NEWS OF THE DAY, AS COULD REASONABLY BE expected, was no longer the arrest of Domenico Cuntrera, a.k.a. Mimmo, at the border, but the mysterious murder at the home of Deputy Chief Schiavone. The press conference at the district attorney's office had veered toward that story which, in just minutes, had magnetized the attention of the entire city and the television news broadcasts.

For the first time in nine months, Rocco Schiavone found himself in the office of Chief of Police Andrea Costa, sitting in front of his boss's desk, looking at a man whose face was as pale if not paler than the face in the framed photograph of the Italian president on the wall behind him. Costa was feeling uncomfortable. Nine months of coexistence with Rocco and he was starting to like that strange Roman policeman. He'd never have expected it, that first day they met in the parking lot behind police headquarters, when the deputy chief introduced himself with a muted smile and eyes veiled in sadness. Costa knew all about Rocco's past, about the reason he'd been transferred from Rome to Aosta. But he'd made inquiries with a colleague in the Palazzo del Viminale, in Rome, national police headquarters. Rocco Schiavone had done outstanding work in Rome on the staff of the state police. And now here he was, sitting across his desk from him, with the same sad eyes he'd had nine months ago.

"What's its name?" he asked, pointing to the dog that lay in Rocco's lap, fast asleep by now after his gentle petting.

"Lupa."

"Did you find it?"

"No, some of my colleagues found her when we were searching for Chiara Berguet."

"What breed is it?"

"Just take a wild guess. She's such a mix that you'd be certain to get at least one right."

"Are you going to keep it?"

"When a dog finds you, you have to keep it. You never run into a dog in life just by accident. Someone always has sent it to you."

"Who sent you this one?"

"I have my suspicions. But I can't tell you."

Costa smiled. "Let's talk about what happened. Do you have any ideas?"

"No. Not yet."

"Were you the target?"

"No doubt about it. Adele Talamonti works at her parents' bar in the Balduina section of Rome. Her record is cleaner than the pope's, and as far as I know she's just argued with a neighbor or two. She was the girlfriend of Sebastiano Carucci, a dear friend of mine."

"And is he someone who stays out of trouble, too?"

"No, sir. Sebastiano has had plenty of trouble with the law."

Costa nodded. "Could he have been the target?"

"Impossible. That Adele was even here, in Aosta, at my

place, was something that only Adele and I knew, along with Furio, another friend of mine from Rome. A friend of mine and Sebastiano's. A close friend, like a brother."

"What about this Furio. . . ."

"Don't even think of it, sir. We're talking about a brotherhood that goes back forty years. We always shared everything. If there were scores to settle, we settled them amongst ourselves. Dottor Costa, whoever unloaded the clip of a 6.35 mm handgun into Adele Talamonti thought they were unloading it into me."

"There's a question I have to ask you. Where were you last night?"

"At Anna's place. I slept there."

"And why was Adele staying at your place, if I can ask?"

"Minor troubles between lovers. She was hiding out at my house to try to make Sebastiano crazed with concern so he'd try to find out where she was. This was supposed to prove that he loved her desperately. The kind of thing you'd expect from teenagers, but that's just the way Seba and Adele were."

Costa started folding a sheet of paper. "You do realize, Dottor Schiavone, that . . . ahem . . . it certainly doesn't testify in your favor, much less in favor of Aosta police headquarters, that one of our men should have been involved in a story that's so . . ." he struggled to find a suitable adjective, ". . . so very . . . ?"

"I do realize that, but I'd like to remind you that in this case, I was the intended victim."

"I know, I know. And I'll try to explain it to the newsvendors and also to the Ministry of the Interior in Rome. But. . . ."

"But certainly, it would be better to have a clean deputy chief who doesn't have any history with anyone, and especially who doesn't have guests who get murdered in his apartment."

"I couldn't have put it better myself."

"What do you want me to do?"

"For now I'd like you to see if you can figure out who did it. In the meantime I'll try to plug the various leaks. You know what? You have a lot of enemies in Rome."

"I have to admit it."

"No, I don't just mean murderers and various criminals. I mean at the Palazzo del Viminale, too."

"I'm politically bipartisan."

"And when they find out about what happened, there's a chance, and I'm just saying it's a chance, that they'll start exerting pressure to get you transferred."

"Do you seriously think it could be worse than Aosta?"

"My friend, I think you might find that you miss Aosta."

Rocco nodded. Lupa was awake now.

"What do you feed it?"

"I'm going to take her to the veterinarian now. Then we'll see."

"I had a German shepherd who ate as if he was one of my children. He *was* one of my children, actually. That dog was very sweet."

Rocco nodded.

"But there's one thing you have to promise me."

"Tell me."

"If you catch whoever killed this poor unfortunate Adele, you'll come to the press conference. No ifs, ands, or buts."

Rocco smiled. He nodded. Then he stood up. "I'm not going to shake your hand. Mine smells of dog."

But Costa stuck his hand out anyway. "Bring me good news."

"Same to you, Dottore."

LOCKED IN HIS OFFICE.

He didn't feel like lighting a joint. He didn't feel like an espresso. Lupa was fast asleep, which is a puppy's main occupation. Someone knocked at the door.

"Who is it?"

"Ernesto!"

It was Farinelli. Rocco opened the door. "Ciao Ernè . . ." he said.

Ernesto came in. "I'm so sorry, Rocco."

"Thanks. Take a seat."

"I don't have a lot to tell you. Eight shots, a 6.35 mm handgun, not a very common weapon but deadly effective if used at close range. The murderer was just six feet away from the bed when he fired."

"Have you figured out how he got in?"

"Yes. From the balcony. He climbed up the drain pipe."

"How can you be so sure?"

"We found that the central section of the drain pipe had been pulled away from the wall of the building. So I'd suggest a person weighing well over a hundred fifty pounds.

Skilled at breaking and entering. The window panes were left intact. He used some kind of device to open the lock. A precise little job of work, clearly someone who knew what they were doing."

Rocco and the deputy director of the forensic squad looked at each other.

"We've never seen so much of each other."

"True. . . ."

"Do you know who had it in for you?"

"No. But the list is long."

"I'm going to stay in Aosta for a few more hours. This time, I'll go to see the judge. I swear to you. Has he already called you?"

"No."

"But have you thought it might have been someone involved in the kidnapping?"

"You see, Ernè? There are three things that don't add up. The first thing is that they don't usually move this fast. If they're going to make you pay, they do it at their own pace, when they're good and ready. And then, why climb up into my apartment late at night like a burglar? I walk around like anybody else, all alone, and there would be every opportunity in the world to shoot me out in the street. Third, it lacks the usual signature, the head shot. They usually finish you off with a bullet to the head, execution-style, as the saying goes, to make sure you're done for. No, this guy snuck in, emptied his gun, and didn't even stop to check. It's no one who's involved in the kidnapping. It's some dickhead who has it in for me. And who's afraid to be seen out in the open. Someone who was behind bars, or maybe somone who's wanted by the police."

"Is this going to mean trouble for you?"

"There's going to be an investigation. An adjunct is going to be sent up, and he'll get to work on it. What can I tell you?"

"I'm here if there's anything I can do."

"Thanks, Ernè. . . ."

For the first time, Ernesto shook Rocco's hand.

"The person you're looking for, could it be someone out of your past?"

"Yeah, something like that. Only that's like sticking your nose into a bottomless black hole."

"Take a red thread with you."

They exchanged a smile. "Yes. No matter what, that's where I'm going to have to search."

He'd always thought it, he'd always known it. Sooner or later the filth would overflow, coming in the window and dirtying everything. And now, there it was, in front of him, a sea of mud and shit he could dive into, wallow in, camouflage himself with in order to identify the shadow who had crept into his home and taken the life of Adele Talamonti, thirty-nine years old, and with a much longer life expectancy ahead of her. She was dead, and it was his fault. She had died in his place.

That was his curse.

SITTING ON A LOW WALL OUTSIDE THE HOSPITAL, Rocco waited. The afternoon had settled over the city, and with it, the traffic noises. No rain, no wind, just a stack of clouds that came and went incessantly in the midst of the mountain summits. A baby blue Mini Minor pulled up and parked a few steps away from him. The first to get out was Sebastiano. Then Furio, who locked the car.

They walked toward him. Moving slowly. Sebastiano, tall, with a head of curly hair and the body of a bear squeezed into a too-small short leather overcoat. Furio, unshaven, with sunglasses, black gloves, and tight jeans. Rocco got up and went to meet them. Seba threw open his arms. He hugged him so hard it took Rocco's breath away. The big man was shaking, sobbing, and he clutched at Rocco as if he were the only buoy on a stormy sea. Furio lit a cigarette. Once his two friends had finished their impassioned hug, Furio too exchanged a more restrained but still brotherly hug with the deputy chief.

All three of them were crying.

"Let's go see Adele," said Sebastiano.

ALBERTO HAD OPENED THE DOOR TO THE MORGUE without a word. Only Seba went in, and he walked over to the sheet-covered corpse. Furio and Rocco stood in the door. The last thing either of them wanted was to see Adele. They wanted to remember her the way she'd been when she was alive. The medical examiner lifted the sheet. Rocco watched as an earthquake shook his friend's broad back. Sebastiano took Adele's hand, raised it to his face, and kissed it. Then he laid the hand back down. He turned around. He no longer had eyes. In their place were a pair of dark wells. He said nothing. They left the morgue. Rocco exchanged a glance with Fumagalli, who had already laid the sheet back over Adele Talamonti's corpse, then he turned and, with Furio, followed his friend out.

"I'M TAKING HER TO ROME."

Sitting on a bench, they smoked cigarettes and looked at the buildings.

"As soon as the proper authorities issue their approval," said Rocco. "Do you believe me when I say that I wish it had been me instead of her?"

"I just need to know who the fuck it was," Sebastiano muttered through clenched teeth.

"Could it have been someone from here?" were the first words out of Furio's mouth since he'd set foot in Aosta.

"No. No way."

"So this is something from Rome?"

"I think so. And the fact that Adele should have had to pay the price for my bullshit is a knife to the heart."

"For *our* bullshit. Who says it's not our fault, too?" asked Furio, flicking the cigarette butt far away.

"In that case, they would have settled matters down in Rome. They wouldn't have come all the way up here. It seems as if anyone who gets involved with me, winds up paying for it sooner or later." And Rocco put his face in his hands.

"I'm the one who killed Adele," said Sebastiano. "She should have stayed clear of me. I always knew it. Now what am I going to tell her mother? Her father? I just feel sick. And I can't even manage to vomit. What am I going to do now?" He'd asked it as a question but Seba wasn't talking to his friends. Or even to himself. It was hard to know who he was mad at. "Is it hard to forget, Rocco?"

"It's very hard. It's practically impossible."

"I'd like to bury Adele near Marina."

"Certainly. She can have my spot."

"Swear to me that if you find out who did it, you'll leave them to me."

Rocco didn't answer.

"Swear to me!"

Rocco nodded.

"I want to hear you say it, Rocco!"

"I swear to you, Seba."

AFTER DROPPING SEBASTIANO AND FURIO OFF AT THE residential hotel, Deputy Chief Schiavone was sitting at the Chalet bar, in front of the Roman arch. Lupa lay in his arms, sleeping peacefully. She smelled of popcorn.

"So who is she?" Marina asks me.

"She's Lupa. Do you like her?"

She pets her. "Her tummy is pink," she says.

"Right. And so is her nose."

"Is she going to pee and poop in the apartment?"

"No. Don't ask me how or why, but she's perfectly trained. She goes outside to poop and pee."

She looks at her with her enormous eyes. Marina's enormous eyes.

I got lost in them the first time, and I never did find the exit.

"*What are you planning to do?*" *she asks me. She's not talking about the dog anymore.*

"*I don't know.*"

"*Are you going to go after him or will you wait for him here?*"

"*I don't feel like thinking about it.*"

"*Do you have any idea of who it might be?*"

"*No. And something strange happens to me. When I think about it, I can't seem to concentrate. My thoughts all just scatter.*"

"*That happens when you think about things from the past. Look, Lupa woke up!*"

It's true. She's opened her eyes. Only now that a ray of sunlight catches them do I realize that they have golden highlights. "*Look at the sky, Marina. It's beautiful. Blue as can be.*"

"*Not a cloud in sight. You'll see all the flowers that bloom.*"

"*You think?*"

"*That's what happens. Snow helps. Because it has nitrogen. Soon your jaw will drop. You know what? Looking at you like this, in profile, you resemble your father.*"

"*Do you think that's odd?*"

"*No. Don't take this the wrong way. But he was much more handsome than you. He was taller than you, he had blue eyes, and he had much better manners.*"

I laugh. "*Did you know him all that well?*"

"*Not well enough. But when I fell in love with you, I looked at him and said to myself: if that's what he'll look like when he gets old, then I'm there with bells on!*"

"*And how did it go?*"

"I don't know. How did it go?"

"It went that I'm getting old all by myself."

"Why don't you let me go, Rocco?"

"I can't, Marina."

"It's been seven years."

"Don't ask me again."

"Please, Rocco. I can't take it anymore."

"Me either, I can't take it anymore either."

"You see? The sun has set, but it's not nighttime yet. Look at the people out in the street. They don't have shadows anymore. And it seems as if they're flying. They lose their substance. They seem like dreams, like fog. Abandoned rags."

"It's true. Memories have no substance either. But there they are."

She looks at me seriously. I don't like it when Marina looks at me seriously. "Memories slip away, my love. Day by day, you might not even realize it, but they slip away. The beautiful ones, and the terrible ones with them. The night devours them, and they drift off, mingling with other people's memories. Soon enough you can't even find them, try as you might. Until you too become just another memory. And then everything will become much easier for you."

"Give me your hand."

She reaches out to me. Lupa wants down. She shakes herself, she takes a little run. She chases a pigeon that takes to the air, but she's not fast enough to catch it. She barks in her sharp, sweet doggy voice. She comes back to me. She wags her tail and tilts her head. Soon it will be dark. Lupa wants her dinner.

ACKNOWLEDGMENTS

I am both obliged and pleased to thank Paola and Giampi, my family (Toni, Laura, Giovanna, Francesco, and Marco) the first and toughest readers of the manuscript, the acumen of Valentina, the invaluable efforts of Mattia, the indispensable support of Marcella, Maurizio, and Francesca. A special thanks goes out to Olivia and Antonio (*daje*—you know we can do it!). A warm welcome to Emma, my number 5, and a fraternal embrace to Picchio "don't-worry-I'll-be-there-any-minute," to Pietro "sure enough," and last but not least, to Fabrizio "*na-ssediata-nun-te-la-toglie-nessuno*: Signor No-One-Can-Keep-You-From-Sitting-Down-For-A-Second." A. M.

Antonio Manzini is an actor, screenwriter, director, and author. He studied under Andrea Camilleri at the National Academy of Dramatic Arts in Rome. He is the author of five murder mysteries featuring Deputy Police Chief Rocco Schiavone, including *Black Run*, *Adam's Rib*, and *Out of Season*. Manzini lives in Italy.

ALSO BY
ANTONIO MANZINI

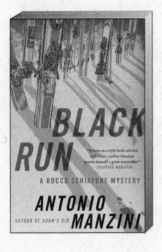

BLACK RUN
A Rocco Schiavone Mystery
Available in Paperback and eBook

A sly, sizzling mystery—the first in a sensational crime series—set in the Italian Alps, reminiscent of the works of Andrea Camilleri, Donna Leon, and Henning Mankell. Antonio Manzini writes with sly humor and a dash of irony, and introduces an irresistible hero—a fascinating blend of swagger, machismo, and vulnerability—in a colorful and atmospheric crime mystery series that is European crime fiction at its best.

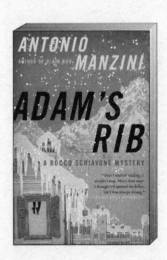

ADAM'S RIB
A Rocco Schiavone Mystery
Available in Paperback and eBook

"[Schiavone] brings the case to a solution out of Agatha Christie as satisfying as it is unexpected here . . . Schiavone continues to make a memorable companion in crime." —*Kirkus Reviews*

In this stylish international mystery, Antonio Manzini further establishes Rocco Schiavone as one of the most acerbic, complicated, and entertaining antiheroes crime fiction has seen in years.